THE BONDS THAT TIE

Broken Bonds

Also by J Bree

The Bonds That Tie Series

Broken Bonds

Savage Bonds

Blood Bonds

Forced Bonds

Tragic Bonds

Unbroken Bonds

The Mortal Fates Series

Novellas

The Scepter

The Sword

The Helm

The Trilogy

The Crown of Oaths and Curses

The Throne of Blood and Honor

THE BONDS THAT TIE

Broken Bonds

J BREE

Broken Bonds
The Bonds that Tie #1

Cover & Interior Illustration by Emilie Snaith
Cover Typography by Bellaluna Cover Designs
Edited by Telisha Merrill Mortensen
Proofread by Samantha Whitney
Interior Formatting by Wild Elegance Formatting

Broken Bonds/J Bree – 2nd ed.
ISBN-13 - 978-1-923072-00-8

J BREE

Prologue

The dream is always the same.

We're all in the car together, traveling on the highway. I'm arguing with my mother, who's sitting next to me, and it's because I'm so angry that she's making us move again. I'd made friends in Connecticut, real ones, and for the first time in my life I felt... normal. Average. Just one of the girls and not like some freak of nature.

It was the last time I would feel that way.

My father is driving, our looks so similar that there's no mistaking I came from him. He's listening to the news and frowning, always glancing back at me to check that I'm okay. He always has an eye on me, his beloved daughter.

Andrew, another of my mother's Bonded, is in the

front passenger seat with his laptop open as he works. He's a very serious guy, cold and aloof to anyone outside of our family, but he's very affectionate and loving to me. He calls me his reason. The reason he works hard, the reason he's always striving for more.

Vincenzo is the third and final of my mother's Bonded and he's sitting in the back with us, holding my hand tightly as his thumb strokes down my thumb in comfort. He's always been the kind one, the one who was affectionate and loving no matter where we are. Often, when we're living among the non-Bonded, people assume he's my biological father because he would spend the most time out with me. He's a stay-at-home dad, the type of man who is happiest taking care of the house and his Bond.

I'm angry but it's also the last time I felt at peace... and safe.

I'm struggling not to cry; I've always been the type to burst into furious tears. My mother is trying to get me to talk to her, quiet words I can't remember, but the sound of it is soothing to the deepest depths of my soul. That's the last I remember of them and the last moments of the dream.

Right before it turns into my nightmare.

The one I can't wake up from, the one that tells me that this isn't a dream at all. It's the memory of a day I can't scrub from my mind, no matter how hard I try.

Something hits the side of the car at a high speed, pushing it over until the car flips and flies down the side of a ravine.

In my shock, my gift flows out of me.

I panic and try to pull it back into my body but I hit my head, dazing myself so badly that there's no stopping it.

I'm the only survivor.

And I will never stop hating myself for it.

Never.

J BREE

FIVE YEARS LATER

The interview room is as cold as ice.

I'm still wearing the same clothes I had on when I was grabbed off of the streets by the Tactical Response Team, stuff that I really should have thrown out months ago, but I never wanted to waste my money on new clothes when these still did a decent job. Life on the run wasn't easy, or cheap, and I wasn't expecting to be dragged out of the heat of the South and into the chillier state of Oregon.

I'm also pretty sure they're trying to put me on edge.

What I did... running away from your Bonded, the people fated to be with you, that isn't something that happens a lot. Or ever, really. Running away from the people that complete your soul, only a fucking crazy person would do that.

I am that crazy person.

But I did it for a reason... actually, I did it for a lot of reasons, and all of them completely sane. They're just not something I can talk about without risking my life, my Bonds, and every other person on the goddamn planet. Seriously.

I can't tell them that though.

Guess I have to keep my mouth shut and face whatever consequences my actions have brought about.

I try not to rub my arms or make it so obvious that I'm uncomfortable, because that's exactly what they want. My skin crawls with the need to leave, get out, run until I find myself in a big city where no one knows me and could ever attempt to lock me down again. My eyes dart back to the door, but I know for a fact there's a giant guard on the other side, waiting for me to try something.

They made sure to tell me all about him, and his abilities, when they'd thrown me in here, just to be sure I'd keep my ass in this seat like a good little girl. The thing is, I *will* keep my ass here because being paralyzed isn't on my to-do list today. Nope, not at all. An icy drop of dread works its way down my spine at the very thought of it.

I seethe about the attitude of the men again for a second before the door finally opens and a man steps through. He's tall and imposing, a wall of man, really, and hell, I hope he isn't one of my Bonds.

He'd probably strap me down and torture me just for his own sick pleasure.

"Ah, Miss Fallows. I don't think we've met yet. My name is Brian Noakes, and I'm here to go over a few key details before your Bonds arrive."

I swear I feel beads of sweat start to form on my forehead despite the chill in the room. "Sure, it's not like you've given me much choice."

He takes the seat opposite of me and slides a file across the table. "I don't think you fully grasp the situation you are in, Miss Fallows. It's highly unconventional for a Bond to run away."

I try to keep my face calm and blank. "I haven't broken any laws, you can't keep me here against my will."

As his eyes pick me over, the man smiles, but it's not a nice thing, more a baring of teeth, like he's a predator preparing to go in for the kill. "The Council has voted. While there may not be any laws against leaving your Bonds behind, there has to be special consideration taken in this case. North Draven is on the Council, he's a pillar in our society, and with his social standing, this entire... 'adventure' of yours has been quite embarrassing for him."

My teeth clench, my jaw locking up so there's no way I could answer him even if I wanted to, but let's be real, there's not much running through my head except exactly how badly I wish I could choke him out with nothing but my mind.

That would be an amazing gift to have.

He nods at me like I've spoken and continues with his condescending drivel. "So you see, we had to make a decision. You can't go running off again, not with your Bonds being who they are, and your deceptions over the years mean that we cannot trust you."

It takes more will than I thought I had but I force my jaw to relax to spit out, "So you're going to lock me up here then? You're putting bars on the windows and I'm going to be kept as a fucking pet? It doesn't matter who my Bonds are, forcing me to complete the bond is *rape* and I won't just bend over for them like a good little slave."

All pretense of civility drops away from him as his garish smile turns into a grimace. He mumbles something about my terrible manners and the door opens again, this time the hulking guard walks in and I shrink back in my chair. I hadn't realized just how outmatched I really am now without being able to use my gift.

Despite it being the worst thing to do right now, I start to panic.

The thought of being paralyzed in this room with those two men... there's no stopping the dread from taking hold of me. The sweating gets worse and my hands begin to shake as I grab my knees under the table so they don't see it, but it's no use. The guard smirks at me, spotting my terror and probably getting off on it. Fucking sicko.

"Ah, Jennings, thank you for coming. I'm hoping Miss Fallows agrees to this without having to use extreme measures."

Agrees to freakin' what?!

He pulls out a small leather pouch and unzips it. All I see is the scalpel before I freak the hell out. "What the fuck do you think you're going to do to me?"

Jennings smirks and then I feel the scalding touch of his power wash over me, my muscles lock up, and I'm fucking trapped in my own body.

I can't even move my eyeballs to glare at him or to see what's coming. I just have to sit there and take it.

I will never forget this man. Someday, I'm going to make him pay for this. If it didn't jeopardize everything I've been running from all this time, I'd unleash my own power onto him, see how he fucking likes it, but instead I have to just... take it.

For now.

"Now, now, Jennings. I thought we'd give her a chance to be good, though I'd rather get this over with without her smart mouth getting in the way. I'm not envious of Draven at all."

Jennings laughs and they move around me, standing behind me so I have no fucking clue what they're doing.

"I dunno, breaking her in sounds like a good time. It's always the ones with a smart mouth that break open so pretty."

Holy fucking shit.

That's it, I'm going to have to use my power and run, there's no *fucking* way I'm being raped by this guy today. Nope. Never fucking happening.

My hair is lifted off of my neck and the panic really starts to squeeze my chest. My gift swells in my stomach, straining at the restraints I've locked it in, wanting to come out and protect me. I can't freaking think. I can barely breathe. If this isn't over soon, I won't be able to hold it back. Like a reflex, once it's been triggered, there's no stopping your gift from coming out as protection.

"Can you soften her muscles here a little? I won't be able to get it in if you don't."

My vision starts to white out, I'm definitely hyperventilating.

"I can soften her up a bit."

Then I feel a sharp pain over the back of my neck that snaps me out of the panic. The fucker is slicing me open! He pushes and pulls at my skin, opening the wound and then pushing something inside. What the actual *fuck* is going on?

Jennings leans forward so I can feel his breath on my neck. "Just a little something so we know where you are at all times, Oleander. If Mr. Draven needs any help with you, I'll be the first to volunteer."

A GPS tracker.

They've put a freaking GPS tracker *into my skin.* I haven't even met my fucking Bonded yet and already I hate them. I know I ran away but I did it for a reason. Not that I could ever tell them that, not without risking their lives again. They don't even know everything I fucking gave up for them.

Besides, I'm a human being. A Bond. I have my own mind and I'll make my own decisions. They can't force this shit on me!

One of them actually stitches my wound back together, I don't see which of them but I'm hoping it's Noakes, and then they both step back around the table where they're in my view again.

They're both on my list now. The list of people I'll fucking come after some day when using my power isn't too freaking risky. I'm going to hunt them down and make a freaking show of my payback.

"You can step out now, Jennings. I can deal with the rest of the briefing."

His power tightens around me like a vise before he finally lets me go, like he wants to remind me of just how much control he has over me right now. I take a deep, shuddering breath.

At least they didn't actually try to rape me. I'm sure I can get the GPS out if I need to.

"That device can conduct enough volts of electricity to kill you if you attempt to take it out. I could also knock you out with it if I wanted to; your entire existence is in the palm of my hand now, Fallows. Your Bonds will be arriving shortly, but I wanted you to be muzzled before they get here. Draven is a close, personal friend of mine. There isn't much I would consider off-limits when it comes to keeping his Bond close. You would do well to complete the bond with him sooner rather than later. Just lie down and *submit."*

Okay, maybe not.

Bile creeps up the back of my throat even as the angry tears start.

He smiles and stands again, gesturing to the file he's left for me. "There's all of your rules and guidelines of what we expect of you now. I suggest you memorize them, live by them. The quicker you get into line, the better this will go for you."

And then he leaves.

I'm fucking trapped here.

I don't bother looking at the file for now, mostly because I don't want to know a thing about the men I'm stuck with and what they can do. Instead, I run my fingers over the stitched wound on the back of my neck, wincing at the sharp, throbbing pain of it. Fucking *bastards*.

I have to get a hold of myself, to find that calm within myself so I don't lose control of my gift. It might sound sick, but I imagine how I would use my abilities to get out of here to get calm again. I plan every little moment of how I would get out and how I would get payback on those men who had just touched me. I walk through those plans, over and over, until I feel calm once again.

Minutes creep into hours and eventually I know the sun has gone down and I'm still fucking stuck here. I desperately need to pee, but I'm not going to knock on the door and ask for a toilet break. My stomach begins to growl. When had they found me and grabbed me off of the street, two days ago? Maybe three now. I'd been on my way to work, late and having skipped breakfast.

No one has given me food since. One of the drivers had shoved a bottle of water at me that I'd guzzled down greedily, but that had to be at least a day ago. These guys aren't at all afraid of torture because I feel like a freaking prisoner of war right now.

The door opens again and this time an older, stem-looking woman walks in. My leg starts to bounce nervously under the table, an old tick I can't let go of.

"Follow me, I'll take you to freshen up."

Freshen up? I glance down at the mess my clothes are in. I probably stink too after days in the same clothes. "Oh, yeah. Thanks."

My head spins when I stand up. Blood loss or hunger, I don't know, but the lady doesn't notice me swaying on my feet at all. She just wrinkles her nose at me and then turns on her heel to lead me out of the room.

The building we're in looks like an office building, everyone wearing suits and ties. As we walk through the halls together, my skin starts to pull tight as I feel the eyes of the workers here on me. There's a lot of interest and it's pretty obvious they all know who I am.

Oleander Fallows.

The runaway Bond.

The murderer.

Not that they know I'm a murderer, I'm sure this would all be going very differently if they did. A lump forms in my throat as I think about it. Hell, that's the quickest way to freak out and lose control. I give myself a shake. *Stop fucking thinking about it, Oli!*

The bathroom is clean enough and the shower is an actual stall, thank God. The woman shoves a bag at me, one I hadn't noticed her carrying thanks to my freak out, and snaps, "I don't have all night, so you better be quick. I'll drag you out naked if I have to."

Right.

Fuck this bitch.

I give her a dirty look and take the bag, stomping into the stall as if I'm four years old and not the mature nineteen that I am. Well, I think I'm mature. I've survived five years on the run, living on the streets when I've needed to. It hasn't been easy, but it's better than the alternative.

This is the alternative.

Being chipped and forced to live with the men who are biologically fated to be mine... that's the worst fucking hellsphere I can think of. Not that I've met them. I've only seen photos of them, little headshots that were handed over to me the day after my family was killed. I can barely remember what any of them look like, but I remember their names.

I strip off and scrub down, wincing at the state of myself. I'm covered in bruises. The Tactical Team hadn't been kind in their takedown of me, three fully grown men had slammed me to the ground. I'm not exactly tiny but fuck... One guy grabbing me would have done the job.

My hair is a mess, so I wash it and then dry it carefully. The clothes they've left for me are ugly, sweatpants that are at least three sizes too big and an old sweatshirt. The smell of cologne on it makes me want to hurl, my bond is so freaking picky about scents.

I hear the woman start to tap her foot and I roll my

eyes. What a bitch.

I leave the stall with my old clothes bundled up in the bag and the hairbrush in my other hand.

"There's no time to try to pretty yourself up. I doubt you'd be able to do much anyway," the woman snaps.

I'm a stubborn girl, the quickest way to get me digging my heels in is to throw those sorts of insults at me.

So I stand there in front of the mirror and I brush out my hair, slowly and meticulously, until it's knot-free and then I braid it. I do the most complicated braid I can manage with only one hair tie to secure it. I have to focus to make sure my hands don't shake at the sight of the silvery strands, I don't think I'll ever really get used to this color.

She huffs and puffs under her breath but I ignore her. She doesn't know what I can do, so she's hesitant to actually try to drag me out. That's a good thing because I can't use my abilities, so I'd be forced to punch her in the throat.

And I would.

I would enjoy every freaking second of it too.

Finally, when I can't procrastinate any longer, I follow her back to the tiny interview room that is now my hell on Earth. Nothing has changed, the file is still sitting there, waiting for me. The woman leaves me there without another word.

I finally crack and open the file.

Fuck.

Big mistake.

There's updated photos of my Bonds in there. Hell, if my life weren't such a giant freaking mess, I'd be ecstatic. Every photo just gets hotter and hotter. They're all ridiculously good looking, too good looking for someone like me.

Okay, I know I'm not, like, hideous or anything, but the photo of Gabriel is of him jogging shirtless and I think the guy has an eight-pack. I have to tell the bond in my chest to settle the hell down because I can't have him. I certainly can't complete the bond with him.

I definitely don't have an eight-pack. I have a little pouchy tummy that says I enjoy chocolate too much when I'm hormonal and let me tell you, I'm not ever giving it up for a flat stomach.

Nope.

I also didn't realize two of my Bonds were brothers. That's going to be... different. The Councilman and his scholar brother. Hell, this entire thing is a fucking mess.

I sift through the other photos, hellbent on finding some sort of escape route. I mean, the killer GPS tracker means it'll be tricky but I've gotten out of shit before. I'm sure I can figure it out, and I need to do it soon. It takes me a second to realize there's something vital missing from the documents and I scour each page just to be sure.

Their gifts aren't listed.

There's a field on each of the documents that says 'gifts' but on each and every page, it's been left blank. There's not even a clue to tell me what any of them is capable of, and I suddenly find myself insanely desperate to know what they can do.

I'm still fixated on the documents when the lock on the door turns, and I feel the tug in my chest that tells me one of my Bonds is here. Every muscle in my body turns to stone as I wait.

My entire body is practically vibrating with tension as the door opens and I glance up, making eye contact with the eight-pack hottie himself, but he looks away immediately.

Hell.

I had always assumed they'd be upset or disappointed in me, but I am not at all prepared to see the pure, unadulterated loathing in their eyes when four of my mates walk into the interview room.

Freaking loathing.

I swallow and duck my head.

One of them scoffs at me but I ignore it, keeping my eyes glued to my hands where they lie folded on the table in front of me. I don't need to see more of their hate. I hate myself enough for all of us, any more and I might end up finding a fucking bridge to jump off of.

Murderer.

Nope. Can't think about it right now, not when I'm already on edge and freaking out. Where had the fire in me gone? It's like it was sucked out the moment they all stepped into the room.

I hear the scraping of chairs and I grow a spine, glancing back up. I stare around at each of them, slowly taking them in. It's easy to distinguish them all from each other, even without the photos spread out in front of me on the table.

Gryphon is scowling and grumpy looking, the scar running through his eyebrow standing out even more. He looks exactly like his photo, right down to the frown.

Gabriel fusses with the coffee cup in his hands, just as nervous about this as I am, apparently. The smiling hottie is nowhere to be seen. I mean, he's still hot but he looks... miserable.

Fuck.

North, the Councilman and the reason for my GPS chip, sits there in his perfectly tailored suit. He's the only one who's trying to mask the loathing a little. He's failing at hiding it but I appreciate the effort, I guess.

Nox just keeps staring at me like I'm the worst thing that has ever happened to him. And, fuck, maybe I am, but at least I won't be the worst thing to ever be unleashed on the entire population of the country.

I can live with being hated. I hate myself enough to know just how easy it is to loathe me.

We sit in complete silence for what feels like hours but I'm sure it's only ten or so minutes.

It's excruciating. A living nightmare. Sitting there with four of the five men who are supposed to be drawn to me, to someday love me the most in the world, while they stare at me with utter contempt... I get it. I do, I know what I did, but that doesn't mean it doesn't feel freaking unbearable.

Finally, Gabriel huffs and snaps, "Should we even bother asking where the hell you've been? Or why you left?"

It's hard, but I hold in my flinch at the betrayal in his tone. North and Gryphon both watch me closely, but it's the smirking glare on Nox's face that has the hair on the back of my neck rising. It's not just that he hates me... he's ready to torture me, to find some sort of payback for me leaving him.

I take a deep breath and blow it out slowly, ready for whatever venom he's going to spit at me. I can see it slowly filling him up and it's only a matter of time before he bursts out with it.

"You have been very hard to find. I've wasted a lot of resources tracking you down," says North, picking at some invisible fleck of dust on his suit.

He and Nox look very similar, all dark eyes and pitch-black hair. North's is cut short and styled perfectly, where Nox's is longer and curling softly around his cheeks. Both of them are cold as ice, completely cut off" to what is happening.

My bond is keening in my chest but I tell it to knock it the fuck off.

I did what I had to do for us all.

Gryphon doesn't say a word. He just scowls at me like he's trying to find something written under my skin, something he'll find if only he looks hard enough. I'm too freaking good at staying the perfect blank canvas though, so he's getting nothing out of me today.

Nox sneers at me. "I did wonder at how you were surviving out there. I'm assuming you were selling yourself, there's nothing else you have to offer. I'll have to wait for the test results to come back before I complete the bond and get what I'm owed from you."

Ex-fucking-cuse me?

What he's *motherfucking* owed?

That helps me to deal with my mourning bond, because there's no fucking way I'm letting some entitled rich-boy Bond tell me all I'm worth is a quick fuck to complete our bond and give him more power.

Not fucking likely.

I grit my teeth and try to speak civilly. "That assumes I want you to touch me. Not fucking likely, Draven."

The smirk only gets wider. "And how exactly will you stop me, Bond? Your blood work didn't show your ability, what teeth are you hiding from us? Or are you Ungifted and a total fucking waste of space?"

Did he just... say he's going to attack me? I'm about to slam my foot into his dick and call it a day but his brother comes to the rescue.

North slides a large, bulky envelope across the table in my direction while he's looking down his nose at me. "This phone is also to be on you at all times. If I call you, you will pick up. If I have to call you a second time, there will be hell to pay. If you fail to pick up, I will assume you have either run or been kidnapped and I will send every resource under my command to find you. Is this understood, Fallows?"

Fallows, like I'm one of his subordinates. I speak through my clenched teeth, "Understood."

Nox scoffs. "You're pretty agreeable to him. Looks like you'll get to bond after all, brother."

My eyes snap back over to him. "I'm not touching any of you. If you try to lay so much as a finger on me, then you'll be committing a crime, and I'll happily stand in front of the Council and tell them exactly how much I don't want any of you."

Gabriel stands abruptly and walks out, the door slamming shut behind him. I'm too fucking furious to feel bad about it, my attention is entirely on Nox and his shitty attitude.

Me not wanting them touching me, it goes beyond just the emotional stuff. I mean, I don't want guys who hate me trying to drag me into bed just so their abilities strengthen, but if my abilities heightened?

Fuck. No.

Absolutely not.

"I'll be back tomorrow morning to take you to your dorm room. The file Noakes gave you has everything you need to know about your life now. Read it, learn it, and live by it. There's no other path for you now, Fallows."

Then he stands and the other two stand with him, walking out the door and locking it firmly behind them.

I'm trapped in this fucking room all over again.

And still, no one has fed me.

I barely sleep.

The bed is horrendously uncomfortable, springs sticking into my back and the thin blanket doing nothing to keep me warm.

A different woman comes in the morning to take me to the bathroom, the clothes she hands me much better than the sweatpants and sweatshirt nightmare from yesterday. There's clean underwear, a dress, and ankle boots. My stomach is aching with hunger, the dry crackers from last night were nowhere near enough food to keep me going, and after a night in the braid, my hair is looking like a mess.

This woman is a little nicer though. She helps me with my hair and even slips me a little bag with makeup in it.

I smile at her. "Thank you. I'm sorry you got babysitting duty."

She smiles back, shaking her head a little. "I don't mind it so much. I'm sure Olivia made it a nightmare for you yesterday."

Olivia, so that's the bitch's name. "Yeah, she wasn't very happy with me. I'm not sure why she hates me so much."

The woman grimaces. "She's... in love with one of your Bonds."

Oh.

Oh, fuck.

"Sorry. I know it must be hard to hear that. I'm not sure if Gryphon ever... reciprocated."

Gryphon. My silent, scarred, biker-boot-wearing Bond who looked at me like I was nothing to him. Like he didn't care if I came back or not.

I have to ignore my weeping bond again and, fuck, I hope this isn't going to be a regular thing now. Am I always going to have to deal with it fucking keening in my chest for men I can't have? I think I'd rather die. I shove it down in my chest, further and further, until I can breathe again.

"Thanks for letting me know. I just thought everyone in our community hates me for running. I know it's not... something that happens a lot."

The woman, fuck, I should ask her name, she shakes her head. "It doesn't happen a lot but... ultimately, it's your decision if you don't want to complete a bond."

I give her a smirk. "They have me chipped like a stray dog, it's not my decision anymore."

She ducks her head, obviously uncomfortable with what her superiors have done but not quite enough to help me, and I let it go. She was nice enough to me and the makeup means I'll be heading into college today without looking like a complete mess.

I'll take what I can get for now.

She walks me back to the interview room where we find North waiting for me, another immaculate and freshly pressed suit on and his phone in his hand.

"Thank you, Carrie. She looks much better today."

He speaks without looking at me once, but the smile he gives *Carrie* is warm and kind. So there is a soul somewhere there under the suit and tie.

His eyes are much less kind when they finally touch me. "We have a meeting with the dean of Draven University, then I'll take you to your dorm."

I give him a sharp nod, it's not like I can say no to him anyway, and then I follow him out of the building. He waves and smiles at most of the people we pass, all of them looking at me like I'm some sort of science experiment. My skin prickles uncomfortably with all of the attention. I've done everything I can to blend in for the last five years, suddenly being the center of attention is... jarring. Uncomfortable. Fucking *weird.*

There's a Rolls Royce with a driver sitting at the curb, and I take a second to *pray* that it's not here for us.

Of course it is.

North freaking Draven has a driver for his Rolls Royce. I want to puke. No wonder everyone hates me. I knew he was a Councilman but I wasn't expecting this sort of...

wealth. The sort that comes with drivers and suits and hell only knows what else.

My parents had been well-offbut even they didn't have a freaking driver.

"Are you getting in the car, or do I need to force you in? Are you going to fight me at every step today? I'm attempting to be civil."

This is civil? Fuck me. "I got distracted by your obscene show of wealth."

He opens the car door to usher me in, a completely fake show of chivalry. "Obscene? This is a necessity."

My stomach rumbles as I move into the car. "So glad your driver is a *necessity* but letting me eat isn't."

He slides in next to me and glances at me. "They didn't feed you?"

I squint at him. "They're your people, right? You should know then that it's been four days since I last ate. I have a little money, I offered to buy something myself but was told I had to wait for you. So yeah, can we hurry this up because I'm about to fucking pass out."

He doesn't react at all, just blinks at me. "They know better than to just starve you. If you're aiming for sympathy, then you're woefully mistaken."

Right.

Fuck him, I'm done being *civil.*

I cross my arms and shut my mouth. I don't speak

another word to him for the rest of the drive over to the college campus, the scenery outside beautiful but not enough to cheer me up. Fucking Bonds. I knew it was going to be bad but I wasn't expecting to feel so... much. I feel everything through the bond inside, every glare and harsh word cuts through my soul like a knife.

When the car finally pulls up, North gets out and opens my door for me again, the perfect mockery of a gentleman, because I'm now feeling woozy with hunger.

Fuck him.

I'll just keep thinking it until he disappears.

He walks me up and into the building, charming his way there with those same warm smiles, and I start to feel like I could puke watching him. It's all so freaking fake.

The dean sees us straight away, seating us and then hurrying out of the room to grab paperwork. I guess this is the best time to tell North that I dropped out while I was on the run and there's no way I can get into this place, not even with his help.

His name is on the freaking building.

North's eyes are cold as he takes me in. "What do you mean you didn't finish high school?"

Despite all my efforts, my cheeks heat with embarrassment. Damn him, why do a few simple words from him have the ability to cut my freaking heart to ribbons? "I moved around too much to stay in school."

I spent all of my spare time in libraries, doing what I could to always stay learning, but I don't want to say that to him. What if he laughs at me? What if I just look freaking pathetic to him, even more than I do now?

His jaw tightens and I wait for his scathing comment, my heart back in my throat no matter how hard I swallow to move it. I need to find my freaking spine around this guy. Why do the others not affect me like this?

The door to the office opens again and the dean walks through, a stack of papers in his hands. "I have everything you need here to enroll, you just need to supply your SAT scores and identification."

Neither of which I have.

I open my mouth but North cuts me off. "We will have everything to you by this afternoon. If it's ok with you, we have other appointments we must get to today."

The dean nods and hands the files over as we both stand. I'm not sure how North is planning on handing stuff over that doesn't exist, but I keep my mouth shut. No need to poke the bear.

I wonder if he *is* a bear? I don't know why they'd make such a big secret of him being a shifter though, so that doesn't really make sense, but also maybe that's why I'm so terrified of him. Maybe it's my own instincts telling me that Bond or not, he's bad freaking news. Fuck.

He places a firm hand on the small of my back and

directs me out of the room. I flinch but manage to stop myself from scrambling away from him, thank God. He doesn't notice, just pushes me out of the building and into his car, the driver opening the door for us both and shutting us firmly in the backseat together.

I want to crawl out of my damn skin.

"Something wrong, Miss Fallows?" he asks, his eyes firmly trained on his phone. I really don't matter to him at all, just our fucking *bond.*

"Nothing at all. No problem whatsoever." I can't help but let the sarcasm drip from my words.

His eyes narrow at me. "I understand that you are a petulant teenager but if you could attempt to be civil, this will go far more smoothly for us all."

It nearly fucking kills me not to tell him, to keep my secrets and not throw them in his face, but my lips stay sealed shut.

"Nothing to say? I wonder why is it that I've been cursed with a selfish Bond? Bad enough that you're practically a child, simple and plain. With the power of all of your Bonds, I assumed you were going to be something... spectacular. How disappointing."

I will not cry. I fucking will *not* cry.

The driver pulls over in front of the student accommodation and quickly gets out to open our door.

I blink back the tears. "Is there a reason we're here? I

can't attend the college."

North gestures for me to get out before him, his eyes steely and cutting. "You will be attending. I will make the necessary arrangements. I suggest you spend your time here wisely, I will not tolerate laziness and if you think having wealthy Bonds means you don't have to work and provide for yourself, well... you have misjudged us all."

My cheeks sting as if he's slapped me. Did he just—did he just call me a fucking gold-digger? The fucking *gall* of this man.

I would rather fucking die than bond with him.

"Thank you for the ride and for pulling strings for me." I nearly choke on the words, but I'll be damned if he gets to call me a petulant, selfish *child* again.

He steps out of the car after me, dammit, and nods to the driver. "I'll see you upstairs. There's other things we have to discuss about our situation."

Oh, hell fucking no.

If he thinks he's going to form a bond right now, to just take the extra power he so desperately wants, he has another thing coming.

Why don't I have a knife or a gun or something? I need to protect myself against these guys.

I follow him up the stairs, sizing him up carefully. He's taller than I am by at least a foot, and he fills out the suit nicely. When I'd tripped and he'd caught me earlier,

I hadn't felt any softness to him at all, his entire freaking torso was rock hard. What part of his office job makes him so damn ripped?

Basically, short of using my gift, which I cannot do under any circumstances, I don't stand a chance against him if he tries to force the bond. I need some pepper spray or, fuck it, a gun. I smirk at the picture my mind conjures up of his face if I pulled a gun on him.

It's pretty freaking good.

We get a lot of curious looks as we move through the dorms and more than a few flirty smiles. North's entire face changes into a stunning, smiling, warm mask of schmoozing councilman. I can't contain my eye-roll. Of course he's beloved. Of course he's the type of guy the other woman will drip for.

Of-fucking-course.

He leads me up a set of stairs, why the hell isn't there an elevator, and then to a room at the end of the hall, ushering me in ahead of him. The room is plain, nothing but an old, spindly looking bed in the corner and a cheap, pine desk.

"This is your room and where you will spend your evenings. You will be in here by six every night, and you will not leave again until at least seven in the morning. Any exercise, study groups, or socialization will take place outside of these hours. You will attend all of your classes, hand in all of your assignments, and you will pass every class. I was unaware of the holes in your education when I signed you up, but I'm sure you'll be able to catch up."

My cheeks bum again and I swallow back the rage that builds in my gut at the sheer fucking nerve of him. "And if I don't stick to these little rules of yours?"

He turns on his heel to face me finally, running a hand down the line of buttons on his perfectly tailored jacket. "Having you here where I can keep an eye on you is a means of freedom for you. The alternative is to chain you by the throat to the floor in my cellar. I won't be pleased to do that but make no mistake, Fallows, I will keep you here."

The air leaks out of my lungs in a wheeze.

My Bond is a fucking psychopath.

He steps forward to the door again, his hand around the door handle as he casts me one last look. "You cannot possibly grasp the damage you've wrought by leaving us. I intend on ensuring that will never happen again. You'd do well to learn your lesson here and submit."

Then he's gone and I'm left staring blankly at the empty doorway.

Sub-fucking-mit.

I think I'd rather *die.*

I had once dreamt of being able to attend Draven University. Out of all of the colleges in the country that cater to the Gifted, Draven is well known for being the best. It offers all of the usual classes that the human schools do, but with classes specifically structured for us too, like History of the Gifted and Impulse Control 101.

I had given up any sort of hopes for a higher education when I was forced to give up school to go on the run so, while I am angry and frustrated at being forced here, I guess I'm also pretty thankful that I have the opportunity to be here and learn at such a distinguished college... for as long as this lasts. It doesn't mean that I'm not trying to find a way to escape, as long as the Resistance is after me,

I will never truly be comfortable staying in one spot, but I'm going to soak in as much information and knowledge as I can.

I wake up early on my first day, my stomach a riot of nerves, and I take extra care with my appearance. My bags were already in my room when North had dropped me off, I hadn't even known the Tactical Team had grabbed them when they found me.

I don't have designer clothes like most of the other girls in my dorms but I can look clean and well put together, which is what really matters. I hope I don't stand out too much, I just want to blend the hell in until I can get out.

By the time I'm braiding my hair, my phone buzzes with a text from North. My stomach drops when I see his name, but the text itself isn't too bad.

Gabe will pick you up from your dorm to escort you to your classes this morning.

So I get my own guard to walk me into the building. Great. Out of all of my Bonds, I guess Gabe is the one I'd choose to walk me in though. He looked as miserable as I felt last night, so hopefully that means he won't try to talk to me or anything. We can just get into the building together in total silence. Yay.

Once I'm ready, I sit on my bed and stare around my sparse room while I wait for him to arrive. I can do this, I can totally catch up to everyone around me. It's not a big deal, I've spent so much time in libraries reading and using the internet there, I'm going to be okay. I keep telling myself this, over and over again, and freaking pray it's true.

The knock at my door startles me out of my daze.

I stand and sling my bag over my shoulder, fussing with the hem of my shirt for a second to delay opening the door for a second longer. I take a deep breath and throw it open, plastering a fake-ass smirk on my face.

My heart stutters at the perfection that is my Bond, and then I remember he hates me and I need to get the fuck out of here before we all get slaughtered by the Resistance while our guards are down.

Fuck, I can't think about them right now.

Not without my hands starting to shake and my entire body breaking out in a sweat.

His eyes drag over my outfit, a little too much like he's assessing me for my liking, and then he says, "Better than the last time I saw you, I guess. How was your first night in the dorms?"

Fuck him, I'm not rising to the bait. Instead, I shrug. "It was fine. I've slept on the street before, it's much better than that."

He grimaces at me, his lip curling a little, and then jerks his head at me to follow him, as if I'm a fucking puppy. We walk down the hallway together and I notice all of the interest he gets from the other girls here. Now my mind doesn't care about this, I know he hates me, I know they all hate me, but it's like I can feel my bond in my chest protesting at the attention. The lack of concern he's showing me is like salt in the wounds, and I'd love nothing more than to rip the bond out of myself and watch it fade. If only *that* was my power. Instead, I do what I do best and shove my bond out of my mind and leave my face carefully blank.

Gabe doesn't notice this internal battle I'm waging. No, he's too freaking busy flirting his way down the halls, winking at girls on the staircase, and blowing a fucking kiss at the building TA. He's a fucking player, clearly having bedded half the girls here, and a plan already in action to do the rest later.

When we get outside I'm not expecting him to turn on me, all of the easy smiles and lit up eyes gone. "Do you even fucking care? Do you care about anyone else but yourself?"

I hold in a flinch and roll my shoulders back, looking around like I don't know which way we're heading, when really I obsessively Googled my surroundings last night. "If you have something you need to get off your chest, then you may as well do it now."

He grabs my arm and shoves a piece of paper under my nose. "If a guy shoved his phone number into your pocket around me, I'd rip his fucking throat out and yet you're standing there, unbothered and ready for fucking class?"

I blink at him like an idiot. Is he kidding me? "So you want me to be pissed off at girls flirting with you? It's not like you tried to stop them. Why should I give a fuck about where you're sticking your dick?"

If I thought he looked seriously pissed before, I had underestimated his rage. "Nox was right. You are just a selfish bitch. What the fuck did we do to get a Bond like you?"

He drops my arm like I'm diseased and stalks off, not waiting for me as he crosses the road.

I tell myself this is a good thing, that the more my Bonds hate me and want to get away from me, the quicker I can be on the move again, but my own bond inside me is freaking devastated by his words.

I have to run to catch up to him because I really don't want North up my ass for getting left behind this early in the day. We make it to campus just in time for my first class, and it soon becomes very obvious that everybody at this college knows *exactly* who I am.

No one wants to look at or speak to me at all. It only gets worse as the day goes on, every time I take a seat in class, I find that all of the seats around me stay empty. Gabe has the exact same classes as me all day, something I know was meticulously planned, but he sits as far away from me as possible at all times, and every student here follows his lead.

It's as if I have the plague.

After five years on the run, I've never felt so lonely in all my life as I do here. It started as a nervous flutter in my stomach as we walked around, but by the time we let out for lunch, that flutter had turned into a cavernous void. I want to throw up.

I think about calling my Bonds out on it, telling them that I will never complete the bond if this is the way they're going to treat me, but instead I clamp my mouth shut and ignore it all as best as I can. It doesn't get any better once we make it to the cafeteria for lunch. Gabe continues to laugh and flirt his way there, giving me side eyes and filthy looks that I do my best to ignore. I don't even bother looking at the food choices for the day, I just grab platefuls mindlessly. Food was hard to come by and I would never let anything go to waste. I had never gotten to the point where I was starving, thank God, but I'm also going to enjoy having the easy access to it.

Gabe is much more selective about how he feels his plight. He looks like the poster boy for nutrition; protein, vegetables, and a small amount of starchy carbs. I shake my head at him without even realizing I'm doing it.

"What? You think I look this good while eating crap?" he says, and it almost feels like he's flirting with me. This boy could give me whiplash.

"I really couldn't care less about anything you do," I say giving him an apathetic look.

His eyes narrow at me in a glare and he mumbles, "Cold-hearted fucking bitch."

Yeah, that's totally me.

So cold that I ran away from the people fated to love me to try to stop the end of the freaking world as we know it. Total fucking bitch.

I take the closest table with an empty seat and the three students already sitting there get up and walk away. I roll my eyes, kind of getting immune to it now, and dig into my food. The pizza is a little overcooked but still delicious enough.

Gabe sits down with me, dammit.

"Is there something else you need?" I say around my food because I doubt his opinion of me can get any lower.

He smirks at me over his healthy plate. "You've been getting some interest today. I'm making sure that everyone knows you're off limits."

I can't stop myself from gaping at him. "Interest? People have been treating me like I'm diseased, I doubt there's anyone that holds any sort of interest. What's your real angle here?"

He shrugs. "I told you, I'm making sure you don't think about running off with anyone else. You might not think your bonds are good enough but you dressed up today to catch someone's eye."

Ok, he's clearly fucking with me.

There is no way he could possibly think my jeans and an old thrifted tee is dressing up. God, why does he have to be such a dick? I get it, they all hate me, but just leave me alone then.

I go on the defensive, my smart mouth always kicking in when I need it to. "When do you want to bond then? I can schedule you in for next week."

His head jerks back. "What?"

I smirk. "You want me, right? That's why you got so pissed that I left? Well, I'll fuck you and get this over with. Just tell me when."

It has the exact effect I was looking for, his head jerks back like he's been slapped. He's clearly a romantic, someone who was crushed when I left, he probably had our whole lives mapped out together before he even knew I existed.

"I think I'd rather have any fucking Bond but you," he hisses, and I shrug.

"I feel the same way. Leave me to my food, it's not like I can go anywhere now that you've fucking chipped me."

His brows draw in and then he shoves his plate away, stalking off toward the door.

Finally. Peace and quiet.

It lasts for about a second.

A quiet, mousy girl creeps up and slowly slinks into the chair across from me, her head down and her hands shaking just a little as she reaches for her coffee. I try not to stare at her too much, clearly something is up with her, but my eyes just keep drifting over to her.

"I hope it's ok to sit here," she mumbles, and I nod.

"Of course. Are you sure you want to sit with the social pariah?"

She shrugs and a smile tugs at the comers of her lips. "The elbow room here is pretty great and no one will come over here, thanks to Gabe."

My mood turns sour. "You know him?"

She winces at my scathing tone. "Everyone knows your Bonds, sorry. We're not friends or anything, I just know about you running away because... well, everyone knows about it."

This isn't news to me, but it still stings. I wonder how much shit they all got for me leaving, and then I think about North's cold reception and Nox's loathing-filled eyes. Nope, I don't think I care.

At least they all had each other. I had no one.

"I didn't mean to make you uncomfortable. I just wanted to eat in peace," she mumbles and snaps me out of my thoughts.

I frown at her. "Why wouldn't you eat in peace?"

She pokes at her salad. Her food looks even sadder

than Gabe's had. "I'm kind of a pariah here too. My Bond prefers his other Bonded. Riley has made it clear to me that I'm not good enough for him. He's already graduated, but *Giovanna* still attends Draven. She hates that she wasn't the center of the Bond, so she's made it her mission in life to freaking ruin me. There, I think we're even now. You know all my shitty stuff too."

I don't miss the distinct word usage there. *Bonded.* In our world, there's always one Central Gifted person in the bond who is fated to be with two or more people. Once the Central has completed their bond, with sex, they become Bonded, something revered and highly sought after. Your power grows and you forge an unbreakable connection.

Her Bond has chosen that with the other girl but not her.

I already hate him.

My skin prickles under my clothes. "Do you really want to hang out with someone who rejected her Bonds though? I mean, you're kind of on the other side of that."

I should just shut my mouth and accept the friendship, because it'll probably be the only one I have offered to me, but I've never been good at faking this kind of thing.

She smiles at me and nods. "That fact that you have no idea who I am, or anything about my mess of a bond, means you're the perfect person to be friends with here. My name is Sage, by the way, and I really wouldn't mind hanging out with you. I could help you with your assignments, I know it must be hard coming in halfway through the semester. Besides, having the entire table to ourselves will be... nice."

I guess that's one way to look at it.

Because my day is freaking cursed, my first class after lunch is History of the Gifted. Normally, that would be right up my alley. I love learning about where we came from and how our abilities have evolved. The problem here?

My timetable shows the lecturer is Nox Draven.

Fucking kill me now.

Of the four of my Bonds I've met so far, he's been the most vocal in his hatred and loathing of me.

As I walk with Sage into the lecture hall, my eyes are immediately drawn to the front of the room where Nox is talking to two female students, one of whom is caressing his arm and giggling.

Great.

My stomach drops and I tell my stupid bond to get over it; he hates me and I think he's a self-centered dick. It doesn't help that every eye in the room is on me as I slowly make my way down the stairs to sit as far away from Gabe, who is smirking openly at Nox, as I can. I take my seat and ignore it all.

Of course I'd have to end up with Bonds who are super freaking hot and popular, pillars of our society and renowned for their acts of service.

Of course I'm the villain.

I mean, I *am* the villain in this story right now. Even if they were to find out about what the last five years have been like for me... even then, I'd probably be the bad guy. Not that they will ever find out. If they do, they'll be dead. It'll be right when the Resistance comes here and murders us all. Not me though, nope, they'd keep me.

I'm too fucking valuable to die an honest death.

Thank God Sage is here with me and I have someone to roll my eyes with over the utter bullshit of this room. The whispers aren't even subtle, they're just openly talking about how shit I am.

Oh well.

"Wow. He's really pissed off at you, isn't he?" Sage whispers as she unpacks her laptop and settles in.

I shrug. "Pissed means he might get over it. I'm pretty sure we're beyond that and firmly in the 'I wish Fallows would die' phase."

Sage grimaces. "That's... really freaking awful.
Giovanna is like that too."

I shrug again. There's nothing I can do about it except

to find a way out of this hell-hole before I get us all killed.

Even as the room fills up, the seats around us stay empty, as though we have the plague or something. The whispers aren't even a little bit discreet, no one here gives a fuck about what I think of them all talking about me.

I enjoy the fuck out of the elbow room this bullshit affords me.

The girls at the front finally step away from Nox and take their seats in the front row, their flirty giggles loud in the room, even as everyone starts to quiet down. My bond squirms deep in the pit of my gut, unhappy with the entire situation, but I squash it down.

"Alright. Settle down, everyone! We have a lot to cover today."

The room quietens down pretty quickly, the guys all seem to respect him and the girls in the class are all making eyes at him. Even the girls who are bonded are looking at him appreciatively, which I get.

He is *really* fucking hot but he's also a dick, so I guess it cancels itself the hell out.

He doesn't look up at me once as he starts the lesson, but he shoots flirty grins at the girls in the front row the entire time he speaks. "So last week we left off at the beginning of the Gifted split and the rise of the Resistance. Does anyone remember the very first thing the Resistance did as an act of violence against the Gifted?"

One of the girls raises her hands, pushing her chest out and arching her back like she's on a pom set and not in a lecture hall. Hell, the thought of spending the next three years trapped here with these girls... nope, that's a whole new layer of fucked up.

Nox smirks at her as he calls on her and she beams at him as she answers, "They found all of the Ungifted that were bom from the Gifted. The anomalies and those without Bonds. Then they hunted them and killed them, claiming they were unworthy of our bloodlines."

Fuck.

I know exactly what Nox is thinking but nothing prepares me for him turning that dark gaze of his over to me. Sage shifts in her chair, uncomfortable with his blistering glare now that it's pointed in our direction, but she shouldn't be worried. It's my blood he's after.

"Fallows, join me for a demonstration." Nox's eyes bore into me, a branding challenge, and my skin prickles as I feel the entire class turn to look at me as well. I raise my chin, even as uncomfortable as I am, I won't back down to the asshole.

He has no idea of what I've sacrificed for him.

I stand and walk down the rows until I'm at the front of the class, the entire lecture hall staring down at me. The giggles of the girls in the front row are bordering on asinine and they sound like twelve-year-olds.

"Ungifted Bonds are rare but, unfortunately, they do happen. Oleander here is a prime example of when things go wrong."

It's a struggle but I keep my face blank as the giggling and whispers start up. Gabe rubs a hand over his face but he doesn't move to stop Nox, their friendship and loyalty to each other far stronger than the weak bond we share.

The one he thinks I've turned my back on.

"She has five Bonds, all with above average strength and abilities, and yet she has... nothing. No ability, no affinity, absolutely nothing worth keeping her around for."

The whispers get louder and I fight to block them out. I know what they're thinking, rejected by my own Bond in such a grand freaking spectacle, but it's nothing he hasn't already said to me.

"We're not like the Resistance, so we don't kill people for being bom lacking any real use in our society, but it's important to remember our history, don't you think, Fallows?"

I stare up at them all and memorize their faces.

I could kill them all right now without breaking a sweat, but I'm not a fucking monster, no matter how badly they all treat me. I'm above this shit.

I repeat my mantra in my head again. *Better to be hated and alive, better to be in pain than a murderer, better to be alone and safe.*

Sage invites me to go back to her dorm room to study, but when I check the location on my phone, it's outside of the perimeter North gave me and there's no way I want to deal with that asshole today. Not after his dick brother just shamed me in front of half the fucking freshman class.

Fuck.

I can't think about it without feeling that special sort of rage that means my ability wants to come out to play and that can't fucking happen. I do let myself think about it though, for like a second. Just to bum off the rage a little.

So instead, I head back to my own dorm room to... sit and fucking mope, really. In the light of day, the room looks even more bleak. Bare walls, empty cupboards, and the shiftiest bed known to man. For real, I've slept in homeless shelters with better mattresses, and the blankets are a scratchy nightmare.

I also only have about eight dollars to my name, so buying new shit isn't in the budget.

I unpack my bags and go through what little clothing I have left. There's a little makeup and three pairs of shoes. Not great, shoes are kind of my life and the Tactical Team left behind a pair of leather ankle boots that were the greatest thrift shop find of my life. I refuse to admit how much that loss hurts me.

There may be tears.

Then I spend a few hours on my phone researching jobs that fit into the perimeter North gave me, but none of the hours work with his stupid curfew. Looks like earning money is out and I'm stuck in this shitty room the way it is.

Fuck my life.

Even on the run, I managed to find little pieces of art and trinkets to cute up my spaces. I had a car too. I'll have to talk to North about it because it's registered in my name and I don't need to be racking up tickets for abandoning it.

Fuck, if only I could get my car back.

The real problem here is the killer GPS chip. If I could get it out then I'll be out of this place on the next bus... or, hell, I'll hitchhike my way to the East coast. Or maybe Canada. I'd need a passport for that.

Fuck.

Eventually it gets dark outside and I get bored enough in my shitty little room to get ready for bed. The showers at the dorms are a special sort of hell thanks to all of the whispers and gossip, but it doesn't take much brain function to realize that there are times of the day when this place is a ghost town and I use that to my advantage.

I'm drying off my hair in my room when my phone pings with a text.

Strange.

Only Sage has my number and she's at work right now. She's already given me a basic rundown of what her week looks like so we can find time to study together. I steel myself for whichever one of my Bonds is starting a whole new campaign of hate against me, because I'm sure North gave them all my number, but when I check it, I find a message from my last Bond, the one who's been missing so far.

I slump down on the bed as I read his text once, twice, eight times.

Fuck.

I think we should meet here first. The name is Atlas Bassinger, and I live on the other side of the country. I'm finishing out the semester and then coming to you, my college wouldn't let me transfer mid-unit, otherwise I'd be there now. Hope you can understand that.

Oh God, I think he's asking me for forgiveness for not dropping everything and coming to me. Me! I stare at my phone for a another second before replying, trying to find the words to tell him I'm the worst fucking option for him.

Have you spoken to the other guys? I'm sure they have plenty to say about why you don't need to drop everything to come to me.

His reply is much faster.

I don't give a fuck about their opinions on my Bond. I spoke to them when my bloodwork came back and they told me you ran. I'm not a dumbass like the rest of them, you ran because you had to. I know it. I'll be there as soon as I can and if that isn't fast enough for you, I'll come now and start the semester over again.

My stomach drops. I drop the towel I was drying my hair with to the ground and focus entirely on my phone.

You can't do that! I made you wait for long enough and, honestly, I'm still not too keen on sticking around.

I could cry, just fucking sob at my phone at this tiny scrap of kindness, but that might just break the dam inside me and at this point, I'm a freaking expert at compartmentalizing my own trauma. I hesitate when my phone pings again in my hand, then take a deep breath and look.

Introduce yourself, Bond. I don't want to talk about anything but you and I. That's what's going to get me through the next two months.

I swallow. What's a little honesty going to hurt? I can tell him enough that he doesn't hate me but not enough to put either of us in danger. Also, the text messages help me to be a little more honest than I usually am, like the fact that he's thousands of miles away means that nothing I say here really... matters I guess. All of it is future Oli's problem and, fuck it, I really don't want to think about her right now because with any luck, I'll be gone before he makes it here. I've always been more of a live-in-the-moment person.

You have to be when you're running for your life.

There's nothing really to say about me. My name is Oleander Fallows, I'm nineteen, and I don't want to be here. I was found by a TacTeam and the Council had them bring me back here. They've put GPS trackers in me now, so theres no way for me to leave here. Yet.

The text had barely shown up as delivered when the phone rang. Oh God. I stare at it for a second and then, with a shaking hand, answer his call.

"Hey, what do you mean a GPS tracker?"

His voice is like warm honey, all liquid and soothing. I try to keep my own voice calm but it's a trying situation to be in. Fuck, why did I say anything to him? What exactly was I expecting?

I clear my throat. "The Council held me down and

implanted a GPS tracker under my skin while I struggled. Well, I would have struggled if the Gifted in the room hadn't paralyzed me. It's got some safeguard on it so I can't just dig it out myself. Apparently, one of my other Bonds is a very important man and I've pissed him off enough to have my autonomy taken from me."

There's a beat of silence and then he says, "I'll come now, fuck my college classes."

My cheeks heat up. "It's my own doing. I ran. They won't ever let me forget that either. Fuck, I'd probably hate me too if I were them."

He grunts and I hear him rummaging around in the background. I pray he's not looking for, like, car keys or a laptop to buy plane tickets. "You had a reason though, right? You didn't just leave for the fun of it."

I scoff. "How exactly can you be so sure of that? I could be a total asshole here."

He scoffs back at me and I imagine a wry grin on his face. I mean, I have no clue what he looks like, other than the tiny little photo on the file North had given me, but there's something in his tone that tells me he's full of smugness and flirting right now. "Don't try to distract me, Bond. There's no way you were leaving me behind, not on purpose."

His calm and unwavering belief in me knocks me off of my feet and I slump on my bed. "That's pretty arrogant of you to assume, I might just be a total fucking bitch. Fuck, it doesn't matter anyway. I can't talk about any of it, no matter how nice you are."

He grunts down the line at me. "Okay, fuck this, I'm booking a flight right now."

I squeeze my eyes shut. "You can't, they'll only hold that against me as well. Just... maybe we can just call and text sometimes? It would be nice to talk to someone who doesn't... hate me, I guess."

He chuckles down the phone and my knees go weak. "Yeah, I'd like to get to know my Bond. This way we can do it without all of the sex getting in the way, though I have to admit, I'm a lot happier knowing I'm not the only one missing out. I'd rather they all stay pissed at you so I can taste you first."

Fuck.

Well, isn't that just great?

Too bad exactly *none* of them can taste me.

Not ever.

Not without risking everything I ran away to keep safe.

I fall asleep in my tiny, uncomfortable bed with my phone in my hand and sweet messages from Atlas bouncing around in my head. He's so... normal. Scarily so, he just flirts with me and takes an interest in my life, as if we're two normal people meeting for the first time and not Bonds with a shit-tonne of baggage.

I don't want to know what my other Bonds will think about him if he makes it to Draven before I figure out how to get out of here.

I make it through the next few days of classes without killing anyone, which is a freaking miracle because this place is teeming with assholes and rude bitches. Sage sticks with me in all of our shared classes and in the cafeteria while we eat. She's still quiet and kinda broken looking but the more we hang out, the more open she gets.

Her Bond is an actual fucking asshole.

Like, beyond mine even. Okay, maybe his mouth isn't as bad as Nox's and he's not as domineering as North but the fact that he's dropped her for Giovanna after they've spent their entire lives together... absolute scumbag. At least I know my Bonds have a reason for hating me. I betrayed them... in their eyes, I abandoned them.

Sage is the sweetest freaking human, and the shit she gets from everyone is fucking vile.

I wake up on Friday in a grumpy-ass mood and not at all ready to tackle the day, mostly because after my morning classes I only have one afternoon class, but it's a three hour block, which sounds like torture. What class could possibly need that much time? Something that's been abbreviated to 'TT', like I'm supposed to know what the hell that means.

When I question Sage about it, she winces and chews on her lip like I'm being sent to the freaking executioner's block.

"What? Oh, God, what the hell has North signed me up for?"

She fumbles over her words. "It's- uh, TT stands for... Tactical Training. You only take that if you're planning on... joining the Tactical Teamforce someday. It's pretty, uh... brutal. I know you don't have an ability so... I don't know why you'd be enrolled."

Fuck.

Fuck me sideway, upside down, and twice on Sundays.

Someday, once I've gotten really freaking far away from this place and my Bonds, I'm going to send North a letter and tell him exactly what type of utter fucking asshole he really is. I'll do it in my best penmanship, on proper stationery, because I feel like that shit would cut him even more, the freaking psychopath.

"Right. So I'm going to be put through really hard, like, workouts or whatever?"

Sage grimaces. "Yeah, for the first few hours. Then they'll... run some scenarios. That's— ah— that's where I think you're going to hate that class."

Scenarios?

She sighs at the face I pull and continues, clearly hating being the bearer of this awful news, "There's three different training courses on campus. They're all full of dangers and you have to join a team and work your way through it. You have to pass all of the courses to graduate so... here's hoping they put you in a really good team."

There's no way I'm getting into a good team.

Even if the teacher isn't friends with Nox or North, there's no way I'm going to be put with people who have experience with this sort of shit and be dragging them down. I'll be put with other inexperienced and lacking students and I'll get my ass handed to me every fucking class.

Gabe follows us both to all of our morning classes, our usual scowling shadow. I've gotten so used to him being around that if it weren't for my bond keening in my chest for him, I wouldn't notice his presence anymore.

I wonder if I'll ever get used to the feeling, if the sharp and vicious pains in my chest at the gaping chasm between us will ever fade into background noise in my body and I won't even notice it anymore.

I desperately hope so.

The time I've been forced to spend in my room alone and studying is already starting to improve my classwork. The overwhelming feeling I'd had on my first day has eased up and I'm no longer drowning during the lectures. Sage even comments that my notes are better than hers, which makes me a smug bitch because she's a total brainiac.

It's good to know I didn't completely ruin my life while on the run.

Gabe's brooding presence keeps the chairs around us empty, but I don't give a fuck about making a heap of friends. Sage is sweet, kind, and hilarious once she opens up a bit, and that's all I need.

We sit together at lunch and when time's up she hesitates for a second. "I can... walk you over to the training center, if you want?"

I give her a half smile and jerk my head in Gabe's direction, where he's already heading our way. "I'm pretty sure my prison officer will direct me over there, but thanks. I'll message you later to cry about how freaking bad it is."

She winces and glances at Gabe. "I do not envy you. My parents wanted me to take it this year just so I had a grasp on self-defense but I pointed out that I can literally set people on fire, so I'm good. Hell, I almost killed my little brother by sneezing a few years back, so I need control, not encouragement."

I cackle at her, because I highly doubt it was really that close, and wave her off. She's heading to a politics class that sounds insanely boring that I would give my left kidney to transfer into. My eyes narrow as I watch the other students giving her a wide berth, like she's diseased, thanks to her asshole Bond.

Fuck the lot of them.

Maybe I'll try to talk her into running with me when I figure out how to get the hell out of here with this stupid GPS chip... except she'd be in danger then and not just social targeting.

"I'm starting to think you're in love with her," Gabe grumbles, and I roll my eyes at him.

"Are we going to the torture sessions or not? I'm guessing you love this class, it's your favorite, isn't it? Gross."

He huffs and stalks off, his strides so big that I practically have to jog to keep up with him. "I'm acing it, doesn't mean I love it. Vivian is a hard-ass and tries to kill us all. I hope you're in shape, or this is going to suck for you."

Considering that I'm puffing just keeping up with him, I'm going to die today. I'm going to just run myself into the ground and freaking die.

The training center is on the far side of campus and there's an outside training course fenced out in the front that looks like it was built for Navy Seals and definitely not college students. I gulp, freaking the fuck out, and Gabe laughs at me like an asshole. There's that edge to it, like he's really freaking enjoying my terror, and if I wasn't doing my best to make sure I don't touch him, I'd probably punch him.

It would also probably be like punching a wall.

The other students surrounding us are all very athletic, tall and muscular, and it becomes very obvious that I'm not just going to die here, I'm going to be utterly humiliated as well.

Fuck my life and damn North Draven to hell where he belongs.

I know before I open the door that one of my other Bonds is in the classroom. I figure out pretty quickly that it's Gryphon, because he's the only one of the four Bonds here in Oregon that I haven't spent any time around. I feel weirdly nervous about him being here, out of all of my classes for him to show up to, he chooses the one I'm most concerned about?

I'm not going to be the fastest girl there, or the strongest. I have a handle on self-defense but very little knowledge about actually fighting someone, and the moment we're put into some sort of scenario or fight, I'm going to fail because I'm doing everything I can to keep anyone from knowing I even have powers.

He's going to watch me fail.

There's something about him that makes my bond want to impress him. It's fucking stupid. I don't care about Gabe or North or that asshole Nox like that. Hell, Nox had pulled me to the front of the class and shamed me in front of all of the other students like it was nothing and, while my bond was pissed off, I was also expecting it from him.

There's something about Gryphon that might break me.

Gabe pushes the door open and ushers me in with a smirk.

I follow Gabe's lead and walk into the changing rooms to dump my bag off in the locker that has been assigned to me, a tag with *Fallows* already stuck on there. There's a uniform and a slip of paper with the combination to the locker on it.

The other girls are all laughing and talking as they change into their uniforms and I can't help but notice that they're all very toned looking. I've never cared enough about other people's opinions of me to feel self-conscious of my body but, hell, I've never been so aware of my own short-comings before.

I'm going to die.

The shorts are too short and the shirt is too long, so

it almost looks like I'm not wearing bottoms at all. None of the other girls attempt to speak to me but all of them give me a once-over like I'm diseased, whispering and murmuring without even attempting subtlety.

I take a deep breath before I walk back out into the training room, just to pull myself together and attempt to find some inner strength to get through this but... nothing. There's no secret well within myself overflowing with fortitude and confidence.

There's a heap of grumpy and self-loathing though, so I might just pull on those instead and hope for the best.

Gabe is lounging against the wall outside the changing room, laughing and joking around with some of his friends from the football team. They all fall silent when I walk out, throwing looks around at each other like they're all talking telepathically about how shit I am. Fuck, they might be, for all I know and care.

"I was about to come in there after you. You can't hide from Vivian, you know. He'd just come in here after you."

I shrug and try to hide my shock at this hard-ass *Vivian* being a man. Of course it would be another man here to push me around and ruin my life. Gabe rolls his eyes at my silence, putting on a show for his friends because he obviously doesn't want them knowing how badly my rejection hurts him. It's so obvious to me, but they all start cracking jokes about his defective Bond like I'm not standing right here listening.

Fucking pigs.

I stalk away from them, out to the front of the group, to find Gryphon standing there in Tac gear with a very old, very round man who looks like he's mad at the world that he woke up this morning and has to deal with college students.

I recognize it because I feel the exact same way.

Gryphon looks me over with cold, disinterested eyes and then glances away, which my bond does *not* like at all, but I shove the feeling aside. Vivian takes way more interest in me, frowning and staring me down.

"*You're* the Bond? You look about twelve years old, are you sure you're old enough to be here?"

I cross my arms over my chest. "Nope, can I leave now?"

Gryphon ignores my sass and walks around me to start barking out orders to the rest of the class, directing them into a training circuit that I'd rather have Sage set me on fire than complete.

Vivian looks me over again as Gryphon stalks back over and says, "I was expecting more. What's your gift? You'd better have something good for me."

For him? That's fucking weird. I shrug. "Nothing. I've got nothing for you."

Gryphon's eyes flash over to mine as he frowns but

he doesn't comment on me finally confirming all of their worst nightmares; a giftless Bond.

Fuck, I wish it were true.

Vivian's eyes narrow even more at me until they almost look closed, his mouth turning down, "I'm going to work this attitude out of you, you know. You'll break before the end of the day, I'm sure."

God, probably. I'll be lucky to last ten minutes, but I don't give him the satisfaction of saying so. I just wait for him to start directing me.

It's so much worse than I thought it would be.

Vivian makes me my own circuit to go through so he can assess where my fitness is at and my lungs are screaming within a minute. By the half hour mark, I can't feel my legs. By the hour, I can taste blood and see white dots in the comers of my vision.

It's only by my sheer stubborn will that I keep going.

When Gryphon blows a whistle sharply to signal the end of this part of the training, I'm shocked to find out I'm the only one still working out, everyone else is sitting around drinking water and watching me sweat my ass off on the elliptical.

I want to collapse onto the ground in a heap but then Gryphon calls out, "That's your warmup over with, get your asses into the control room so we can go over today's lesson plan"

Warmup?

You've got to be shitting me.

I want to kill someone, I want it so badly that my gift stirs in my chest and I have to tell it to simmer down because I can't actually lash out right now, or ever.

It takes me three tries to get my legs to work, but I stumble after the group and through the building until we 're in the control room, which just looks like a meeting room filled with security screens. They're all on and showing the empty obstacle courses, the images flicking through until I want to weep, each of them looking impossible to get through.

Gabe leans against the wall next to me, his eyes on Gryphon as he sips at his bottle of water. I'd kill for some but there's no way I'm asking him. Not when we're jammed in this room with at least fifty other students, all of them listening and judging me, because the whole campus would hear about him telling me to shove it.

So I focus back on Vivian and my scowling Bond at the front of the class.

"We're sticking to something easy. You'll be splitting into two teams and the first to get everyone through the course wins. Simple," says Vivian, scowling around at everyone, but he doesn't fool me for a second.

There's nothing easy about that. It looks impossible, freaking impossible, and when he calls out the names of people on the red team, I'm not shocked at the sounds of groans and bitching when he calls out mine to place me in the group.

I'm probably going to be the deadest weight my team has ever had.

When the teams have been named, everyone moves into the next room, grabbing armbands in either red or blue and tying them on. More than one person on my team makes snide comments about being doomed thanks to my presence but even if I felt like starting a fight, I can't.

There's no freaking way I'm getting through the course, not without help, and there isn't a single person here who isn't looking at me with open contempt.

Not even my own Bonds.

Okay, probably not the best example to use because of course the Bonds that I rejected are both looking around like they'd rather peel their own skin off than be in the same goddamn room as me. The second I get out of here today, I'm walking over to the dean's office and demanding a schedule change. I'm not doing this shit all year. I could handle the training and the workouts— it's brutal but doable— but working with other students who all would love nothing more than to watch me croak?

No.

No fucking thank you.

I'm the last person to grab an armband and Vivian

watches me tie it on with a scowl. When it's secure, I look up at him and he jerks his head to motion me over to where he's standing. I take a deep breath, preparing myself for whatever bullshit he's going to throw at me.

He's an older man, his face a little haggard and scarred, and when he talks, the thick white line through his top lip distorts the sound a little, giving him the slightest lisp. "You're at a disadvantage here because everyone else has done the course before and knows their way around it. I'll pair you with your Bond just this once, so he can get you through it."

Dear God, no. "I doubt he wants that. It's fine, if I die, then at least I don't have to do this again."

He squints at me like he thinks I'm joking but then he glances over my shoulder at whatever face Gabe is pulling right now and shrugs. "Suit yourself, I don't get involved in bond bullshit. There are three other people in the class with low-level gifts, they all do fine, but they all have their Bonded with them and are in better shape than you are."

Great.

Excellent. Perfect. I nod and slink back over to the wall where Gabe is scowling at the ground like it's personally pissed him off. The room is so loud that I almost miss it when he mumbles, "Fuck, I wish you'd never come back."

The blue team gets let in from the left side of the course, while the red takes the right. I stay towards the back of the group, mostly to stay out of the way, but also so I can see exactly where people are going. The aim here is to run the whole course and not be taken out and I'm at a disadvantage to everyone else right now, so whatever edge I can give myself will help.

There's a group of guys at the front, jostling and jeering at each other with that over-exaggerated bravado that has my eyes rolling, and a bunch of girls giggling over their antics. All of them are dressed in teeny-tiny shorts and tight tank tops, with a whole lot of toned skin on show. I'm jealous, honestly, of how great they all look, while I'm over here looking like a sack of potatoes in the oversized uniform. I've always cared about my appearance but being here, surrounded by the whispers and judgmental stares of everyone, I'm suddenly hyper-aware of every last one of my flaws.

My ass looks nothing like the amazing one the girl eyeing Gabe is rocking. He meets my eye over her head for a second before he winks at her, constant in his efforts at baiting me into jealousy. My bond isn't happy but I shove it down in my chest again because *fuck him.*

He's already made it clear he doesn't want me, all of his antics to get a rise out of me are just freaking childish.

I'm still busy picking out all of the features I'd love to have from the other girls when a buzzer sounds and the doors open. Gabe is one of the first guys to enter the course, bounding out of the room and disappearing into the thick cluster of trees right at the door. I approach slowly, glancing at Vivian and Gryphon's broody figures before I finally cross into the course.

It's so much bigger once you're in it.

I'd known that it covered a lot of ground, the fences went on for miles, but the moment the door shut behind me with a resounding *thump,* I know I'm in way over my head.

The only upside is that we're not supposed to use our gifts, so it's an even playing field for me. Wait, no, it's still not fair, because everyone else has run the course before and knows what to expect and there's also the small fact that they're all ripped and I'm not, but at least no one is going to be throwing fire balls at my head or shapeshifting or, fuck, becoming invisible and slitting my throat.

Okay, that last one might be my dramatics coming out.

The first thing I have to do is jog down to a river that I'm sure can't be real. The funding that must have gone into this program is insane. If I didn't already know that the Dravens are freaking filthy rich, I would now. The other students are all crossing it together, laughing and joking with each other because it's all normal shit to them, and I glance down at my shorts and shoes in sadness.

Running the rest of the course in wet shoes is going to be actual torture. I could take them off, who the fuck cares about the time that'll take me, but what if there's sharp rocks or... *creatures* in there?

If I think about any of the *creatures* that might be in the water, it's entirely possible I will run away screaming, which is too freaking embarrassing, so I guess I'm leaving my shoes on, soggy feet be damned.

I wait until everyone else has made it through the water, watching them as they make it across. There's a sinkhole if you head straight through the middle of the path, and everyone is avoiding the left-hand side, so there must be a reason for that.

Once they've disappeared through the thick trees again, I get to work, wincing at the freezing temperature but gritting my teeth and just walking straight in. I really, really hate it. The mud is thick enough that I can feel it seeping into my shoes and when I finally get to the other side, I have to pull my shoes off to attempt to empty the slime out.

When I've done my best to empty them and tied my sneakers back on, I glance up to find Gabe bounding off into the trees, as if he'd stopped to watch me. My bond crows in my chest, like it's a victory that he gives a fuck about me making it through, but for all I know, he was hoping to see me drown.

The sadness that clings to him when I'm around says he's worried about me, but I don't want to think about that.

I then have to run for another quarter mile, the ground far more rough and dangerous in wet, slimy shoes. I'm freezing and my thighs are chafing, thanks to the water and the shorts, and I kinda want to die.

I'm going to call North and tear strips off of him for this stupid class.

The trees clear again and I find most of the other students running away from the next obstacle, already having completed it and gaining more of a lead on me. I can spot Gabe's back as he leaves me behind, without a second glance this time, and I take a deep breath.

Barbed wire is strung up along posts, low to the ground, as the students all army-crawl their way under it. By the time they each make it out on the other side, they're covered in dirt and mud, scrapes and cuts along their arms because this isn't about pushing us all, it's about destroying our wills and breaking us down.

I don't wait around this time, the longer I look at the barbed wire, the less I want to crawl under it, so there's still other students making their way through it in front of me. Granted, they're all taking it a lot better than I am, barely making a goddamn sound while I'm grunting and panting my way through, but I try not to focus on that.

At least being out of shape helps me shimmy my way under the wire, thanks to my complete lack of ass. I take the lead over the girl in front of me, thanks to her having to watch out for her amazing bubble butt. I'm no longer jealous that she has one.

Okay, I'm still just a little jealous.

My arms are tom to pieces when I finally get to the end and I have to do my best to brush away the gravel and sticks that are glued to the wounds. The girl I shimmied past doesn't bother cleaning herself up, she just throws me a savage look and sprints off down the path like this is all a regular Friday afternoon for her.

What a freaking psycho.

I take the next quarter mile at a slow jog, every part of my body screaming for me to stop. There's definitely going to be blisters all over my poor, soggy feet when this shit is over with. I focus on my breathing and tell myself that this is all going to end soon. I could be wrong, there could be fifty more stupid things to climb under and over and through, but my mind might break if I think about it too much.

When the clearing finally appears out of nowhere, tears are prickling at the comers of my eyes and my nose is running. I must look like a complete mess and I'm grateful that no one is around to see me like this.

The next obstacle is an A-frame with netting over it and a large pool of muddy water underneath it, a smell wafting up from it that turns my stomach. If I fall in that, there's a one hundred percent chance of me ending up with a flesh-eating bacteria, so even if I'm going to bomb out of this shit today, this is not the obstacle I'm going to tank on.

I'm not sure any of my Bonds would believe I need medical care before I freaking died.

My arms shake and my fingers are completely numb as I try to grasp the rope netting, so I slow down, race be damned, and gingerly test out my grip until I'm sure I'm not going to slip and fall before I start the climb over the A-frame. I don't give a damn if I'm the last person to cross the line, getting there is enough for me.

I can think about the team when the team starts to give a fuck about me.

When I reach the top, I have to take a second to choke down the vomit climbing up my throat, the coppery tang of blood in my mouth, and I just sit there and take some deep, gulping breaths. I can see the end of the course from here, the line of trees right before the gate to get the hell out of this hellhole, and I give myself another deep breath before I climb down the other side.

I'm almost done, almost out of this place and back to my dorm room to die in peace, away from all of these judgmental eyes.

Not that there's anyone left in this place.

I don't think anyone else is having the trouble that I am getting through the course, and it's been at least an hour since I last saw someone. Considering this is supposed to be a race, that's not so strange, but as the ropes dig into my hands as I slip and scramble my way down, I find myself a little frantic to get out of here. I'm so close to being done, so freaking close, and I don't need to fall into a trap now and ruin everything.

I have to jog for another quarter mile before I finally see the fence and the gate through the trees. I want to yell out in victory but my lungs are screaming in my chest and I think I'm going to vomit everywhere the second I cross the finish line. I need to get in shape if this is going to be my life now but knowing that I've actually managed to survive my first class without dying or making a fool of myself?

Incredible.

The moment I reach the tree line, my guard is down, so I don't see the shadow of the girl until it's too late. The fist to my head knocks me out cold.

I wake up in a white room.

White walls, white floor, white sheets on the white bed. Jesus, it's like a nightmare I've woken up in and I have to tell myself that being knocked out means I must be in the medical bay area of the training center.

Then the white door opens and it's definitely a freaking nightmare.

North walks through, a sour look on his face as he stares down at me with disapproval. "If you're planning on hurting yourself to get my attention regularly, I should warn you that I'll be happy to throw you in a padded cell until you grow out of the compulsion."

It takes me a second to realize that he's angry at me,

that he's not here out of some sort of concern for me and that he thinks that I was assaulted on the freaking course as a way to act out against him.

"I know you're not here to ream me out right now over some bitch taking a cheap swing at me. I know you wouldn't be here for that because if you are, I'm going to lose my fucking mind."

His eyes narrow at me as he watches me struggle to sit up, one of my hands clutching at my pounding head and sure enough, there's a lump where the girl's fist connected with my skull.

My head is spinning and I can feel my stomach churning, bile creeping up the back of my throat as he takes a second to look me over properly. It's clear he doesn't believe me and that he's not at all impressed with this supposed charade.

I could freaking *scream.*

"Why would I wait until the last quarter mile to pull a stunt like that? Why would I wade through the river, crawl on my belly over rocks and dirt, and climb that stupid, stinking frame if I was planning on... wait, what exactly do you think I did to knock myself out? Jesus fucking Christ." I fling my arm at him in frustration and instantly regret it when my head starts screaming again. I gag a little and have to swallow quickly to stop myself from puking all over his shoes.

North is hard to read with his cold eyes and expressionless face but for a second, I think I see him doubt himself, but it's such a fleeting thing that it's gone before I'm sure I've seen it. "I'm not so easy to fool, you're desperate for attention and with two of your Bonds present, you couldn't help yourself."

If there was ever a time I needed my gift, it's right the fuck now. I no longer care about his shoes, if chewing him out means I'm puking on them then so be it. "How was I getting attention from either of them if Gabe ran off ahead of me and Gryphon didn't even acknowledge my existence?"

The look on his face says there's a nerve there I've hit, but hell if I know what it is. "You should be thanking him. Gryphon had you run the easy course."

The easy course? Fuck this, I'm not going back to that freaking class and I'm not sitting around for this utter bullshit interrogation he's conducting. I grit my teeth again and pull back the sheet that's covering my legs, wincing at the mud and grass stains all over them. I look like a mess and it takes me two tries to get my legs steady beneath me, but the second I'm sure my legs won't collapse, I high-tail it out of the room.

North barely has to adjust his stride to keep up with me, his hand wrapping around my elbow to tug me in the right direction when I was about to make a wrong turn.

"You can't just storm out whenever you're called out for toxic behavior."

Icy rage trickles down my spine and when I rip my arm out of his grasp, there's too much force in it because my gift slips the tight hold I have on it just a little. North frowns at his hand like he's questioning if he really felt the extra kick of power, and I freak out a little.

Distraction.

I need to get his mind off of it right the hell now.

"You'd know a lot about toxic, did it ever occur to you that maybe you shouldn't threaten your own damn Bond? That maybe telling me you'll chain me to your basement probably isn't the way to go about this whole... mess?"

I say it loud enough that some of the other students loitering around hear me and start murmuring amongst themselves and not only does North notice them as well, but for the first time, I think I might see him look embarrassed.

Not at his actions, but that people are talking about him.

His lip curls and when he grabs my arm again, I feel his gift thrumming through his fingers, pulsing like a warning of the power he hides underneath his polished suits and perfectly sedate smiles.

He's careful with the way he drags me out of the building, making sure no one can actually tell that he's physically dragging me through the building and out to his waiting car. "I think that if you hadn't run away like a selfish, manipulative, childish little girl, we would've given you the world. There wasn't a thing on this Earth you could've asked for that we would've refused you, but now you're facing the consequences of your actions for what I'm sure is the first time in your life. It is very clear to me that you've been nothing but spoiled your whole life and can't think of anyone but yourself. Clearly your parents—"

I barely hold myself in check. "Don't you fucking *dare* speak about my parents. I will dig the tracker out with my bare hands and be gone, don't push me."

The driver hears all of this as he opens the door in time for North to shove me in without comment, shutting it firmly behind me as his asshole boss steps away and then they stand together, ignoring me completely as they have a nice chat about the weather or some other useless bullshit.

I'm raging mad.

That's a really freaking bad idea, I know it is because my gift starts stirring in my gut, my skin is tingling, and my vision slowly starts whiting out.

I turn into a freaking glow bug and there's no freaking way I can light up in this goddamn car today with one of my Bonds standing right the hell there. I screw my eyes shut and slow down my breathing, counting and humming under my breath so I have something else to focus on, but

I've been fighting against my gift for too long for it to quieten down easily.

The panic that soaks through my skin will only make things worse but I can't stop it from happening. I can feel the sweat starting to bead on my forehead and my breathing starts to stutter and shake so badly that there's no hiding the spiral I'm in. I might pass out.

There's a buzzing sound that breaks my concentration.

I blink rapidly, trying to clear the glow from my eyes but even though I can only just see the bag sitting at my feet, I recognize it as my own immediately.

It's my cell phone buzzing.

I dig around in there with shaking hands until I find it, a text from Atlas there for me and even though my stomach is still a mess of rage and anxiety, the comers of my mouth lift up at the sight of the little blue dot next to his name.

How does he always know when I need something to pull me out of a spiral?

I know the Dr avens are filthy rich but what are the rest of the Bonds doing for cash? I'm one more shitty Econ class away from dropping out and mooching off of them. Tell me one of them is decent and loaded, I need to figure out which one to befriend.

I snort at him, mostly because thanks to our constant messaging I know he's joking and would never accept anything from any of them, and send a text back.

I'd rather stick pins in my eyes than take anything from any of them but if you 're fine selling your ass to them for an easy life, then -who am I to judge? Who knows, you might actually get along with them.

I'm still grinning down at my phone, the three dots popping up as he starts to type out his reply, when the passenger door opens and North slides into the backseat with me. My vision is back to normal, so I think I must have my gift back under control, but it doesn't matter anyway because North doesn't look at me, not so much as a glance.

I should feel relief but honestly it just pisses me off how quickly he can dismiss me, just block me out like I'm freaking *nothing* to him, while I'm still struggling with all of the bullshit he's thrown my way. I huff under my breath, sounding exactly like the petulant child he thinks I am, but he ignores me for his phone.

Two can play at that game.

I chat with Atlas, more flirting than anything else, and focus entirely on my screen. At first I'm only doing it to fuck with North, but Atlas is too good as a distraction and when I tell him that I'm messing with the other Bonds because they're being assholes, he's more than happy to keep me busy.

I'm not sure he's ever going to get past them sticking that tracker under my skin.

When the car finally comes to a halt and the engine stops, I glance up and startle at my surroundings because we are definitely not at the dorms. Hell, we're not even on campus anymore! The house we've stopped in front of isn't a house at all, it's a freaking mansion, and it only takes a quick glance around to see we're clearly in a gated community of mega-mansions.

North has brought me back to his house.

I glance over to find him staring back at me, his eyes like a cold void as the contempt he has for me oozes out at me.

Fuck him. I cross my arms and slump back in my seat. "I am not getting out of this car."

The driver immediately gets out of the front seat and steps around to open my car door, like he's hoping I'll cave to his boss just because of this one little act of consideration.

Joke's on him, I don't give a fuck.

"I don't know why you enjoy being threatened, Fallows, but rest assured that I will do whatever it takes to get you out of this car. We're here to eat dinner with the rest of your Bonds, put the phone away and get moving."

I get out of the car but only because I can't argue with North once he gets out unless I follow him. The driver shuts the door behind me and locks it, as though he's afraid I'm going to try to climb back in it at any moment if spooked.

Irritation creeps up my spine but before I have the chance to snap and snarl at them both, North dismisses him with a polite nod of his head and says, "I'm sure you can eat here tonight without being a complete brat about it if you try hard enough, Fallows. No self-mutilation required."

He turns to walk up the path that leads to the front door without a glance back at me while my brain fusses over his words. *Self-mutilation?* What the hell does he mean by that?

Then it hits me.

I'd rather stick pins in my eyes than take anything from any of them. That's what I'd just said to Atlas and North wasn't close enough to have read the message over my shoulder. MotherfwcA;e/-.

A hot flush starts over my cheeks and works its way down my body. "You fucking asshole! You have my phone tapped?"

He straightens his tie and stalks off toward the house, his long stride meaning I have to jog to catch up to him, but I'm not letting him just walk away from me. "That's a gross invasion of privacy—"

"No, it's the consequences of your actions. That's my phone. I provided you with access to it so that I can contact you, not so you could whine to Bassinger about the privileges that I've already afforded you. You attend school thanks to me. You have a bed to sleep in, food to eat, access to your Bonds and that phone *thanks to me.* And what do I receive in return? A brat for a Bond who wants to sit around complaining about the people she betrayed."

He opens the front door by pressing his finger against a scanner, because of course he'd live in a pompous, avant-garde house in an exclusive gated community, and then he stalks in without so much as glancing my way to make sure I'm following him.

I could run.

The chip doesn't even matter to me anymore, death doesn't sound so bad when the alternative is staying here with this fucking asshole of a man who thinks he *owns me* just because we share a bond. Who does he think he is? Being a councilman doesn't make him a god, for fuck's sake!

I'm either about to bolt or tear North a new asshole when I spot the driver, who is now holding the front door open for me with his eyes averted away from the spectacle we're making, like this is all such a shameful thing.

My cheeks heat.

Would he run after me and stop me, tackle me to the ground, and berate me for being the villain to all of these upstanding men in our society? Now I'm imagining an entire TacTeam appearing out of nowhere and taking me the hell out. God, my bones still ache from when they found me and dragged me here, I don't want to go through that again.

I step into the mansion and try not to gape at the sight of it. Marble floors, plush rugs, art on the walls, everything looks so goddamn expensive that I'm afraid to breathe on something and break it.

"This way, Fallows,"

I startle at North's savage tone and scurry after him, trying not to look as freaked out as I am. There's paintings of a lot of old, rich-looking guys on the walls, probably generations of Draven men, and I feel too freaking intimidated to function.

The hallway is long and wider than my room back at the dorms, with doors leading off to other giant, ornate rooms. By the time we both arrive at the dining room, I can definitively say that I couldn't make my way out of here if you paid me, and that just might be North's angle here.

I freeze in the doorway at the sight of the huge table, easily big enough for thirty people, and North takes the opportunity to hook his fingers around my elbow and tug me over to one end, depositing me into a seat next to Gabe, who is already piling a plate full of roast meats.

He barely glances at me but grunts out a greeting to North, who takes a seat at the head of the table to my right. No one speaks and I sit there sullenly, fuming over the phone tapping and the fact that this is my life now. North fills a plate with a little of everything and then slides it over to me without a word.

Controlling asshole.

I don't want to eat it just on principle, but the moment the amazing smell hits my nostrils, my stomach growls and I give in, tucking into the food.

The table is silent, only the soft sounds of our cutlery gently scraping our plates can be heard. The food is amazing but I can't enjoy it with all of the tension in the room. I kind of want to just inhale it down and then ask to go back to the empty shell of a room I now call home, but with everything that's happened today, I'm not sure that's an option.

"How are your classes, Fallows?"

I glance up at North but he's still not looking at me. I push my carrots around the plate as I wonder why the fuck he even bothers pretending to care. "They're fine. I've already caught up. I've made a few friends."

His eyes narrow at Gabe. "Who?"

My mouth drops open. Well, I guess I should be happy my suspicions have been confirmed. He's been hanging around me to spy for North. Freaking perfect.

"Sage Benson. She's a Flame, she seems nice enough. Hasn't encouraged any adventures," Gabe mumbles, looking miserable even as he eats enough food to feed me for an entire week.

North's head tilts as he frowns at him. "Benson? Maria's Bonded daughter? Isn't she one of Riley's Bonds?"

Gabe nods again, sighing as he looks over at me. "Yeah, her and Giovanna. She fucking hates Giovanna as well, so she's trying to focus on her studies. Oleander and Sage have been pulling extra hours in the library."

I put my knife and fork down. There's no way I'm going to sit here and listen to the freaking debrief.

North notices straight away. "Not to your liking, Fallows? I'll let the chef know for next week."

"Next week? I'm not coming back again."

Gabe stiffens, his movements getting jerkier, but he doesn't stop eating. I'm not sure anything would stop him at this point.

North watches him and then turns to me with a sharp glare. "You'll be here every Friday for the foreseeable future. It's taken a few weeks for me to nail down a day that works for us all but now that I have, this is going to be a regular occurrence."

I scoff. "I can see everyone seems to be taking it seriously. Can I leave now? My curfew starts in ten minutes and I don't want to be late."

Gabe winces and takes a big gulp of his beer. Of course he gets alcohol and I get freaking water. What I wouldn't give for a vodka soda or a beer or something right now. Anything to take the edge off because I can feel the bullshit in the air, like things are only going to get worse.

"Your curfew isn't an issue during our dinners. My chef put a lot of work into cooking us all dinner, Fallows. The least you could do is eat it."

My lip curls and I'm about to rip him a new asshole when the door opens and in walks Gryphon. He ignores me entirely and takes a seat further down the table where he won't have to look at me.

I roll my eyes— can any of them at least pretend to be civil— and then Nox stumbles through the door with one of his many little groupies tucked under his arm, giggling like a child.

My idiot, traitorous bond keens in my chest.

I don't fucking care what the asshole does but apparently my bond does.

"Oh, if it isn't my little poisonous Bond. Are you here to ruin dinner for us all? How about you do what you do best and run off and leave us all to our meal in peace."

Two minutes ago I desperately wanted to leave this table, and now I'm going to eat every last thing on my plate, even if I freaking choke on it.

Fuck Nox Draven.

The groupie giggles as she slides into her chair. North ignores her presence entirely but says to his brother, "You're late. If you're not going to be able to make it to dinner, please tell me beforehand. I can reschedule."

Nox shrugs and the little giggling bitch slumps into the chair next to Gryphon, leaning into his body to grab a plate.

My bond doesn't like that.

Not one little bit.

Gryphon glances up to meet my eyes and I hold his gaze for a second, completely transfixed by the rage in my chest, before he glances away and breaks the moment.

He doesn't push her away.

I grip my knife so hard my fist shakes. I think about everything I want to say right now, all of the home truths I could give these arrogant, ungrateful, asshole bonds, and then I swallow them back down.

The high road is definitely not for me and walking it just might kill me.

I manage to get through dinner without stabbing any of my Bonds or the giggling nightmare that Nox had brought with him, which in itself is a miracle because after we finish the main course, there is an elaborate spread of desserts brought out by a horde of North's household staff.

Everything looks amazing and anything chocolate is an absolute must for me but on principle, I once again attempt to refuse.

North fills me another plate to the brim.

I don't know if this is just him trying to prove his dominance over me or he's trying to say something about all of the extra curves I have compared to the gorgeous, rail-thin women he likes. Okay, I'm generalizing a helluva lot here because I've only seen one of North's hookups and you can't pick a man's taste from a pool that small, but there's something about him that screams 'fussy, pushy billionaire with a taste for models' to me.

I eat a little of everything.

The chocolate torte is a religious experience and I have to smother a moan of delight because there's no way I want any of them knowing just how much I love it. I realize I must make some kind of noise because Gabe startles next to me and shoots me a look like he's never seen me before.

Interesting.

"So, Oli, I heard you have no gift. That's gotta suck."

There goes my chocolate high. I turn in my seat to look at the giggling groupie who's staring back at me like I'm a bad smell in the room. Gryphon is blatantly ignoring her, talking with North about new training programs he's starting with the TacTeams, and Gabe is focused entirely on the plate of dessert in front of him. It's actually the first time I've seen him eat something that isn't super healthy and he's scarfing it down like it's his last meal on death row.

Nox stares me down from across the table like he'd enjoy nothing more than picking the meat from my charred bones.

Maybe he's a shifter, because the look in his eyes is all predator.

I stare the girl down as I shrug, keeping my voice casual and unaffected, "I'm not losing sleep over it."

She giggles again and I swear the sound of it is going to haunt me. "I just can't believe it, being the Central Bond to these guys and having *nothing.* How shameful. No wonder they all get around, no one would stick around for a defect like you."

My hand clenches around my fork again, but this time I can't hold myself back from snapping back at her, "What's your gift? When I stab you with this fork, will you heal straight away, or can you only do something shitty, like talk to pigeons or shit gold?"

Gabe snorts and then slaps a hand over his mouth like he's been caught cavorting with the enemy, glancing at North like he'll get grounded. I roll my eyes but I know how to take my wins where I can and 1 lean in to mockingly whisper, "She looks like the type of girl who can change her nail color at will."

Gabe clears his throat and replies, "Ashlee is an Elemental. She can conjure water but only enough to fill a jug."

I burst out laughing. I might look like a bitch to them all right now but I was always taught to not start fights, just be sure as shit to finish them. "Wow, that sure makes me envious of you, *Ashlee."*

Her eyes flash at the sarcasm dripping from my

words and she snaps back, "Big words from a girl with nothing. Do you really have no shame for being such a disappointment?"

It might be stupid but I shrug. "I guess you'll never know."

Gabe pushes the plate away from himself and clears his throat. "I'm heading back to the dorms. I'll drop you back, Fallows... unless you want North to?"

Fuck no I don't.

I try not to look as eager and relieved as I am as I push up from the table, gritting my teeth as I choke out a terse, "Thank you for dinner," to North so he can't accuse me of being a brat again.

No one else acknowledges that we're leaving, so I turn my back on them all and practically run after Gabe. He might be an asshole to me at Draven but right now, he's my only ally since he's getting me the fuck out of here.

I barely take in any of our surroundings as we weave our way through the giant maze of a house. My phone vibrates in my pocket as I step out into the sprawling garage, just barely pulling my attention away from the millions of dollars' worth of vehicles stored here. As I follow Gabe over to one of the motorbikes, I dig my phone out of my pocket.

I miss you, Oli.

I have no idea how to even answer that. No freaking

clue at all, and then when I remember that North is reading all of the messages, my stomach sinks like lead a little more.

I shove my phone back into my pocket just in time to see Gabe grab a helmet from one of his packs and hold it out to me. I stare at it and then up at him, but he smirks and shrugs back.

"If you don't want North or Nox to drive you home, then this is it, Fallows."

He makes a great point.

I take the helmet and pull it out, fumbling with the strap a little to tighten it. He watches me, looking like he wants to reach over and help, but restrains himself, and once I'm set, he climbs onto the motorbike, holding an arm out to help me on as the garage door opens in front of us.

I haven't been on one for years.

I can't think about my father and his love of dirt bikes right now. I can't think about being six years old and sitting in front of him on one, my long dark hair whipping around us both as he drove around the tracks. I remember feeling as though we were going so fast when we were probably only going a few miles an hour.

There's still a moment of deja vu as I slide into the seat behind Gabe, hesitating for a second before wrapping my arms around his waist and pressing myself against his back as the engine roars to life underneath us. He kicks the stand up and away and then we're off, flying out of the garage and down the paved driveway without a care for anyone around us.

Gabe drives like he's ready to die and that's something I can get behind.

Even after years of being on the run and doing everything I could to survive, there's some deep and dark part of me who hears the call of messy vehicular death on the asphalt and desperately craves it. I wonder how badly my Bonds would hate me then, to know that I'd choose a grisly death over being forced to stick around the lot of them.

Imagining their reactions keeps me busy the entire ride back to the dorms.

Gabe kills the engine the second we pull up, but he doesn't move from the seat as I swing off. I hand him the helmet and clear my throat a little, awkward as hell now that I have to acknowledge him helping me out.

He saves me from trying. "Ashlee is a fucking bitch but you should be prepared. Nox is going to bring someone every week and you can't threaten them all. Crystal is a Flame and she'll singe your eyebrows off the first second she can. Also, Yasmine is a living Voodoo Doll and she'll stab herself without a second thought."

I scoff and adjust my bag on my back. "Of course he fucks crazy, he seems like the type."

Gabe shrugs and looks out over the street so he doesn't have to look at me as he replies, "You can't blame him, you're the one who ran away and ruined everything."

When my alarm wakes me the next morning, I feel a pooling of dread deep in my gut.

I lay there in the pokey bed to try to figure out why my entire body feels like lead, why the thought of climbing out of this bed fills me with the icy tendrils of fear, but there's nothing, no reason for me to be dragging my ass today.

So I push the feeling away and get up.

The communal bathrooms are busy and as much as I hate being in there, I never actually got to shower after the mess that was the TT class yesterday and my legs are still covered in dirt, so it's a nonnegotiable.

The longer I'm here on campus, the better I'm getting at blocking out the shit these petty girls have to say to me. Most of them have taken to pretending I don't exist, like the crimes I committed by running away mean that I'm not worth a second of their time, so they're all shunning me.

I can handle that.

It's the four or five of them who are petty, mouthy assholes that make living here a nightmare. I scrub down as quickly as I can and dress in the stall. I'm not dumb enough to walk out in a towel because even with the campus-wide rules about appropriate gift usage, I wouldn't trust any of them not to mess with me while I was vulnerable like that.

By the time Gabe arrives at my door to walk me down, I'm too busy fussing with my bag full of assignments to take much notice of him or the fact that he's absolutely seething with fury.

It's not until we reach the cafeteria that I find out that the entire student body is subdued. I'm not used to standing in line without there being nasty jibes in the giggles of ridiculous gossip following me. But all of that is missing now.

I glance back and finally spot the mood Gabe is in.

"Something happened? I just thought you hated being around me, but now it's pretty clear that it's not just you," I ask hesitantly. I'm fairly certain that even with me leaving him on read last night, Atlas still would have told me if whatever happened was big enough for news to hit the East Coast. This must be local.

"You know that some of the Bonds and Bonded are going missing now, right? Well, three more were taken last night. A fourth person was found dead."

He sounds miserable, so I leave it for a second, until we're both seated at our usual table, and then I ask, "Did you know the person who died?"

He shoves his plate away from himself and rubs a hand

over his face with a sigh. “He was on the football team with me. He was one of the seniors, but he had taken me under his wing because he was shifter too and he knew how hard it is to control the change in such a violent game.”

Right.

I can’t even enjoy the fact that he’s just told me his gift, because bile is creeping up the back of my throat. The Resistance was here last night, they took people and I, for one, know exactly what’s going to happen to them.

It takes a second for me to be able to choke out, “I’m sorry. I know what it feels like to lose someone like that, I’m really sorry.”

The words are too revealing, the shock making me less careful, but he’s too distracted to see it. He just shakes his head as if to clear it and says, “Brayden was a good kid; he didn’t deserve it. It’s pretty obvious that he was killed because he was trying to stop them from taking the others. The Resistance aren’t after shifters. One of his Bonded was taken, and I’d like to get her back. I know he’s dead and it doesn’t really matter to him anymore, but for his memory, I’d like to get her back.”

A fine tremble starts in my fingers at the thought of him getting too close to those people after everything I’ve done to keep them away. Even if he had noticed the changes in me, he’d have no clue that’s why I’m so shaken.

A few of his football buddies walk past and they give

him a slap on the shoulder as they go. He grabs his plate again to try and eat something and once he is no longer folded over in misery, I find myself able to eat as well. I'm so lost in my thoughts about the Resistance and how desperately I need to get out of here, that I don't notice when Sage approaches until she pulls the chair up beside me and takes a seat.

"You heard about Brayden, then?" she murmurs, and I nod my head.

"Is Riley okay? I know he lives over in the boys' dorms."

Sage grimaces. "He is living at Giovanna's house at the moment. He has been for months."

Gabe pegs her with a stern look. "They're Bonded, he's supposed to want to live with her."

Sage flinches, but it's only really noticeable to me because I know what it looks like when you're trying to hide it. My fingers start to tremble with something that isn't fear. "Do you have to be such an insensitive dick about it? It's not like she was saying she was pissed off about it."

He smirks at me. "Oh, so you're a bleeding heart about your girlfriend but don't give a shit about your Bonds? Maybe Nox is right and you really are a lesbian. That would explain a lot."

Fuck, I wish I was. I bump Sage gently with my shoulder and give her a little smile. "I'm glad he's safe and

I'm sorry you guys are still... struggling."

Sage smiles at me and shrugs. "It is what it is. I'm glad he's safe too, as long as he's alive I guess there's a chance we can work things out."

Gabe winces a little. "Sorry, Sage. I didn't mean to be a dick about it. I'm just... fucked up over Brayden and my own mess of a bond."

Ouch.

I ignore it and give her a smile back instead. "Do you want to hit up the library this afternoon? I'd love some help with the Econ assignment we both have. You're like a freaking genius with that stuff."

Sage giggles and shrugs, but it's clearly forced. "I'm really not. Plus, you're doing so great catching up. There's no way I would be where you are if I'd dropped out freshman year of high school, you're amazing."

Gabe's eyes snap up to mine. "You dropped out of high school?"

I squirm in my seat. I'd assumed North had told him and the rest of my Bonds but apparently not. "I was on the move too much to still attend. I spent a lot of time in libraries though."

I don't know why I'm even explaining myself to him. It must be something to do with the raw look in his eyes after his friend's death, but I should've known better.

"You were that fucking intent on escaping us all that

you dropped out of high school? Fuck, Fallows, you're a real fucking bitch."

He shoves his plate away, still half full, and storms off. I rub a hand over my face and finally give up on my own plate. What's the fucking point?

"Sorry. I just keep getting you into trouble with him, I need to learn to shut my mouth," Sage mumbles, and I want to hug her to me to get rid of all of that self-loathing she has trapped inside her. It's an echo of my own but I'm better at hiding mine around everyone.

"If it weren't you, he'd just find something else to take out on me and you know what? I did run away from him. He's not wrong about that part, so I guess I deserve his anger."

Sage stands and grabs her book bag, waiting for me to do the same, and then walks with me to our Econ class. "I've only known you a few weeks and already know something else must have been going on, Oli."

I give her a side-eye and she shrugs again. "I'm not asking for details, I know it must be really bad if you don't want to tell your Bonds and get them off of your back. I just want you to know that I believe you're a good person, no matter what they say."

I must be hormonal or something because that makes me want to bawl my eyes out in the bathroom for a few hours. Instead, I link my arm through hers and whisper back, "You'll be the first person I do tell. If I ever can, that is."

Sage and I spend two hours after our classes let out for the day at the library together and it is honestly the most peace I have felt since arriving at Draven University. The panic I was feeling about my assignments starts to ease once she has walked me through her previous assignments with our Econ teacher and I know what to expect. I have a decent outline and a plan on how to get it done, I'm going to freaking kill it!

I can't wait to see North's face when I bring home an A. That'll teach him to assume I'm some brain-dead dropout.

My stomach rumbles loudly and I check my watch and notice that my curfew is only a half hour away. I sigh and give Sage a self-loathing smile, pissed that I'm going to have to flake out on her once again. "My jailer will be pissed if I'm not locked up back in my tower soon. Sorry, I'd really love to stay for a few more hours if I could. This has been so great."

Sage chews at her lip for a moment and then gives me a shy smile, her dimples flashing. "How do you feel about margaritas and tacos?"

My smile brightens. "I feel amazing about those things. We have to do it in my room though; North knows exactly where I am, so I can't even use the common rooms at the dorms."

Sage winces. “That doesn’t seem very... normal. I think your Bond might be a possessive dickhead.”

I burst into laughter. “Yeah, I sort of get that feeling too. If you don’t mind my boring-ass room, I’d love to hang.”

She looks so happy and shocked that I’m down that I wrap my arm around her shoulders to give her a little squeeze. She’s so freaking broken, so much more than me.

Or, I guess, she just wears her damage where we can all see it. I bury mine as deep as I can, as far down below my skin as possible, so I can pretend it’s not killing me slowly, painfully, constantly. Even now, just thinking about the fact I have damage, not even what that damage is, makes my blood run cold. Fuck.

I shake it off as I try to hand Sage some cash, what little I have left from my time out there in the world by myself, and she shrugs me off. “My treat this time. I know North won’t let you get a job, so it’s the least I can do.”

I roll my eyes at her. “You’re the one who is helping me out. I should definitely be buying dinner.”

She giggles at me as we both stand and start to make our way out of the library together. “Oh, yeah? How good is your fake ID to get us those margaritas?”

Damn. I forgot about that. I sigh dramatically, lifting my hands up to the sky like I’m imploring some benevolent god in the sky. “It *was* fantastic, but then North got a hold of it and now it is no more."

Sage laughs and threads her arm through mine. "Yeah, I guessed that. No worries, Riley hooked me up with a good one."

The smile slides right off of her face at the mention of his name. I kind of want to meet him just so I can see if he is as great as she thinks he is underneath all of this drama.

I'd also like to chew him out a bit for her, just tear into him for not seeing how freaking amazing she is.

I squeeze her arm. "Ok, rule one for the night: no more talking about our idiot Bonds. Let's stick to the important stuff, like what color I should dye my hair next. I'm thinking lime green streaks."

I don't add that I'm thinking lime green because I'm sure that will piss North off the most, because I'm serious about keeping the conversation away from the guys. I haven't had the chance to hang out with other girls my age since I was fourteen and my whole world changed, so I'm so freaking excited about having the chance now.

Plus, Sage is a really great person. An A plus, amazing human being that doesn't deserve the piles of shit Riley and Giovanna keep heaping on her.

They should count their blessings that I can't use my powers, otherwise they'd both be royally fucked.

We have to part ways outside the library so I can make my curfew and Sage can grab our food. She jumps into her cute, rundown little VW Bug and I take a quick photo on my phone at how freaking adorable she looks in it. I save the photo on her contact in my phone and grin at it a little more. Shit, having a friend is so much better than I remembered.

Mostly, my pre-teen friends were all about the drama. We used to fight over clothes and boys, none of the other girls were Gifted, so they didn't understand why I insisted on crushing on like twelve guys at once.

I remember one of the girls saying I was going to be a whore like my mom and that she'd seen guys coming in and out of our house all the time. My mom was the Central Bond and I had three dads. I can't remember why we lived amongst humans, I feel like it had something to do with my mom's job, but they tried their best to be discreet about it.

I kind of blew it that day when I told Alexandra Hargraves that all three of my dads could kick her scrawny dad's ass if she didn't learn to shut her petty gossiping mouth.

My mom was not happy with me.

I got three consecutive high-fives from my dads though.

Worth it.

The memory keeps me happy and warm inside the entire walk back to the dorms.

"A lavender rinse? You want me to turn my hair the same color as the old bitties at the milk bar?" I choke on the margaritas and Sage giggles at me uncontrollably.

There's bags spread out over my bed and the floor all around us, overflowing with snacks and beauty products because Sage decided on her way over that a girls night would only work for us both if she got to mess around with my makeup.

I wonder how long it's been since she got to do something like this, because it's been years since I have. I also kind of think she's guessed that and wants to do something special because she's too sweet like that.

"You told me you can't stand the silver look, which is crazy because the last time I tried to go icy blonde it cost me a fortune and never lightened up enough for me to pull it off."

Drinking and talking about this stuff isn't a smart idea but there's something reckless in me about our friendship. Like the years of not having anyone at all to speak to or confide in has made me stupid about her softly spoken kindnesses.

I refuse to look at my reflection in the mirror by the door as I answer her, "It's not about the color, it's the memories that come with it. I tried dyeing it back to black a few years ago but it never really took. It's like my hair... rejected it."

I risk a glance over to where Sage is refilling both of our cups but she's frowning a little at the concoction of alcohol and sugar she's devised. "Well, what's the worst that can happen with the purple dye? If it doesn't take, then at least we've given it a shot and if it does, no more memories about... bad things chasing you."

The rest of the night is a blur of drinks, purple dye all over my sheets, and standing in the communal showers in my underwear with Sage at three in the morning to wash the shit out. It's messy and stupid and completely freaking life-saving.

We both wake up a few hours later hungover and

desperate for food.

Gabe doesn't show up to walk me to class and North messages me to say I still have to attend without my scowling shadow, which is fine by me. I get looks and whispers the whole day but the pounding in my head drowns most of it out and I make it through, thanks to Sage's equally hungover presence.

When classes finish for the day, she glues herself to my side as we walk over to my dorm. The joint assignment we have is basically done anyway but I've quickly figured out that Sage would much rather hang out in my pathetic dorm room with me than go home. She never comments on the pathetic lack of stuff I have or how horribly uncomfortable the bed is, she just acts like this situation is completely normal.

It's vital to my survival.

She's become the rock for me, the one person who is keeping my sanity tethered because if I didn't have her, I'm sure I would be a screaming, raging mess by now.

When we get to her car to drop off her extra textbooks, her phone pings and she rolls her eyes at whatever is on the screen.

"Riley? Or that bitch, Giovanna?"

Sage huffs and says, "Neither, it's my dad. My parents are pissed about how 'withdrawn' I've become. Because in their world, it's fine for me to be shunned but totally unreasonable for me to then refuse to go out to any social gatherings. Mom and I argued about it all this morning and now Dad is pleading with me to go to the football game."

I shrug and hike my bag higher onto my shoulders, "Do you hate football? I could... maybe figure something out and we could both go?"

I don't want to have to call North, but if this is important to her then I'll do it. Sage gives me a shy look back. "I actually sort of love football. My brother plays. I miss going there, but I hate being there by myself because sitting with my parents is like torture. My mom still blames me for ruining things with Riley."

Fuck that. I'm calling my asshole Bond and we're going, no matter what it costs me.

I hit dial and take a deep breath, preparing myself for the fight this will be, and the cold tone of North's voice as he answers sets my teeth on edge. "I'm about to walk into a meeting, Fallows, this isn't a good time."

Don't snap, don't cuss him out, be calm. "That's fine, I'll be quick. Gabe has a football game tonight and I'd like to attend it. Sage is going and we're going to grab hotdogs and bad game food there. I just need to know that you're not going to send a TacTeam in to grab me from the stands while I'm watching the game."

There's a pause, like he's weighing out each of my words and testing how honest I'm being with him, and I take another long, deep breath to keep my cool.

Finally he says, “Fine. I’ll keep a close eye on you and Gabe will meet you after the game and get you back to your dorms. If this is an attempt to run away again, I am going to make your life miserable.”

Fuck him. “You mean like it’s not already?”

I hang up before he can get another word in and shove my phone back into my pocket, giving Sage a smirk, but she’s still grimacing in my direction at overhearing that entire... mess.

“He actually hates you, doesn’t he? God, I thought Riley was bad enough.”

I thread my arm through hers and squeeze it, “Riley is fucking horrible. At least I did something to North that made him a dick, your Bond has no excuse.”

She sighs and glances around like she’s afraid Giovanna is going to jump out of the bushes and attack us both. This is the one topic we didn’t talk about last night but she doesn’t run away from it now. “I did something wrong too. I’m not a six-foot-tall Italian model with legs men want to climb and an amazing rack. I’m just... plain old Sage. God, we need to talk about something else before the self-loathing takes over me and I spend the rest of the night drinking from a flask in the bleachers.”

There’s nothing I want more than to get wasted all over again right now and forget about this entire fucking mess, and though drinking has never been something I've shied away from before, there's something about talking to North that has me hesitating.

I somehow feel as though I'm holding onto my gift harder than I ever have before, but at the same time, it's the least in control of it I've ever been. Every day I've been here I've had to push down, beg, plead, ignore, and stifle the bond's wishes, every day it has called out to the men I'm destined to be with, and every day I've had to smother it until there's no sign of how deeply this entire separation has burned me.

Drinking tonight is off the table, at least until I have a hold of myself again.

I change into a pair of ripped jeans and an old sweater. I'm shocked at how well they both fit me because the last time I tried them on, they were a little on the tight side. I guess all of this time surrounded by people who hate me has slimmed me down. Sage sits on the floor in front of my mirror and does her hair and makeup. She's pretty low-key about it, a few curls and a quick swipe of mascara, but she's so pretty that it's all she really needs.

It kills me how little she thinks of herself thanks to Giovanna.

Nothing would make me happier than killing that bitch, and I honestly think it would be the first death I wouldn't feel so freaking guilty about. She would be the first person I was sure was an asshole.

Is being an asshole enough to warrant someone's death?

Fuck, today has been too long and exhausting to be thinking about this moral bullshit. All that matters is that I shouldn't kill anyone on campus because North is so far up my ass that he'd figure it all out. He'd see right through every lie I've told since I came here and he'd use it as an excuse to chain me up in his basement.

Sage grabs a chair to sit and do my hair for me while I work on my makeup. She does what little she can to tame the newly-dyed tresses, grabbing large chunks to curl in loose waves so it looks a little more natural and effortless... well, as natural as lavender hair can look. She tells me stories about growing up in the tight-knit bonded community, little stories about everyone except my own Bonds, and I have to focus on keeping my hand still with all of the laughing we're doing.

I go all out on my own makeup.

I need a lot more to look half as good as Sage, and it's been months at this point since I've been able to feel good about myself at this sort of level. I choose colors that set off the blue tones in my hair and when I'm done, Sage sprawls back on my bed while I put some product in my hair to set the curls a little.

It's chilly out and I don't want to lose all of her hard work.

"I feel guilty," Sage says, breaking the silence.

I glance over to her but she's too busy scrolling aimlessly on her phone to meet my eye. "Over what? It's not your fault I'm stuck here and you can go out and have a life."

She sighs and puts her phone down. "I'm a terrible friend. There's a part of me that's relieved that North has you on lockdown because that means you'll stick around. I haven't ever had a friend like you. God, even the people I thought were my friends before Riley threw me aside were nothing like you. I'm— God, I'm so sorry, Oli."

Not even my broken Bonds make me feel like this. "Why would I be mad about that? How could I be angry that you actually like me and want to be my friend? Listen, if things were the other way around, I can guarantee I'd feel the same way."

She smiles at me but her eyes are still way too sad. "You wouldn't. You're the most selfless person I've ever met. You take everything that your Bonds are throwing at you and just... move on with it."

I wish that were true.

Would I be this sure about what I was doing if there wasn't such a huge risk? Would I be as strong as I am now if I wasn't already aware of how many people will die if I don't manage to get away from my Bonds, if the Resistance finds me again?

I'm not sure I would be.

I shrug and pile the makeup back in Sage's bag carefully, mindful not only that it isn't mine, but also that it's all high quality and expensive products, stuff I've never even considered before because I'm broke.

"I don't care about that shit, Sage. I care about all of the other qualities you have that make you the best possible friend for me. I care about you showing up here with arms full of makeup without me ever asking because you know there's no way I could dress up without your help. I care about you inviting me over for tacos and margaritas. I care that when I grab notes in classes when you've skipped them, you thank me like I've conquered a kingdom for you. I care that you don't give a shit about all of the things people say about me, you chose to get to know me before you made judgement. I have a million other things for you but let's just leave it at that. You're fucking incredible and someday you'll believe me when I say that."

She grins and ducks her head. "You're pretty good yourself, Fallows. So good that I'd run away with you if you decide to leave again."

We head out to the game early because it turns out that Sage maybe wasn't vehement enough about how much she loves football and because of how much she loves the game, she's extra picky about where we sit. She's at a whole new level of excitement about the whole thing, talking nonstop the entire way over to the stadium about all of the players and stats about the team. She even gushes over Gabe, completely disregarding her usual reluctance to talk about my Bonds in her excitement about us watching the game tonight.

I don't mind at all because seeing her this happy is unheard of. We've been friends for weeks and the most I've gotten out of her has been a shy smile and the occasional dry laugh, but right now she's oozing joy.

We have to stop by her house on the way over to the stadium and I wait in her car, texting updates to North like an obedient little possession. He sends a lot of one word replies, like I'm not really worth his time, so I make my own messages too long and too detailed, just for spite.

I hope he fucking hates it.

I'm giggling to myself like a child when the car door opens again and Sage slides back into the driver's seat.

"I grabbed Maria's season pass for you so we can head straight in. She's working late tonight, so Dad's sending her updates. And we won't have to put up with her," Sage says as she starts the car and pulls out from the driveway, her playlist starting and blaring indie punk bands through the cab.

Maria is her dad's other Bonded and completes her parent's triad bond. She works for the Council as a lawyer, and as one of North's key advisors, and has been giving Sage a hard time about being friends with me.

Sage avoids her at all costs.

I'm also going to do what I can to stay away from her psycho-ass. Can you imagine being so involved with your boss that you'd do what you can to interfere with his Bond's friendships?

No thanks.

We're early enough that parking is easy and Sage chats to everyone we see like they're old friends of hers. Stilted, because they all look at her with pity and thinly veiled mistrust, but they all acknowledge her, so it's half a step up from the other students at college.

Sage sighs and points over to a couple. "There's my parents. They're sitting in my spot, waiting for us."

Oh shit.

This feels like a whole lot of pressure right now that I didn't sign up for, but Sage chews on her lip and I'm back in defensive bestie mode because I'm freaking pissed that even her parents aren't a safe space for her anymore. Everyone has turned their backs on her, thanks to something she has no control over.

Then, as if my shitty attitude was a calling sign to him, Riley arrives with Giovanna on his arm and they weave through the small crowd that's started to form. He's staring at his Bonded like she's set his whole world alight with her beauty and there's this sickening air of smugness around them. As though being together isn't enough, they also have to rub it in everyone's faces.

The moment Riley sees Sage's parents he turns the charm on and schmoozes them like a total creep. They lap it up too, just falling over themselves to speak to him, like he hasn't shoved a knife through their daughter's heart.

Disgusting, the lot of them.

Sage hesitates for a second before she tugs at my arm to grab my attention away from Riley's grinning face. "Can we go down to the locker rooms and see my brother? I need some air."

Yeah, because out here in the open air of the night is freaking suffocating now that her asshole of a Bond is down there looking like an all around stand-up guy.

He's fucking scum.

I nod and walk back down with her, watching as she talks her way through every barrier with ease, ignoring all of the shitty looks from everyone like a pro. I don't take it as well and by the time we make it into one of the training rooms, I'm scowling at every person in there like I'm going to make myself their problem.

Sage bumps my shoulder with hers to jolt me out of my savage look as she texts her brother to come out and meet us both. He doesn't answer her back, but we decide to wait around. Thankfully, it doesn't take long.

Sawyer looks a lot like Sage, his ash-brown hair is cropped short and a smudge of dirt is already on his face thanks to whatever they've been doing for warmups. He's laughing and joking with his teammates but when Sage calls out to him, he looks over with surprise and real affection.

They're close, and he's clearly missed her showing up to watch him.

I honestly don't care how much shit I catch from North and my other Bonds for being here, I'm going to do everything I can to show up to every game with Sage from now on.

Sawyer frowns a little at me as he approaches us but he pulls Sage into an easy hug. "Braving the storm? I didn't think you'd cave to Mom."

Sage scoffs and shrugs. "She wore me down, finally, and I've been craving hotdogs all week. How are you feeling?"

I zone out a little while they talk about the stats of tonight's game, all of the sports jargon flies straight over my head because while I have a general grasp on the sport, I definitely do not understand half of what they're saying right now.

Instead, I look around the hallway at all of the guys

getting ready for the game. Most of them are already dressed and ready for the game, some of them are going through their pre-game rituals, and all of them are grinning wildly.

The quarterback smiles at me, flicking his wet hair out of his eyes, but his eyes linger on Sage for a second before he turns away. He's definitely older than us, probably a senior, and he's hot as hell. Sandy blond hair and clear blue eyes, there's a dimple in his cheek that would melt most girls, but I'm immune to guys and their charms, thanks to my messy bond situation. There's also a sadness that's clinging to him when he looks at Sage that sets my teeth on edge.

Why is everyone so freaking obsessed with pitying her and treating her like shit?

"Shit, sorry, Sawyer, this is Oli. I forgot you two haven't actually met yet."

I blink away from the guy and smile at Sawyer, trying not to be offended at the uneasy look he's giving me. He's probably worried about Gabe giving him shit if he's even a little bit nice in my direction, so I shift back on my heels and give him a tight smile. "Nice to meet you, and good luck with the game tonight."

He gives me a curt nod back and then hesitates before saying, "Thanks for coming with Sage tonight. It means a lot to me that she's here."

I shrug and shift away from him a little more. "No worries, I've been meaning to come see what all the fuss is about."

Sage smiles at me but it doesn't reach her eyes, and I step away from them both to give them a second to talk without me hovering and making things more awkward. I try to blend in with the crowd, which is impossible thanks to my notoriety, and I find myself back out in one of the hallways. I know which direction I should be heading in to get back out to our seats but I stop and mess around on my phone to look busy while I wait for Sage instead. I don't want to run off on her and leave her alone with all of these shitty people.

I'm there for a few minutes before something catches my eye.

The door to another of the training rooms is open a little and I can see Gabe shaking the hand of the captain of the other team. Nothing groundbreaking about that show of sportsmanship except... except there's something in his hands that he's just handed over to him. Drugs? Wait, no, it's a piece of paper. They're both looking around like they're doing something highly illegal and then Gabe's eyes hit mine through the doorway.

He sees me.

I see him.

I have no fucking clue what he's doing but I'm sure

I could walk into the locker room and find his coach and ruin his life right now. The little flash of panic in his eyes tells me I'm not wrong, he's doing something that would get him kicked off of the team... or thrown in lock up for the night.

We just stand there and stare at each other for a beat too long, so much bullshit floating silently between us.

"Hey, sorry for taking so long. We should grab our seats."

I startle and find Sage staring at her feet, her eyes a little red. It snaps me out of the little trance I was in and I look away from Gabe, sliding my arm through hers until we're tucked together as we walk.

I've never been a snitch and I'm not going to become one just because Gabe has been an ass to me.

We walk back up to our seats and Sage introduces me to her parents in the most awkward conversation I've been in since coming here. They both clearly don't want me around their daughter but they smile and pretend to be polite, probably because she came here tonight thanks to me.

I roll with the punches and ignore them, chatting and faking like this is all fine with Sage as the game starts and she really lights up. Sometime after half time, when we've eaten and laughed until my stomach aches, her parents take a call and stand to go grab something to eat for themselves.

A girl I've never seen before slides in next to Sage and she instantly tenses, immediately on high alert.

Why won't the bullshit of tonight ever end?

There's a beat of silence as the cheering around us is deafening but when the crowd quietens, Sage speaks.

"Oli, this is Gracie. Her brother, Felix, is on the team."

She doesn't sound worried or upset, so I follow her lead and lean forward to get a look at the girl. She's pretty, blond hair styled beautifully, but she's wearing a band tee and has a nose ring. She looks out of place here but totally at ease.

Gracie nods at me with a small smile. "Thanks for hanging out with my girl. She's been too sad these days, but she also won't come hang out with me to cheer the hell up."

I glance at her and then Sage but Sage's eyes are fixed on her brother. I stick with loyal bestie vibes. "She's my best friend, I'll always be here for her."

Sage startles, her eyes hitting mine, and then she grins. "You're the one risking a TacTeam to hang with me, I think you deserve a little thanks."

I roll my eyes. "Don't remind me. So, Gracie, which one is Felix? I just barely have the rules straight, I couldn't pick out players to save my life."

She laughs and points out the quarterback, the same one from the locker room earlier. "That's him. Did Sage tell you he's obsessed with her? He's been trying to get her to date him since Riley became the world's biggest asshole, but she's become a ghost."

I look over at her, shocked, but Sage shrugs. "I don't want a pity date. I get that he's Sawyer's friend and cares for me, but I'm not going to make a bad situation even worse."

Gracie rolls her eyes, a mirror of my reaction. "He's been obsessed with you for years. He tore the training room apart when he found out you and Riley were Bonds. This has absolutely nothing to do with Sawyer."

I glance between them but Sage seals her lips shut and refuses to say another word, even after Gracie says a sad goodbye and leaves us again.

It's not until way after Gabe and his team win the game and we're waiting by the locker room for him to take me back to my dorm room that she finally speaks again.

"Someday, he's going to find his Bonds, and I can't take losing someone else. A long time ago... I once thought that maybe I was the Central Bond and I'd get to have them both. Stupid. I try to stay away from Felix now because even if we're not Bonds, seeing him with someone else is going to hurt. I can't know what it's like to have him and then lose him. Riley is bad enough."

I nod because I get it. I get it better than anyone else ever could. Being around my Bonds now, the best protection that I have is their anger and hatred of me. If I didn't have that, I'd crumble under the weight of everything we have against us.

I'd break.

My life finds a weirdly normal pattern.

It's all so freaking strange to notice the mundane patterns that start to take over. Studying with Sage, going to classes with Gabe as my shadow, dying during my TT classes, and sitting at the table in North's mansion in an uncomfortable silence during the torturous dinners. I'm not at all complacent about trying to get the hell out of this place but when I wake up every day and know exactly how my day is going to go, I start to think that I'm going to be stuck here... until my past finds me and everything I've been running from for the last five years will finally swallow me whole.

I'm busy enough not to think about it too often.

When my first paper comes back from my Econ class with a B+, I want to scream from the rooftops because I'm that freaking proud of myself. Sage hunts down a couple of cupcakes with giant swirls of icing on top to celebrate over lunch, and even Gabe manages to grunt out a 'well done' to me as he munches through his rabbit food.

I do what I can to stay off of my Bonds radar, the tentative peace that we find has everything to do with our ability to stay the hell away from each other. I see Gabe every day and Nox during class but I only see North and Gryphon during the dinner once a week and that is A-OK with me.

I get complacent.

I start to forget just how much they all loathe me.

The knock at my dorm room door after classes and dinner rocks the boat. I open it to find Gracie standing there looking hot as hell in a pair of cut-offs and a tiny tank top, a sheepish grin over her face as she looks me up and down in a kind but assessing way that attractive girls do. I look like a pile of shit in an old pair of sweatpants and a cable knit sweater that is three sizes too big for me but comfortable as shit to lay around in.

I hold the door close so she can't see into my barren and shameful room but she doesn't bat an eyelid over it. "Sorry for dropping in unannounced, but you are impossible to find online. Hell, even your phone number is, like, CIA-level protected! Does Sage even have it? She doesn't pick up my calls anymore, so I couldn't get it from her anyway."

God. "Uh, okay... what can I help you with?"

She glances around the empty hallway, looking uncomfortable and a little sheepish, "Can I come in? I'm not sure Sage would want me airing this out in public with all of the bullshit that she deals with on a daily basis."

Dammit.

It's like she knows that Sage is the only reason I would ever let some strange girl into my space, because that girl is everything to me. "Fine, come on in."

Grade grins and steps around me, looking around at the barren space with that same curiosity she'd shown my appearance. The thing is, it doesn't feel like she's judging me, it's more that she's cataloging everything and storing it away in case she needs it, and that's still not something I want to get behind.

"No offense but I'm busy, you have like three minutes before I'm heading back to my books."

She grins at me and then lays it all out there. "Sage's birthday is this week. Her parents are throwing a big party, inviting half the Council and a whole slew of people that couldn't care less about our girl turning nineteen. I need you to come along. I don't think Sage was going to ask you to come because she wouldn't want to inconvenience you, and the whole thing is going to be a dumpster fire, but you have to come."

Sage had mentioned it to me and when I'd offered to come, she'd said no. With her dad's Bonded Maria working for North, Sage didn't want me to have to deal with the animosity that will inevitably be there for me.

I shoot Gracie a look and she winces but immediately jumps in with her reasoning, "Listen, I don't want to ask this anymore than you want to be asked, but Riley and Giovanna are going to show up and make the whole night a living fucking nightmare for Sage, and I'm done taking the backseat on this bullshit. She's... I dunno, not stronger I guess, but more resilient now that she has you, so I feel less weird for trying to support her through this."

I do my best not to openly side-eye the hell out of her because Sage has already told me that all of her friends abandoned her over Riley and Giovanna, so why is Gracie suddenly trying to be all up in her shit?

It doesn't feel genuine to me at all but that only makes me want to attend this party more, because Sage needs backup.

I sigh and wave a hand at her, "Fine. I'll talk to Sage about it and let her know I'm going."

I say it like it's easy, like I'm not going to have to beg pathetically to North to get a pass to go. I don't trust this girl, so I'm not going to give her any details of the mess of my bonds.

The Gifted community already has too much to say about it.

When I call North the next morning he takes my request better than I expected, and that's my first real warning that this isn't a party I want to be attending but when I speak to Sage about it before classes, the look of sheer relief on her face is enough for my inner stubborn bitch to kick in.

I'm going, even if it kills me.

I keep my head down and focus on my classes for the rest of the day, forgetting about the party until I split up with Sage to head off to TT and Gabe jogs to catch up with me. My hackles immediately rise because we've come to an unspoken agreement where I don't lash out and bitch him out for stalking me just so long as he keeps his mouth shut and doesn't get too close to me.

My bond enjoys his closeness too much and it's terrifying to me, the thought that I'm going to leave him again the second I can and lose this feeling of *peace* and *contentment...* unbearable.

So I keep him as far away from me as I can manage without facing North's bullshit wrath and he's been fine about keeping to those boundaries, until now.

"What now?" I drawl, a small concession because it's a nicer tone than the snapping I want to do.

"I'm picking you up for Sage's party tomorrow, don't leave your dorm without me."

I roll my eyes at him but he just shakes his head at me, my attitude not rolling off of him like it usually does. "No, this isn't about me tailing you because I don't trust you, this is— there's a lot of Council members going because of Sage's parents, and none of them are going to... be people you should talk to."

I don't want to talk to anyone who isn't Sage but I also don't like Gabe telling me who I can and can't speak to. "Afraid I'm going to embarrass you?"

He huffs and grabs my arm, pulling me off of the path and over to the side of the building where we have a little cover. "Maybe you should stop being so goddamn in love with the victim narrative you have going on in your head and think about this like a rational human being for a second. The Council aren't all friends. It's not some boys club that North is in that's trying to ruin your life. They're the leaders of our community and the staple of our society... and half of them think North should force you to bond with him because you shouldn't have the right to say no to him. Half of them think *rape* is the appropriate course of action here."

My stomach drops and he nods at me, "They're not all good people. They're just voted in as heads of their families and so they get a seat at the table. I'm taking you and I'll stay with you so you don't end up sitting in a dark comer with Sharpe or Vittorio rummaging through your brain with their gifts."

Sharpe and Vittorio, I take note of their names because there's too many secrets lurking in the depths of my mind that could ruin us all.

I stare up at Gabe for a minute, teetering on the edge of trusting him,and there's a throbbing feeling in my chest that has me swaying into him just a little bit. There's a tick in his cheek as he clenches his teeth that tells me he's just as affected by this closeness as I am and suddenly this entire situation feels dangerous to me.

Remember they all hate you.

I push him away from my body, startling when I realize my hands had already found themselves sliding up his chest without me noticing, and suddenly my brain is full of information I do not need right now.

Like how toned and solid he feels under the shirt he's wearing.

We both just stare at each other for a second before the spell breaks when my brain finally catches up to the fact that my goddamn hands are still pressed against his chest and I snatch them away, turning and stalking away from him.

My tone is scathing and shakes a little as I snap, "I'll wait for you to take me over to the party but I'm hanging out with Sage there. I don't care if you follow us around, but I'm not leaving her behind just because you want to hang out with your asshole friends."

I'm expecting him to snap back at me or bitch me out like he usually does but he just follows me obediently, two steps behind me like usual, as if nothing has just happened. We make it to the TT training building and when I pause to push open the door Gabe steps back up to my body, leaning in close to murmur to me, "Maybe you're not as ice cold as you pretend to be."

I fucking need to be.

Just when I think that I'm getting in better shape during the workout portion of the TT class, Vivian switches up my sets and once again destroys my will to live. I still train away from the others in the class because I'm so far behind them, but I've already started to notice the growing strength in my limbs and the way I'm trimming down a little.

I still lose every last one of the training scenarios.

After the first class that I'd been knocked out of, Vivian lets the entire class use their gifts during the scenarios and there's no way I can compete with them.

One of the girls is a walking dose of chloroform.

She also hates my freaking guts and targets me every damn time we cross the starting line. Vivian works her game plan out instantly and starts to make it harder for her to get to me, mostly to teach her how to strategize and to teach me to evade the bitch, but she's like a goddamn bloodhound.

I hate her.

Naturally, Zoey is in love with Gabe and spends every second she can flirting with him in front of me. This should probably bother me more than it does but there's some pissed off, cruel part of me that enjoys just how badly Gabe wants me to react. Every time I watch Zoey brush a hand across his bicep without so much as a flinch, I can see how much it pisses him off.

He never pushes her away though and that says far too much about how he really feels.

The only silver lining to taking this class with Gabe is that after we're done for the day, he drives me over to North's place for dinner each week, cutting down the time I have to be trapped in a small, confined space with North and his driver.

The motorbike is intimate but the flirting with death makes it my preferred method of being dragged to these stupid weekly dinners. Gabe also doesn't try to talk to me or belittle me for my general existence like North does, more marks in his favor.

He also always sits next to me at the table, adding little comments and snippets of information whenever one of

Nox's guests starts shit with me, which is *all the freaking time.*

I'm convincedNox only brings the most confrontational and completely insane girls that he can find to the table.

Tonight is no different and while Lana is less obvious with her infatuation with Nox, her barbed jabs at me cut a little closer to the bone than the other giggling airheads.

"I heard that you lived on the street for years, selling yourself to eat. It must be hard to go back to living a 'straight' life again after being used like that."

Selling myself.

Gabe stiffens and shoots her a glare, his lip curling up. I already know he's not going to actually do anything about it though and when he glances down at me, there's this hesitancy in him that bums me because there's a part of him that believes that bullshit about me.

I'm about to unleash a whole world of pain on him when North interrupts, "We need to discuss some ground rules for the party."

I almost choke on air. "Why would we need to do that? I'll avoid you like the plague, Gabe will stick to my ass like glue, and I'll hang out in the comer with Sage while both of us pray that death will take us so we can get out of there."

Nox finally leans away from Lana, who is still smirking at me like she's won something, taking interest in the conversation for the first time. "I fucked a Flame once. She came so hard she set the bed on fire. I should call your little friend and see if she needs some... loosening up."

It's the biggest challenge I've had at keeping my gift under wraps and my teeth take the brunt of it, my jaw clenching so hard I feel my teeth crack and grind brutally together.

It's the first time the bond in my chest hasn't keened for him, mourning the thought of him touching anyone else but me, and I'm thankful for the small mercies because maybe it's finally caught on to the fact that there's no way out of this.

He'll hate me until he dies.

I push my plate away from myself, bile creeping up my throat at the thought of him fucking my one and only friend, and Gabe glances at it and then back up at me. "North needs me to look over some paperwork, we can't leave yet."

I look down to find my hands shaking violently and immediately tuck them under my thighs. "I'm walking back then. I'm not staying here with him."

"I'll take you," Gryphon says, and I blanch.

He hasn't even tried to talk to me, never even looked at me, really. I thought he'd do everything he could to get the hell away from me.

"Thanks," I say, and he pushes away from the table

without another word or so much as a glance my way. I don't care about niceties, I just need to get the fuck out of here.

He leads me out to the Camaro out the front and unlocks my door for me before walking around to get in his side. I've never been in a car without central locking before. It looks pristine, the leather seats are older but it's clear he takes good freaking care of this thing. I sit down delicately, like somehow my ass is going to destroy this car just by being in here.

Gryphon slides in with less hesitance but no less care, clearly he loves this car and it strikes me that this is the first thing I actually know about him, other than his work in a TacTeam and the way he dresses.

I know a lot about Gabe, thanks to our forced proximity, and both of the Draven brothers have shown too much of their amazing personalities at the dinner table. Atlas has spent our weeks of having contact with one another sending me little stories and snippets about himself, never pressuring me to do the same in return, but inevitably coaxing them out of me. Even since I told him about North's monitoring my phone, he's been rigorous in his attempts at getting to know me.

Gryphon has done everything he can to stay at arm's length from me.

My bond reaches out to him, straining against the

tight restraints I have on it as I tug it away before I brush against him. There's something about his distance and the way he's kept himself away from me that makes my bond desperate for him.

He's the most dangerous of them all.

When he pulls up out the front of the dorm rooms he cuts the engine, the sudden silence in the cab without the rumble of the engine is uncomfortable. I wait for a moment, but when he doesn't say a word I get out, mumbling a quiet *thank you* before heading back up to my room.

With my bond weeping in my chest harder than it ever has before.

As much as I'd like to wear some cute, tiny dress that shows off all of my hard work in that stupid TT class, I'm also keenly aware of the fact that I'll be getting onto a motorbike with Gabe and it probably isn't the best idea to fuck with him like that, especially since we had that little... moment the other day. I've never been so keenly aware of my own bond and how it's reacting to the world around me.

Something about being here, around these men I'm fated to be with, has lit a fire in me that I'm desperate to smother.

I check my outfit in the mirror one last time as I walk out and sigh because I didn't exactly have a lot of options.

This whole deprivation thing North has me on is the perfect torture because I might just crack to get a decent pair of cute boots and jeans that hug my ass a little better. I don't look bad though, and the jacket Sage lent me covers enough of me that the low cut of my cami is hot without being too much.

When I make it downstairs to where Gabe is waiting, the sight of him knocks the air out of my lungs. Dark blue jeans, a white tee that's stretched out over his wide chest, and his football jacket slung over his broad shoulders, he looks like every college girl's wet dream. His light brown hair is styled for the first time, not a lot, but enough that I know he's putting some effort into his appearance for the night, which raises questions. Is it me or the other people going to the party that he wants to impress? Is it because the council members are attending and he doesn't want to make North look bad? Should he even be caring about that sort of thing?

This is all too hard and convoluted to think about and, God, it's not smart but my bond writhes inside of my chest with jealousy over him being out here, looking like this, with half of the girls from my dorm walking around trying to grab his attention.

I'm not stupid enough to do something about it right now but,/wc£, do I want to.

When his piercing blue eyes meet mine there's a smug

look on his face, he knows I'm checking him out, and I have to scramble to save face.

"Hoping to pick someone up tonight?"

He scoffs at me and holds out his spare helmet. "If I was looking to get laid, I wouldn't have to put in effort. I could fuck any of these girls without saying a word to them."

He grins at someone behind me like he's proving a point and sure enough, I hear the giggling and swooning. It sets my teeth on edge and I snatch the helmet out of his hands, catching myself and pushing the anger down before it becomes too obvious how jealous I am about it.

Gabe holds an arm out to me so I can swing on behind him and he pauses for a second before he starts the engine, just sitting there and staring out across the street before finally shoving his helmet on.

My instincts start screaming instantly. "What's wrong?"

He shrugs and kicks the stand. "It's nothing. Nothing you need to worry about, anyway."

Fuck that, I jab him in the ribs but he's a wall of muscle and barely reacts as he starts the engine and then we're off, weaving into the traffic and flying into the night air at speeds that are definitely not legal.

I can't see anything out of the ordinary without using my gift, which Gabe will without a doubt sense thanks to how close together we are, so I have to just trust him for now.

It's something I would struggle with even if he didn't hate me, but knowing how hurt he was by my disappearance? It makes it almost impossible to sit there and know that there's something going on and I can't figure it the hell out.

Thankfully, Sage's house isn't too far from campus and we make excellent time with Gabe's reckless driving. It's in a gated community like North's and although it's a little smaller than his, it's clear they're also filthy rich.

Most Gifted families are.

It makes sense of course, because there's usually three or more adults to each Bonded group, all of them working and providing for the family unit. God, the earning potential of my Bonds is unreal to think about, even if the Draven's weren't freaking loaded. Six incomes can go a long way and after years of scraping by on the run, that's a tempting thought.

Then I think about North's assumption that I'm a gold-digging brat and the whole little fantasy of not starving and maybe having cute outfits just dries up.

I still haven't really worked out a game plan on what I want to do after college, mostly because I've never considered a future where my life isn't in danger... or *the* danger.

We pull up at the front of the house and I force my mind to clear because that's exactly what Gabe had warned me about. Gifted who can read my mind, rifle around in there and pull out all of my secrets until the Resistance comes calling for me.

I swing down from the bike, pulling the helmet off and handing it over to Gabe to shove into the pack. I hesitate for a second before biting the bullet and just waiting for him. I don't want to cause a scene and have him do something to ruin Sage's party.

She's already so nervous about it.

When he's got everything secured away, he tugs his jacket a little to straighten it and then turns to face me, raising a brow when he finds me standing there. "I didn't think it'd be as easy as asking you to stay close."

I roll my eyes at him even as I follow him like some obedient little puppy. "I'm passing all of my classes thanks to Sage and she's the only reason I'm not a complete fucking nutcase in this stupid place, so if I have to stick with you to get through tonight for her, then I'll do it."

He doesn't knock or ring the doorbell, just pushes the door open and walks in like he's been here a million times before. I know he's on the football team with Sawyer but it still feels weird to me.

"Are you sure you're not fucking her? Nox is—"

I cut him off, "If you want me to stick with you, stop

fucking talking about the Draven brothers. North is a controlling asshole and Nox is a complete freaking psycho. You're at least tolerable when you keep your mouth shut."

Gabe's cheeks flush a little underneath his tan and he speaks through his teeth, "You're such a fucking nightmare yourself, Fallows, you can't exactly talk. What about Gryphon or Bassinger? Are they *tolerable* too?"

They're both entirely unattainable and distant, so they're safe, but I'm not telling him that. I'm saved from speaking by a group of people chatting and laughing through the hallway, loud and oozing that familiar sort of joy that you get from people who've known each other since birth.

It makes my chest ache with jealousy and I guess that's just the feeling of the night for me, goddammit.

I'm happy to just walk on past them to find Sage but one of the guys turns and calls out to Gabe, waving him over. I scowl at him but Gabe just hooks his fingers around my arm and tugs me over to the group, that easy grin of his plastered back on like we're not still at each other's throats.

It's only when we approach that I see Riley standing there with them and freeze, totally out of place standing around *Sage's* hallway, with *Sage's* asshole Bond, as though this isn't a complete betrayal to her.

Okay, I'm being dramatic but it feels like that to me,

and I'm a loyal friend to the end.

"I thought you hated your Bond, Ardem, what are you doing cozying up with her?" one of the girls says as though I'm not freaking standing here with them all.

I'm too busy inching away from them all but then Gabe slings an arm around my shoulders and smirks again. "We had some teething issues but Oli has figured out where she's supposed to be now."

They all laugh like this is some big joke and I decide that I'd rather have North's worst enemy pick through my brain than stand around with these assholes. I tug out of Gabe's arms and start down the hallway, ignoring the jeers and catcalls that the group throws at me.

By the time I make it to the kitchen, picking a door at random and lucking out, Gabe jogs to catch up with me and gets his arm around my shoulders again. "If I'm being forced to keep you out of trouble, the least you could do is take a little heat. That shit was mild compared to what I've dealt with since you left."

"I don't care, and it's your own fault for hanging around those types of people. I'm here for Sage and if you want to go hang out with fucking idiots, then go right ahead," I snap right as Giovanna steps into my path and this is it, this is the moment I get kicked out of this party, because the look on that girl's face sets my teeth on edge and my temper is ready to ignite.

"Idiots? They're all the next generation of council members and leaders of the Gifted community. Every last one of them comes from distinguished families, Bonded that have earned their place here. You're the outsider from sullied stock."

I can handle a lot of shit, being here has proven that to me, but there's *no fucking -way* I'm having her talk shit about my parents. "Shut your mouth before I break your jaw."

Gabe's arm slides away from my shoulders only so he can hook his fingers into my arm again, tugging me back as though he'd be able to stop me from taking a swing at this bitch. Sage has told me everything about her gift and telekinesis means nothing to me right now.

It's not like she's strong enough to use it against me.

She clicks her tongue at Gabe condescendingly. "You should keep a better leash on her, she's insulting the wrong family."

I look her up and down, slowly and with contempt dripping from every pore of my body. "If your family is so important, then the community is *fucked* because you're the most vile, petty little bitch I've ever been forced to interact with."

Her lips curl and I note with a detached little kernel of victory that the slash of red lipstick is a shade too orange for her skin tone. "Why would the opinion of some little runaway whore matter to me? You're nothing to the community, to me or my Bonded."

Bonded, even the word is a slap in the face because she's taken that away from Sage. Gabe tries again to tug me away but I'm too angry now, too out of control of my mouth, and I snap back, "I've done more for this community than you will *ever* do, you pathetic, attention-seeking little whore."

Her hand snaps back to strike me but before she has the chance to swing, a wall of a man steps between us and all I can see is leather, but my bond purrs in my chest at Gryphon's sudden proximity.

He's never been this close to me before.

His voice is rough in all the right ways, goddamn him, as he says "I'm sure you're not trying to start a fight in the Benson's kitchen right now, Giovanna, because that would be pretty stupid— even for you."

Her cheeks flame but she finally stalks off, turning on her heel so her skirt flares to show off her long, tanned legs that Sage is so insecure about.

I don't think they're that great, personally, and the rest of her is fucking disgusting. I don't know how Riley can stand touching her because her looks can't compensate for the shitty personality.

Gryphon turns around, his face as solemn and moody as it usually is, but I have another Bond to deal with right now.

"Oli is—" Gabe starts but I rip my arm out of his grip

so viciously that he takes a step away from me as I tear into him, "You are a spineless asshole and if you lay a hand on me again I will break it, got it?"

His eyes flick over to Gryphon and whatever he sees in his face shuts him down fast, cursing under his breath.

I want to say a lot more on the matter but Gryphon interrupts me, "Pissing Daniella's sister off isn't a good idea if you want to stay off of North's radar."

I shoot him a look but his eyes aren't on me as he nods at some older man across the room, barely paying me a second's worth of attention, even though he came to intervene for me. Well, I'm sure he was coming to make sure I didn't actually body slam Giovanna into a wall for daring to talk shit about my dead parents. I hated her before, but now I want to hunt her down and... well, I can't keep thinking about all the ways my gift would mess her up right now or I'll end up hunting her down and ruining her.

I turn away, ready to find Sage and just disappear for the rest of the night, only to find that Gabe is scowling at us both, surly like a kicked goddamn puppy, but I'm more than over his shitty attitude for tonight.

He didn't even attempt to back me up, and if he's really that intent on making sure I'm safe tonight, then one strike and he's out. I'm definitely not a sports girl and three chances isn't my kind of deal.

"Oli! You made it, thank God! Sage is hiding over by

the pool, can you help me get her out? Oh! Gryphon, I didn't see you!"

Gracie definitely isn't the savior I want right now but I'll take it. I slide past Gryphon and do my best to ignore the bubbly and flirty looks Gracie is throwing him. "Point me in the right direction and I'll find her myself."

She blinks at my savage tone, not at all looking repentant for drooling all over Gryphon, and waves an arm at one side of the room carelessly. Yup, she really did approach me as a way to get in with my Bond, the man I'm fated to be with.

I fucking hate this place.

I stalk off without another thought, definitely without thinking about whether or not Gryphon is reciprocating all of Gracie's charms and flirting giggles. I weave through the other guests easily, spotting North in a comer with a glass of amber liquid and bricks of ice in it, schmoozing some other men in suits like he was bom for this life. I duck my head before he can spot me and pick up the pace until I make it out to the sprawling backyard, complete with a pool, outdoor kitchen, and fire pit.

It's a gorgeous night out, warm air and with the twinkle lights on over one of the hedges it looks like something out of a fairytale. I take a second to just enjoy it before I remember the shark tank I just walked out of and go to find Sage, spotting her huddled by the fire pit with her brother like they're both hiding from the party.

When I approach them both, Sawyer glances up, startled, and then winces at me like it's such a hardship to look at me. I'll admit, it hurts my feelings a bit but I'm also a little too worked up right now to be dealing with anyone's bullshit.

"Oh God, what happened in there?" Sage moans, looking just a little bit tipsy, and I immediately want a drink too.

"I'll give you a complete play-by-play of me almost knocking Giovanna's head off if you find me a drink. I need to forget what that bitch's voice sounds like. Sage, you're a freaking saint. How you put up with her without *lighting her ass* on fire, I'll never know."

Sawyer snorts at me before swooping down to kiss Sage on the cheek and getting up. "I'll grab you both drinks... try not to start a riot while I'm gone."

I nod at him with a tight smile, the wince still stinging a little, but then I launch into a completely true and not at all exaggerated version of what went down with that tanned skank of a woman.

We're both dying of laughter by the time Sawyer and Felix find us there, enough bottles of beer between them to drown a hippo. I pull a face because beer is not my favorite, but Felix grins and shrugs at me. "Maria caught us grabbing the good shit, so we had to compromise."

I shrug back and take one of the bottles from him. "It's fine, I just need the alcohol to forget how pissed off I am, really."

Sage scrunches up her nose but takes a bottle as well, introducing Felix and I properly, even though I'm sure we both already know too much about each other. It's awkward for a second, with Sage trying to scoot in closer to me to make room and Felix's eyes following her with a hunger that he's not even attempting to tamp down, but then I start the Giovanna story all over again, with a few more embellishments and commentaries, and the air clears around us all and there isn't another awkward silence between us.

It's a good night, one I was never expecting.

As I look over at the group of gossips, Gabe once again accepted into the fold, I make a point of leaning into Sawyer to hear his story and the look of pure rage Gabe sends me feels like a victory.

It takes three weeks to get our marks back for the assignments, but the second I walk through the doors and into the lecture hall, my bond tells me something is really freaking wrong with this situation.

I might hate having that weird, almost-sentient calling in my chest but it's also never wrong. I lived in LA for a summer a few years back and it saved me from a drink-spiking incident, as well as a car mugger. Since arriving at Draven University, kicking and screaming, it's gotten even sharper, like even just being so close to my Bonds has made the calling as sharp and accurate as the scope on a sniper rifle.

When my footsteps slow, Sage shoots me a look

and falls into step with me, which I'm expecting, but when Gabe does the same thing, a frown etched onto his handsome face, I start to get worried.

Is there a bomb in the room?

A shooter?

What the hell has all of my hackles rising like this?

Everyone files into the room like there's nothing wrong, taking seats and chatting away to each other, and I start to sweat because how do they not feel this panic like a fist in their chests like I do?

Am I losing my fucking mind?!

Nox steps into the room by himself for the first time in months, and it only takes one look at his face to tell me that the ominous feeling in the room that only Gabe and I can feel is of entirely Draven creation.

For fuck's sake.

I slump back in my seat a little now that I'm not looking around for a freaking terrorist, and Sage gently bumps my shoulder with hers with a sad smile, solidarity in the face of my Bond's bullshit because if anyone in this room can understand it, it's her.

The moment he starts talking, all eyes hit Nox and the talking and gossiping immediately dies down. He doesn't call for attention, his mere presence demands it and, like a pack hierarchy, every student falls into line obediently. There's a respect here that he has cultivated that once again makes me curious about what he can do, what the real danger he poses to us all is, because there has to be more than just a respect for a professor here.

I'm too busy thinking about potential powers to notice Gabe leaning into me until his breath hits the curve of my ear, dancing down my neck and sparking a flurry of goosebumps that I don't want him noticing.

"Whatever it is, reacting will only make it worse. You don't deserve the heads up but I'll give it to you anyway."

I keep my eyes on Nox as I give him a curt nod. I can keep my cool here, I've faced worse than hazing bullshit from some asshole guy. I can't think about the stuff that I've faced here, right now, with my mental barriers ripped to shreds thanks to whatever bad juju Nox has put out into the world and my Bond has picked up on. I feel too... raw.

The class drags on forever.

It's all history that I know about, thanks to my study sessions with Sage. The long-running feud with the Resistance isn't something I take lightly, I can't afford to, but there's only so many times I can hear about the abductions and indoctrinations of Bonds and Bonded without feeling like it's a new and very specific form of torture.

The theories about which family truly started the Resistance is interesting. No one has ever actually taken responsibility for the group, though it's been rumored that one of the older, more prestigious families started it. The Draven's are one of eight Gifted families that run the councils on the west coast and I take some notes about the potential there.

I've seen some of the inner circle of the Resistance.

I could pick people out, their faces have been burned into my brain and there's no way I'd miss them in a line up. It's a long shot but, fuck, what else can I do around here until I figure out how to get my chip out?

When Nox finally calls the class to an end, he announces the assignments have been marked and he hands off stacks of papers to his TA's to hand out. Students start streaming out of the room as they're handed their work back, eager to get to their next classes. Gabe hangs back, his eyes cutting between Nox and I. I ignore him, shoving my crap back into my bag and mumbling with Sage about the Econ class we have next while we wait for our marks back.

When the TA finally gets to our row and hands me my paper with a giggle, I take it from her with numb fingers because there's no missing the grade I've been given.

A giant, red, circled F.

"What the fuck is this?" The words fall out of me, Gabe's warning thrown to the way side, because there's no fucking way this paper got that mark. I glance over to Sage and, yup, sure enough, she has a respectable A- on hers. We'd studied together, made our notes together, read each other's work... there's no way that she got an A- and I've failed.

"It's your worthless excuse of a paper, Fallows. If you don't want to flunk out, you should work a little harder." Nox's voice carries across the room clearly, broadcasting exactly what he's done to me, except no one here will believe that he's lying out of his ass.

Everyone in the room stops and stares. My cheeks heat at the attention, he loves nothing more than some public humiliation, but I lift my chin. "You can't do this. You can't give me shit grades just because you hate me."

A slow smirk stretches over his face even as his eyes shutter and darken unnaturally. Whatever his gift is, it wants out to play. "Such arrogance from a gift-less high school dropout."

My temper catches faster than a forest fire in the heat of summer. "You're a fucking piece of shit, Draven. You're an utter fucking asshole who can't handle rejection with an ounce of integrity. What Bond would ever want to be saddled with a dickhead like you?"

Sage gasps and tugs at my hand but Gabe just turns on his heel and splits, abandoning me as easily as he thinks I did to them. I glance around and there's phones out everywhere, girls openly filming this shit go down.

Nox flicks a dismissive hand at me. "Follow me to the dean's office, Fallows."

I refuse to acknowledge it or feel bad about my reaction but I sit in front of the dean's office with hot tears coursing down my cheeks. I'm not scared or upset, they're completely triggered by the impotent rage filling me up.

Impotent because there's nothing I can do about this except use my goddamn, useless words and pray that it's enough to get my paper looked at again, but I'm also keenly aware that this is *Dr aven* University. Like there's any real chance that the dean will side with me over the freaking namesake of the institute.

When a group of giggling students walk in to sort out some pep rally bullshit, the dean's assistant ushers them out before they get a good look at me, tucking a small packet of tissues into my hand as she passes me. She's an older woman, older than my mom would be if she were still here, and it only makes the tears come harder.

I glue my eyes to the scuffs on the old trainers I'm wearing, once again thinking about those stupid shoes the TacTeam left behind when they grabbed my shit because I don't feel like myself here. I don't have any of my prized possessions, I don't have any of the freedoms I enjoyed even while on the run and struggling to make money to feed myself. My entire identity was ripped away from me to come here and for what?

Bonds who would do *anything* to ruin me.

Maybe I should start to fight back. Maybe I should risk the little time bomb they buried in my skin and just pack a bag, get out of this place. Things couldn't get worse, right? I'm doing everything I can to pass all of my classes, I'm showing up to TT every week and almost freaking dying every time for no reason other than to keep me within spitting distance of my Bonds at all times.

Nothing I do matters here.

"Thank you for calling, Sherry. I'll get this sorted out so you don't have to look at my weeping Bond any longer."

I freeze, of course things can and have gotten worse, because North has just arrived, looking like a wealthy wet dream in a suit, smiling tightly at the assistant as he breezes through the office.

The assistant, Sherry, grimaces at him and shoots me a kind look. "She's no bother at all, Mr Draven, it's just that I think she needs some backup."

Backup.

As if he's going to do anything here to help me.

He murmurs something back to her, low enough that I don't catch it, but I also don't want to know what it was when Sherry gasps a little and says, "She's so young, and with no parents! It's good she has you."

My God, I want to scratch his eyeballs out for that.

Coming in here looking like my savior, some white knight here to save the day, when really he's here to prolong the torture.

North stops in front of me and I look up to find him frowning. "Sherry said this is over a paper, do you have it with you?"

I nod and he doesn't say another word as he turns to enter the dean's office. I'm stupid enough to glance into the open doorway and my eyes meet Nox's, the dark glint of satisfaction there chilling me to the bone.

He's feeling pretty smug about this mess.

I want to die.

My phone buzzes in my pocket but I can't pull it out here, not with North's spies everywhere and it being the new phone that Atlas sent me. I press my hand against it through my pants, that weight of it like a comfort because Atlas is a safe place for me. He's a Bond I can speak to without having to worry because he's thousands of miles away, he's someone I can have at least a little bit of honesty with because I'll be out of this place before he ever makes it here.

He's the tiny sliver of a silver lining.

When the door opens again, Nox walks out without a word or glance at me or Sherry and I deflate like a balloon, all of the tension that was keeping me upright just sizzling out of me until I'm slumped over in my seat.

"Miss Fallows, please join us," the dean says, his tone a little warmer than it was when Nox dragged me here in the first place.

Sherry smiles at me as I follow him in, taking the seat Nox just vacated as I try not to vomit with nerves at the scent of him still clinging to the fabric. Why does he have to smell nice? Why does he have to ruin Aqua di Gio for me?

Asshole.

The dean takes his seat again and fusses with some papers on his desk for a moment, clearing his throat and puffing up his chest like he's so important. The posturing is so obvious and definitely not for me, the looks he gives North are bordering on obsessive.

"Miss Fallows, this is a highly unusual situation we've found ourselves in and I'm taking that into consideration with my decision here. While Mr Draven is your professor and should have final say on your grades, I understand that the— *delicate* particulars of your Bond mean that there will be some changes required."

The only thing around here that is *delicate* is Nox's fucking ego.

I nod and keep my eyes on him, my resolve not at all strong enough to handle even a glance in North's direction right now. The dean's eyes do flick over to my asshole Bond as he continues, "Councilman Draven has the same qualifications as his brother and has offered to mark your assignments for the remainder of your classes with Mr Draven. Given the circumstances, I'm willing to go to the school board with this and I'm confident that they'll agree to these terms. You will still be required to attend your classes and workshops, all of your due dates will remain the same, the only change here will be that your assignments will be sent over to the Councilman."

I want to flip the table.

I want to unleash my gift on them both and just watch them face the wrath I have building in my veins.

I want to punch North and his gutless fucking brother in the faces.

Instead, I say, "Thank you, Dean Myers. I appreciate your leniency and efforts on this *delicate* issue."

I can't stop the sarcasm from oozing out of me but the dean doesn't notice, he just grins at North like he's done an outstanding job on this and we all stand as one.

I'm ready to stalk home to walk some of my rage off, then North comes out of the left field and says, "Oleander, I'll drive you home."

My name. He says my actual, full first name without any of the derisive, controlling bullshit he pulls with my last name and, *goddammit,* I shiver at the sound of my name coming out from between those pouty lips of his.

What the fuck was that?!

Okay, I need a brain bleaching the second I get back to my room because I'm definitely *not* going to be thinking about that domineering asshole like that, no matter what my bond thinks. Fuck. I remember where the hell I am and give the dean an appreciative nod before following North out of the office building.

He doesn't attempt to slow down for me and once again, I find myself jogging to keep up with his stupidly long legs. I have to huff out the words, breathless and exasperated, "I know you hate me and, honestly, I'd feel the same damn way, but I worked my ass off for that paper. I have done nothing but study and stick to your bullshit rules, I have no freedom, no fucking life, and still you're going to sit there on your high horse and tell me all about how much of a useless little brat I am? No, fuck you, North. I don't deserve this."

He stops when he gets to the car and holds the door open for me, ushering me in, and I'm distracted enough by the bullshit in my head that I don't notice Gryphon until I'm already sitting down. He's already buckled into the middle seat on the rearward facing row and I scoot along to get as far away from him and North as I can, shame curling in my gut that once again my humiliation has to be a spectator sport. His eyes roam over me with cold apathy, pausing for a second on my cheeks, and I quickly scrub a hand over them in case I've done something mortifying like cry in front of them.

North slides in after me, sitting in his usual seat. "Nox isn't known for his subtlety, you've wronged him and he's going to make sure everyone knows about it. You can't blame him for assuming you'd do a terrible job, he knows you dropped out of high school on a whim, Fallows."

I speak through my teeth, "It's not like I had a choice, *Draven.*"

North glances over to Gryphon, his brow furrowed, and Gryphon shrugs back at him. "She's telling the truth."

I snort. "Well, thanks for your vote of confidence there, Gryphon. Why the hell are you even here? Shouldn't you be off torturing people somewhere else, somewhere that's nowhere near me?"

He stares me down until my skin is crawling and I desperately want to look away from him, but sheer stubborn will says I have to keep his gaze until he's the one to break it. I'm totally winning the stare-off too and then North startles me with his grumpy, asshole tones.

"We weren't expecting the detour here to deal with you, there are Bonds and Bonded going missing, you know."

Like a knife slicing right through my heart, he could never know how much those words hurt me. I choke out, "I'm aware."

A frosty silence takes over the car and I resist the urge to dig my phone out to mess around with as a shield. North will just spy on whatever it is that I do and I can't sit here with his smug ass while this is going on. The drive over to my dorm only takes a couple of minutes and when the driver opens my door, I hesitate for a second before I open my bag, digging around for the assignment that started all of this shit.

The big fat F written in red and circled is like a beacon for us all, every eye hitting it and judging me for once again coming up as a defect.

Except this time I'm not.

I'm not going to let my own anger at this bullshit situation undo all of my hard work. I swallow around the lump in my throat and hold the papers out to North. "I appreciate you offering to mark my work for Nox. If you agree with his assessment of it, then I will accept it and apply for a make up assignment. I can... do that, right?"

North doesn't look impressed by my words or the paper as he plucks it out of my hands. "You have no choice but to pass all of your classes. You'll rewrite it until it's adequate."

I refuse to give him an answer, straightening and slamming the door shut before the driver has a chance to close it for me. It's a long walk up to my room ignoring the other students who have already heard about what happened today. I change into some comfortable clothes and lay back on my bed for a second to breathe. The springs dig into my back but at this point, I'm so used to the feeling that it's almost a comfort to me.

I give myself five minutes to wallow in my rage and spite.

Then I get up and start working on my make up assignment because I'll be damned if I let Nox fucking Draven win.

North emails me a week later with a B- grade and even though I'm positive that it deserves a higher mark than that, I email him back to say thank you and then I hit the books even harder.

Sage gets us a permanent table booking in the library and joins me in my mission to destroy Nox fucking Draven through my grades alone. Well, she tells me that her parents only let up on her about avoiding the whole world if she says she's studying. I'm happy about it for half a second before she adds that her family is hoping Riley will change his mind about rejecting their Bond if she graduates with honors and gets a high paying job... like if she can earn him a lot of money she might be useful to him.

Someday, I'm going to kill them all.

I can feel it brewing in me, like someday it'll boil over and I'll have no choice but to just ruin them all. I mean, I'm already there with Giovanna because Sage was not exaggerating about how fucking evil the bitch is. If anything, she's too nice about her. Something about her smug looks and smirks digs under my skin and irritates the ever-loving fuck out of me. I've never been a power elitist, my time with the Resistance drummed that into me, but there's something about a girl who's skating by completely on her looks that just eats at me.

After the first week of us hanging out at the library together, Sawyer shows up and studies with us. He's polite to me but is still stiff and distant about it. Sage notices and offers to tell him to leave but I'm stubborn and want him to like me, so I work at charming him instead. I'm not sure it works but he's never rude to me, so I'll call it a win.

Grade attempts to sit with us once but Sage shuts her down so swiftly that I have to hold back tears of laughter. When I told her about Gracie drooling all over Gryphon, she hadn't been surprised, just rolled her eyes and cut her out whenever she tried to join us.

The real complication is when Felix and Gabe show up.

For one, they show up together, which instantly loses Felix all of the brownie points I'd mentally given him after

Sage's party. For another, Gabe stares Sawyer down like he's about to drag him outside to beat him to death when he sees us sitting together.

"We're all pretty sure Oli is a lesbian, Benson, no point trying to hook up with my Bond," he snaps but before I have the chance to deflate his ego and remind him that Bond or not, I will never touch him, Sage cuts in.

"If you start shit with my brother, Gabe, I will bum down everything you love. Your bike, your football stadium, your dick... *everything."*

I turn to stare at her because who the hell is this badass and where the fuck has Sage been hiding her all this time?

Maybe I am in love with her instead.

Felix glances between them and then shoots me a look. "Are you going to step in or should I?"

I shrug and smirk at him, propping my chin up on my hand, "I'd rather watch Sage murder everyone in this room than smother this attitude of hers today. It's probably why my Bonds are obsessed with the idea of me fucking her... or maybe it's a fetish thing, I don't care enough to figure it out."

Gabe's eyes flash at me and I know I've hit a nerve but he started it, so he can live with the consequences. Felix looks around at each of us again before pulling out a seat next to Sage, sitting down and opening up his own textbooks. She side-eyes him but when he doesn't attempt to lean into her or talk to her, she lets it go.

I actually think he's perfect for her and the world is a terrible place for not fating them to be together.

When we all ignore him for long enough, Gabe finally huffs and pulls out a seat of his own next to me, spreading his books and papers out on the desk until he's taking over half of my space as well. I'm sure he's doing it to get a rise out of me but I just do my best not to shift into Sawyer's space and spoil whatever progress I've made with him.

Sage watches all of this with narrowed eyes but I just shake my head at her because fighting with Gabe never actually gets me anywhere. The best I can hope for is for him to get sick of being around me and leaving me the hell alone. I'm sure he can convince North to sign off on it, it's not like I've tried to run away.

Yet.

When our study break is over with and I have to head off to my Torture Training session, as Sage is now calling TT, I pack everything away and pull her into a quick hug, squeezing her for a second and hoping she can feel how grateful I am to have her fiercely protective friendship.

I'm shocked when Sawyer also pulls me into a quick hug, ignoring Gabe's moody huffing behind us, and then he ushers Sage out, Felix giving me a nod and then following them both out.

I desperately wish I was heading to class with them

but maybe an afternoon of destroying my body on all of those torture machines will actually make me feel better. Great, Vivian and his training program has somehow indoctrinated me into loving the feeling of my entire body burning up and turning to jelly.

Gross.

I make it out of the library and into the sunshine outside before Gabe jogs to catch up with me, falling into step instead of the three steps behind me like he usually does. I grit my teeth and ignore him, picking up my pace so I can hide in the locker room in the TT center until the class starts and Vivian will be too far up his ass for him to bother me.

The problem is that something has clearly crawled up Gabe's ass about me today and he's not going to let anything go, darting in front of me to block my path, and I have no choice but to stop walking or I'll slam into him.

I can't get pressed up against him again right now.

"I'm not doing this with you today. Wasn't Sage's warning enough for you to let it go?"

"I will never let this go, Fallows. How can I when you're supposed to be my Bond and instead you're draping yourself over any other guy on campus? What the fuck went wrong with you that you can act like this?"

He's lost his mind. My voice comes out like an outraged squeak and I sound fucking stupid, "Me?! All I've done since getting dragged to this shithole of a campus is play by your little rules. What, were you hoping I'd come back and just bend over for you all? Lay back and take it so you could get your bond with me and all the power that comes with it? I'd rather die. Seriously, Gabe, look me in the eyes right now and accept it because *I 'd rather die than do that."*

His lip curls up and all of his usual flinches are gone as he leans down until he's right in my face. "And I'd rather die than sit around and watch you work your way through the freshman class. If your Bonds aren't good enough for you, then you're going to be alone and miserable, I'll make sure of that."

I scoff at him and turn on my heel, ready to sprint to the training center if that what it takes to get away from his crazy today, but he grabs my arm and turns me back to face him, snarling in my face, "You left, you did that, whatever shit you're having to deal with now is because of what you did. You hate us, that's fine, deal with the consequences."

I roll my eyes at him and pull away but his hand tightens on my arm. "Let go of me—"

"What are you going to do, break my arm? How exactly are you going to manage that? Gryphon seems to think you'd be able to do some damage if you wanted to but I'm not seeing it."

Huh. I didn't think Gryphon had taken enough notice

of me to know what I was capable of, but clearly I'm doing something right in TT if he thinks I can take a football player on and survive it.

I don't need my gift or training to best Gabe though, he wears all of his feelings on his sleeve too much for it not to be easy.

I step towards him, pressing myself against his chest and watching as he startles. Whatever was going through his head before to stifle his reactions is long gone now and he tenses up at the feel of my body on his.

"Get your hand off of me before I prove Gryphon right. I might be playing by the rules for now but if you push me, you'll figure out exactly what I'm capable of."

"We're headed to the basement today, so plan your workouts accordingly."

The entire room groans like we've just been told we're about to be sent to hell to fight the devil himself but, like always, I have no idea what Vivian is talking about. Everyone moves onto the gym equipment, dragging their feet more than they usually do, and I stay close to Vivian, preparing myself for whatever circuit he's going to throw me onto today.

He doesn't immediately move over to me like he

usually does, instead he watches the other students for a second, like he's taking note of what they're choosing to do. It's confusing enough that I turn and watch it too but I can't figure out what's so damn interesting for him.

They're all choosing the easier machines, the stuff they all find the easiest. I've spent so goddamn long on the treadmill and elliptical machines watching all of the other students go through their paces while I attempt to forget the pain I'm in that I know that Gabe and his buddies always end up on the weight machines after a particularly rough game of football. Vivian usually barks orders at the guys to move on to cardio and get the hell on with it, but he just stands and watches them all.

When he finally makes his way over to me, he jerks his head at the treadmill and says, "Take it easy today, this is just a warmup."

I frown back at him. "What's so terrifying about the basement? If the Boogey Man is down there I'd like to know now, so I can kill myself instead of heading down there. I was already planning on throwing myself off a bridge, I'll just move it up."

He gives me a hard look, his scars making him look even surlier, but I've been in this class and working with him for long enough that I just bat my eyelashes back at him.

He grunts at me, "I'm a mandatory reporter for students

in crisis, don't say that shit around me because I'd rather not have to fill out all of that paperwork, kid."

I grin at him and shrug, feigning sheepishness. "Got any teachers you hate? I'm happy to mouth off elsewhere as an apology."

He shakes his head at me, grumbling under his breath about his pay scale and dealing with this bullshit, but that's nothing out of the ordinary.

I choose to stick to my usual workout because I'm both stubborn and stupid sometimes. Whatever is hiding in the basement isn't going to stop me from proving myself to Vivian, and it's not like North would allow me to die here, no matter how badly I might want to some days.

I don't think I'll die until he signs off on it.

After the full hour is up, every muscle in my body feels like jelly and my legs are just barely holding me up. I'm so used to it now that I hardly register the shaking, only huffing with frustration when my water bottle shakes in my hand too much for me to get a decent drink.

Vivian only gives us a minute to hydrate before he's barking out orders and staking out the door on the far wall, one we've never been through before and I'd always assumed was just storage.

Guess I was wrong there.

"You're going to regret working out as hard as you did, reject," Zoey snarks as she shoves past me, knocking into my shoulder so hard it wrenches. The tingles that shoot down to my fingertips spell trouble for me but I do my best to ignore it, rubbing at my shoulder and neck as best as I can with my trembling hand.

"She's not wrong."

I roll my eyes at the sound of Gabe's voice but I don't answer him or react, I don't have the energy to spare for him and his bullshit right now.

I need to figure out how to survive whatever Vivian is leading us to today.

"You'll be out in the first three minutes if you don't team up with someone. It's a shame Sage or Sawyer aren't in this class, you might have survived if your girlfriend was around to save you."

We're at the back of the group, so I feel comfortable enough to call him out for his attitude once more. "Your writhing jealousy is showing again. You know, if you stopped being an asshole, we could be friends too. If you want what Sage and Sawyer have with me so badly, all you have to do is stop sucking up to North and just be my friend."

He grunts at me and shakes his head. "I don't want to be your fucking friend, Fallows."

I laugh at him, a dark and mocking sound. "No, you want to own me and take what you think you're owed. You're as bad as the rest of them."

A couple of his football buddies glance back at us, overhearing enough of what we're saying to check up on us. I flip them the bird and Gabe knocks me with his shoulder gently, but thanks to Zoey's rough treatment it jars me and knocks the air out of me.

"Stay away from everyone in the maze. Vivian has people watching the entire simulation but you could still get pretty severely hurt if you're not careful. This is the one place on campus where we're allowed to use our gifts to their full extent and there's a lot of guys who like to flex here because it's safe enough to. The entire basement is bombproof. Unser once went off down there and the place is still standing, so we know it's safe."

Unser? I raise an eyebrow at him but Gabe is still pissed off at me and just smirks, shrugging with feigned nonchalance. I turn away from him so he doesn't see how much it digs under my skin not to know who he's talking about.

What the hell does 'went off' even mean? A living bomb? A flame who has a little extra bang for their buck? The possibilities are literally endless in the Gifted community so I'll have to ask Sage about it later.

The staircase is long and winding, the temperature rising the further we get down until it feels as though the air is made out of soup, heavy and hot in my lungs. There's a small flutter of panic in my stomach, the worst place for it to be because my gift begins to strain at the tight hold I have on it in response.

The last time I was trapped underground like this, I was tortured.

I force myself to think about something, *anything,* except for that time. I force myself to think about Sage and Felix, to wonder whether Felix will be able to find some way to convince Sage to give him a chance. It's something I've been thinking about a lot since her birthday because there was no mistaking the adoration in his eyes every time he looked at her. Sometimes bonds aren't a blessing and they just make things more complicated and those two are a classic example of that.

Gabe staring at me like he's imagining what choking the life out of me would feel like is another.

When we reach the bottom of the stairs, I find a small room. Three of the walls are stone and the wall on the far side is made up entirely of giant fire doors cut out of a concrete door. Whatever is on the other side, it's clear I'll be going in blind.

Vivian waits until we're all crowded in the space and then calls out, his voice echoing in the tiny space, "You'll be split up again, this time into groups of three. No, you don't get to choose who you're with. No, I don't care whether or not you think this is fair. No, there isn't somewhere you can put in a complaint because I don't care about your opinions and feelings here. I care about training you to the best of my ability. I've had two hundred and forty three students leave here and make it into TacTeams and they're mostly all alive today, thanks to this training, so shut your mouths and get to the center alive if you wanna pass this class. First to the flag wins an automatic pass on this class for the year."

Okay.

Get to the center without dying.

I'm not even going to pretend I have a chance of getting to the center first but, fuck, I'm going to at the very least attempt to get there in the next hour. It doesn't seem so bad, and if I have two other students who need me alive and coherent to pass then I should be okay. This isn't so bad.

At least, it wasn't so bad until I got paired with Zoey and some guy I've never heard of before but who grins at Zoey like this is all going to be a freaking party.

Gabe shoots me a look but doesn't attempt to talk to his little friends and get them not to be assholes to me, he just walks over to his own chosen partners and starts murmuring to them. I guess the maze requires strategy, but Zoey and Brenton don't say a word to me as I stalk over to join them both. I also don't mutter a word to them, I already know there's no point.

I'm in this alone.

The moment the doors swing open I see exactly what they mean by *simulation* and honestly? I'm totally and completely fucked.

So just a regular Friday afternoon for me.

The room is pitch black.

As always, I'm the last one to walk forward into the maze, but this time it doesn't really work out to my advantage because everyone else has obviously done this enough to know that the moment our feet cross the threshold of the simulation, all of our senses are tom away.

At least I hope it's all of us and not just me.

I imagine this is how having a stroke must feel. I can't see or hear anything and there's only the vaguest sensation of the ground beneath my feet that says my feet must still be moving. I have no freaking clue how this simulation is possible, how the Draven campus managed to create this hellscape, but I'm utterly defenseless.

I also should've taken it easy on my workout.

I don't know how long I walk through the bleak nothingness, only that when it ends and I can finally see again, the light is blinding, my eyes streaming and my head aching with a sharp pain. My bond immediately reacts to the pain, my gift straining under my control, and I have to stop for a second to regain control. There's no one around me, no sign of the dozens of other people in the class, and I don't know if that's just because I've been going so slow or if the... *magic* or whatever is happening here has put us all in different places in the maze.

All I know is that the walls are all made of black bricks and the ground is concrete, stained in places and very obviously the spilled substance was blood. Fuck, there's a stain big enough that the person had to have died there, no matter what Gabe said about this place being monitored.

Death isn't exactly the worst option here but it's also not my first choice.

I'm too busy freaking the fuck out to notice the sounds of footsteps, but the roar of something definitely gets my attention.

There's a shifter nearby.

I don't know what Gabe can turn into, but there's three other shifters in our class, so I can't assume he's come to find me. Knowing my luck, Brenton is also a shifter and he's come to rip my throat out and make a whole new stain on the ground. We all need to reach the center to win, but I'm sure Zoey is fine with losing me and taking the hit on her point tally.

I step back, pressing my back against the wall behind me and preparing myself for whatever the hell is about to happen when there's a grinding, groaning, snapping sound—

And then the walls start moving.

What in the Harry Potter bullshit is this?! I have to spring away from the wall behind me but it's not the one moving. No, it's the one across from me, rushing towards me and I'm about to be crushed to death if I don't get my shaking knees under control and move my ass.

The panic flooding my entire body is actually a good thing because I'm conditioned to work at my peak performance while absolutely shitting myself, so I manage to get my legs working and dart out of the way. There's a crunch and a thud, then a small flash of light before I hear the groaning of whoever the shifter is now that they're trapped on the other side of the wall, very obviously injured.

Do I call out to them? Do I call out and hope someone will come help them or will I just give away my position doing that and get myself killed for my kindness?

A voice calls out and makes up my mind for me, "Fuck, Martinez, what are you doing getting snapped by the walls? That's rookie shit!"

I have no clue who that is but the panting shifter answers, "I could smell the new girl, I thought we could use her as bait for the pond bitch."

Uhm, first of all, fuck Martinez. I can't believe I was going to help the asshole, but secondly, and most importantly, what the *fuck* is the pond bitch?

I think I'm going to puke.

I also don't have time to let my nerves get the better of me so I push on, choosing the only path I can that appears to circle the entire maze. The only other direction I can head in is backwards and I don't want to go through the deprivation area again, thank you very much. I have to block out the screams of the other students as much as I possibly can as they echo around the room.

I start at a walking pace but then I start to get the creeps about the walls caving in on me and pick up the pace, jogging so I don't run out of steam so early on.

The sounds in this place are kind of terrifying.

There's a flame in here somewhere and every time I see the bursts of light reflect onto the ridiculously high ceiling, I start to panic all over again about air quality and the entire basement burning down. My feet move faster without me even trying, the adrenaline kicking in, and I only slow down when I finally reach the comer at the end of the building.

I stop and take a breath there, forcing my heartbeat to slow down because panic is a great motivator, but I need to use my brain here. I have no access to my gift, and although the training in this stupid class has upped my stamina, I still have very little self defense skills.

If I get around this comer and find myself staring at a fully shifted wolf or cougar or something, I am well and truly screwed.

I strain to try to hear something but there's nothing there, only the distant sounds of students fighting and yelling at each other, so I slowly creep forward to peek around the stone wall.

There's a garden there.

An entire freaking room carved out of the basement with plants everywhere. It's... well, it's kind of stunning, vines growing over the walls and bright blooms of flowers breaking through the deep and gorgeous greenery. It's like something out of Wonderland, like this entire basement is some twisted and sick version of all my favorite tales.

Only the more I look, the more I see that this isn't a paradise.

The vines are moving for one, slowly reaching out towards me like they're about to wrap around my body and take me out. The flowers are all weeping, the liquid coming out of them is eating away at the ground as it drops, and then there's the small matter of the thorns.

They're popping up everywhere.

I look down at myself and curse the shorts and tee I'm wearing because they're not going to protect me from shit but once again, time is working against me here and the longer I stand around indecisively, the bigger and more dangerous the horrors in the room are becoming.

Okay.

Okay, this is fine. I can walk through thorns and acid while dodging creeping vines. Totally reasonable. My gift wouldn't help me with this anyway, so no use feeling shitty about not having it, just zip through this, Oleander.

Self talk doesn't really help but imagining everything I'm going to do to this entire freaking school the second I'm no longer powerless sure does. When the first thorn imbeds itself into my thigh, I think about bringing North Draven to his goddamn knees. When the acid starts to eat it's way through the soles of my shoes, I imagine the look on Nox's face when I show him exactly how I could break him open. I think about proving myself to Gryphon, showing him that I'm not some useless fucking brat.

And Gabe.

Ho boy, the thoughts of exactly what I'd say to Gabe blocks out the tearing pain of the vines wrapping around my wrist and yanking at my injured arm perfectly. The more of the pain I can ignore and work past, the more aggressive the garden gets about trying to stop me, trying to hurt me so badly that I stop trying to get through.

When I finally get to the small opening, the soles of my shoes are completely gone and my shirt is in tatters, blood running down my stomach from the wounds on my entire torso. There's vines wrapped around both of my arms and my thighs, twisting and tightening painfully, and I have to slam myself into the wall and then wrench myself around the comer to pry them off, stumbling to my knees as they finally snap and break away from the main plant. I panic, assuming they'll still be able to wrap around me or that they'll suddenly become snakes, because that's the horror show bullshit I'm expecting here, but they instantly fall away from me as though they really were just vines all along.

I stay on my knees for a second longer, panting and rolling my shoulders back painfully, trying to test the muscles out, and the screaming around me reaches a fever pitch.

Does Vivian have some weird fucking S&M kink I didn't ever want to know about? Does he get off on torturing students and listening to their terror?

I'm definitely going to ask him about it later because I have zero freaking shame about calling him out. This is supposed to be a college class, for fuck's sake. Who in their right mind does this to their students?

The shuffling catches my attention first.

I startle and scramble back before my brain catches on to what I'm actually seeing. In the doorway of the killer garden is what I thought was a tree trunk, but is actually a student wrapped entirely in vines. She's alive, I can see her breathing, but she's out cold. There are cuts all over her body from the thorns and her feet are bare, but she looks almost peaceful now that she's unconscious.

What exactly is the protocol here?

I feel very strongly about not getting myself killed or injured for another student who hates my freaking guts, but if there's a chance this thing is going to kill her— am I really the type to just abandon her?

"Vivian, a little guidance here would've been nice," I mutter to myself, mostly so I don't feel so fucking guilty for just leaving because, let's just face it, I'm going to walk away.

A light blinks to life on the wall.

It's red and is right over the girl, like it's drawing attention to her. I decide that it's enough of a beacon that someone must be coming to get her and I get my ass moving. I pull the remains of my sneakers off and throw them aside, wincing a little at the cold concrete on my bare feet as I break back into a jog. As I look out at the other walls as I jog, I see other little blinking red lights and my heart finally sinks back out of my throat. It must be normal, something that happens when a student has been taken out of the running, and at a quick count from where I am, there's at least ten people out. I can only see a small section of the walls from where I am, so hopefully there aren't many people left here for me to come up against.

The screaming also quietens down a little the deeper into the maze I get, less frequent now, which proves there's less people here being tortured. I have to duck behind one of the comers to avoid a trio of students. One of them was a girl holding a palm full of fire while one of the guys was holding out a forcefield and the other's eyes glowed. They all look battered and bruised, but they're alive and working together, so obviously they're my pick for making it to the center and winning the passing grade.

The guy with the glowing eyes glanced down in my direction but didn't comment on seeing me or noticing anything out of the ordinary, so either he couldn't see me, or he has no interest in *feeding me to the pond bitch* like that dickhead Martinez.

Fucking Martinez.

I'm going to punch him in the face the second I get out of this maze.

When the trio is gone, I get back up from my crouch, every inch of my body screaming in protest, and then I keep working my way through the maze slowly, doubling back after each dead end. It's frustrating and slow going, especially now that I'm on bare feet, and a few times I come across an unconscious student or a mysterious pool of blood that has my stomach dropping.

The real terror starts when I find another room, this time with a huge body of water, and I start to panic that I've found the infamous pond because I'm not sure I can fight a sea creature right now.

There's only one way for me to go though, and it's the doorway cut out of the other side.

There's no fucking way I'm swimming across, even if I hadn't been warned, because the water stinks and I don't want to puke my way across right now. There are rocks and boulders to one side that I could scale my way across but my jelly arms hate that option, so I walk around the water's edge for a second, like I can make a sturdy bridge appear with nothing but my desperation.

No such luck.

Rock climbing it is. The small stones bite into my feet and the larger boulders move a little under my body weight, which is both insulting and unsettling. I scramble to the highest point and then take a second to breathe and attempt to get some strength back in my arms. I know now how much those training sessions have done for me because even me of six months ago would've been wrapped up in the vines.

From this vantage point, I can actually see how close I am to the center and, fuck me, it's close. I memorize the path, and thank God that I climbed this stupid thing because there's three rooms I can avoid if I do this right.

I can't see Gabe but there is a freaking massive snow leopard in one of the rooms fighting against... okay, it's so gross I don't want to say it, but there's a plague of rats in one of the rooms and I suddenly understand all of the screaming because no. No, I would rather face the quiet and absent pond bitch than a million diseased and disgusting rats, thanks.

My skin crawls like I might just pass out and die, so I decide it's time to get the hell out of here and pray the walls don't move on me because, dammit, I need some luck for once!

The second I start to crawl down the other side of the rock, I come face-to-face with the pond bitch and I wish so badly that I could scrub my mind of her because *holy fucking nightmare* is she disgusting.

She was once human, I think. Her skin is grey and sliding away from the bone of her skull, her hair is mostly gone, only little tufts of it sticking up in small patches. Her teeth are broken and sharply pointed as she gapes up at me with milky white eyes, her jaw flapping like she's gasping for air, and I'm officially never sleeping again because this bitch is definitely going to haunt me.

Her hand wraps around my ankle, the dirty pond water dripping from her nightmare body onto the bare skin of my foot, and all I can think is that I'm going to get some flesh-eating parasite from her.

I turn the part of my brain that is freaking the fuck out off and switch my survival mode back on, gripping the edges of the rock and then swinging my free leg up until I can get a good kick in, striking her shoulder first. When that doesn't get her off me, I bite the bullet and kick her in the face, her teeth cutting the heel of my foot, but with a gurgling scream, her hand loosens enough for me to wrench my foot away.

I slide down the rock, skinning the backs of my thighs and shredding my hands, but desperate times and all that. When I land at the bottom, breaking my ass and knocking the wind out of myself, I scurry away as fast as my broken body will let me. Even when I get past the threshold of the room and back out into the hallway I keep crawling, the gurgling sounds of the pond bitch bouncing on the brick walls.

I'm quitting this goddamn class.

I turn two comers on my hands and knees before I finally relocate my pride and struggle to my feet. My nose is running, my eyes are stinging, and my chest rattles with every breath, but I'm alive.

I'm going to need a healer the moment I get out of here and I will break North in half with my bare hands if he tries to stop me from accessing one.

Luckily, blessedly, the walls stay put and I make it to the center of the fucking maze. My body collapses onto the ground in a heaving, shaking mess.

The motherfucking center of this stupid, murderous, dickheaded maze.

I don't even get the chance to feel proud of myself, to feel happy that I made it through by myself and without using my gift once, because I find Zoey and Brenton jogging through the doorway at the other end of the room, their eyes on the flag for a second before they notice me slumped over here.

Zoey grins as she stalks over to me, the crop top she's wearing is tight across her chest and soaked through from whatever she's been up against in the maze so far, but overall she looks a million times better than I do. Whatever she's been up against, Brenton has taken the brunt of it. He's tom up like me but he's still standing.

My eyes flick over to the flag only a few feet away, but with my 'walking-chloroform' here, there's no chance I'm getting it.

I hate this bitch.

I feel her gift take me over, the poison of it touching my skin and floating through my veins. My body is so fucking used to it now, a regular Friday occurrence, that I'm not surprised when my nose starts dripping blood and my mouth fills up with it in response.

It's fucking infuriating.

I spit at her, my blood bright red on her cheek, and her squeal is fucking music to my ears. "You're an absolute cunt and someday you're going to regret this bullshit. I'm patient, I can wait you out."

She smirks at me. "Like I'd be scared of some gift-less reject. Nighty-night, bitch."

And then she knocks me the fuck out.

"I cannot believe Zoey would rather knock you out than win a pass in TT. It's the hardest class at Draven, everyone knows that you don't throw that away!"

I scoff and press the ice against my temple a little harder but there's no use, nothing is going to stop the pounding there.

The moment I'd woken up, bloodied and broken on the ground in the main room of the training center, I'd hobbled over to my bag to message Sage and cancel our plans for the night because there's no way I can possibly study and eat pizza on the floor of my shitty dorm room in the state I'm in right now.

She immediately hauled her ass over to check on

me, dragging Felix behind her because he's a healer. Apparently, my damaged state is enough to get her to call him willingly.

I tried to apologize to him but he'd shrugged and started working on all of the many wounds on my body. There's other healers here but I'm the worst for wear, thanks a fucking lot, Vivian. Gabe is over on the far side, holding one of his friends down as a healer resets the bone in his leg, and he's only looked my way once this entire time. I'm not surprised or disappointed, it's just another strike against the asshole.

"She's a crazy fucking bitch and Sage, I will literally pay you anything if you set her on fire for me. Your bail, getaway money, let's start a new life somewhere far away from here where Vivian can never find me again and force me into a room with the pond bitch again."

Sage stares at me in horror for a second and Felix winces. "You went up against her, huh? She's kind of an urban legend around here."

I scoff again, glaring around at the other students while he resets my shoulder because apparently I'd dislocated it as I passed out, all of the wrenching and pulling of the day finally just popping it out at the end.

I want to die when he finally pops it back in.

"Motherfucking, cocksucking, cunt of a thing, I will honestly carve the skin off of that miserable—"

"Jesus Christ, you've got a mouth on you for such a little thing."

I glance up at Vivian, who is now standing over me with a scowl, and give him a glare back. "We are not friends, I rescind my offer of giving your teacher enemies paperwork for days."

Felix snorts at me, smothering it into a cough at the stem look on Vivian's face as the hardass checks over his handiwork.

"Now, now, you can't pass TT without going up against the worst of what our kind can do. You did good, kid. If you didn't have so many of your own enemies, you'd be free and clear for the rest of the year." He sounds a little too gleeful at this and I'm about to mouth off at him again, when Felix shifts to reset my broken rib and I find myself completely unable to think, breathe, or function, let alone speak.

Sage stops glaring at everyone around us for a second and rubs at my back, slow, soothing strokes that avoid all of the scrapes and cuts. There's even a couple of thorns still imbedded there that I don't want to think about, because I'm sure they'll feel fucking peachy coming out.

Vivian clears his throat and grumbles a little under his breath before finally speaking, "You should be proud of yourself, everything you did in there was perfect. Half the others didn't make it past their first room. Only a handful made it through a second. And only one other student has made it past the pond girl on their first try. She feeds on fear and you barely gave her anything to work with."

Well.

Okay, that does make me feel a little better, I guess. The pond girl looked horrifying but she wasn't really that bad to get past, just so long as I don't think about whatever diseases she has in her mouth that are now in my foot.

Eww.

Vivian glances around at the other students and then drops his voice a little lower, "Thirty years in a TacTeam taught me that what your gift is doesn't mean shit about who you are... it's what you're going to do with it. Look at Gryphon, with his career trajectory you'd be thinking he was a shifter or some other physical gift, but he proves every day that you don't need it. If you've got nothing but your backbone, kid, you're going to be fine out there."

That's too fucking nice and sweet for me today and now I feel shit about how much I cursed the old man out in my head while I was in that hellhole of a maze of his.

I sigh and press the ice to my temple a little firmer, wincing when Felix digs one of the thorns out of my back. "Shouldn't you hate me for rejecting your favorite student?"

He shrugs. "The best things in life don't come without hard work. If he wants you, he should prove himself to you. I've known a lotta bad kids in my time here, you're not one of'em."

Then he turns on his heel and stalks off, barking orders at the other students around us. He's not even a little nice to any of them and that makes me feel better for all of a second before Gabe shows up and collapses on the ground in front of me. There's mud and dirt on him but otherwise he's untouched, which is annoying, especially as Felix finds another thorn in my back to dig out.

"How far did you get? I heard Zoey sabotaged you and she missed out on the flag because of it."

I roll my eyes at him. "Don't come here to rub it in, I'm not in the mood for it and if you think I'm a bitch to you normally, you have no idea of what I'm capable of when I've had a passing grade snatched away from me."

He straightens and blinks at me, the asshole exterior melting away in an instant. "You got to the flag?"

I grit out from between my teeth, "Yes, asshole, I made it there first and then you're little girlfriend—"

"She's *not* my fucking girlfriend. You made it to the flag and Zoey knocked you out there? Are you *fucking* kidding me?"

Oh, of course, because a Gift-less brat couldn't possibly beat all of these amazing and Gifted athletes. Of course I couldn't possibly control my fears and work through my pain like the others. Of course fucking not.

So I smirk and shrug at him, the picture of a smug bitch. “What, like it was hard? I’m honestly a little disappointed in your abilities if you couldn’t get through without help.”

Felix snorts and then glances at Sage for a second, like he’s gauging her response to whatever he has to input here. When his eyes finally flick back to me, he gives me a lopsided grin. “The bones are all set and the thorns are out. If I can put my hand on your chest, then I can fix all of the cuts and scrapes at once... is that okay?”

Gabe’s eyebrows pull down tight and I just fucking snap, “What, you’d rather me heal slowly and painfully after getting through two rooms and the entire fucking maze by myself?”

I don’t give him the chance to answer me. Instead, I yank the neckline of my shirt down and snap, “Thank you, Felix, I appreciate you helping me for no other reason than our friendship.”

Sage coughs like she’s now the one smothering laughter and Felix snorts at the look on Gabe’s face as he presses his palm to my chest, his gift flowing into me and healing everything it touches.

I feel the moment it touches my own gift, skirting around it respectfully.

Felix’s eyes snap to mine.

I give him the smallest shake of my head that I can manage and, bless him, he presses his lips together firmly in silent reply. I decide that I'll back him with Sage if she ever asks my opinion because that right there is a truly good man.

The moment I'm healed and Felix steps away, my entire body checks out for a good nap time. Sage squeaks a little as she catches me, my body slumping down into hers, and my last thought is about how lucky I am to have found friends like her and Felix, with his magic healing hands of gold.

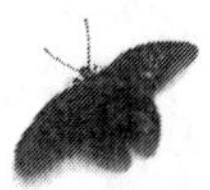

I wake up in my tiny, uncomfortable bed in my dorm room.

I'm still dressed in the rags of my TT workout gear but a blanket has been thrown over me and a glass of water left on my tiny bedside cupboard. I guzzle the whole thing down and then check my phone for the time, finding messages from Sage, Atlas, and North waiting for me.

Gabe carried you the whole way back to your room. Felix and I came too, and I tucked you into bed, call me if you need anything, x

Sage is my favorite, and while Gabe gets points for physically getting me home, he's still an asshole.

I called Draven when you missed our usual call, I'm having something delivered for you in the morning. I told your jailer what it is, so he shouldn't be too much of a dickhead about it.

Atlas has taken to calling North as many derogatory and rude names as he can in our messages and phone calls now that he knows we're being monitored. I'm a little shocked that he called him over something as small as me missing a call but he always has treated me like I'm something precious.

I still feel horrendously guilty over it.

And then there's North's message.

If you are too injured to attend study or classes, I -will send another healer to you. There are no excuses forfailing your classes.

I reply to Sage and Atlas straight away and leave North on read because he can choke on a dick for all I care, then I make the slow and painful trip to the bathroom to pee and scrub the horrors of the day away from my skin. Felix did an amazing job of putting me back together but there's a leftover ache in my bones and muscles that make breathing freaking excruciating. Not that I'm complaining, because this is a million times better than healing without the help but, man, do I want to die the second the water hits me like a thousand burning needles into my raw skin.

Showers are usually my safe space, the one enjoyable experience of my day, and having that tom away from me has me cursing Vivian out again. Just because I like the old asshole, doesn't mean I can't also hate him at the same time for this bullshit. When I manage to crawl back to my room, I immediately pass out and sleep the day away.

I wake up in the afternoon, disorientated and ravenous.

I pull clothes on, whatever is comfortable, and walk down to the campus dining hall by myself to eat an early dinner. I'm expecting to catch shit from someone for looking homeless in my sweatpants and hoodie pulled up over my head, but either no one recognizes me, or they're all too hungover from a great Friday night to notice me here.

I eat enough food to fill a football team up.

Being healed by a Gifted always makes you hungry but, fuck me, three plates down and I'm still thinking about grabbing another breadstick and dipping it in the spaghetti sauce, sprinkling some cheese on it... God, by the time I talk myself out of a fifth plate I think my stomach is in real danger of splitting open.

What a way to die.

My walk back to the dorms is slower now that I'm carrying an extra twenty pounds of undigested carbs and sauces, and there's a package waiting for me at the desk when I get back to the building.

Flowers from Atlas with a teddy, a card that apologizes for being cheesy even though I'm crying over his thoughtfulness, and a box full of candies and chocolates. It's honestly the nicest thing a guy has ever done for me and I have no idea of how to thank him without feeling like I'm leading him on.

The guilt climbs back up my spine and I have to push it away again because... well, I've been honest with him, as honest as I can be. I've told him I don't want to stay. I've told him I can't be with any of them. Is that enough for me to accept these gifts without feeling like I'm the worst type of bitch?

I'm too freakin inept at dealing with bonds and the emotional baggage that comes with them to navigate this without causing damage.

I get back to my room and binge on the candies like I haven't just eaten a huge meal at the dining hall, all of my emotions opening up a black hole inside of me that I need the sugar to fill. I send a fumbling *thank you* to Atlas and then turn my phone off because I'm a coward right now and can't think of how to talk to him.

I'm seriously considering messaging Sage to whine about the bullshit that is my life, when there's a knock at my door.

Who the hell is it now?

Because Sage would message first and no one else that I hang out with would show up here without her. When I step up to the door my Bond gives a little tug in my chest, my hand pausing halfway to the door handle because there's no way I want to face North or Gabe right now.

I'm too sore to verbally spar with either of them, and I don't want North thinking he's broken me just because I'm not in my usual full-glory brat mode.

"Open the door, Oli."

Fucking typical.

Of course it would be Gryphon showing up to mess with my entire freaking day because he's the Bond that can actually fuck my shit up. The butterflies in my stomach are screaming danger at me, but I open the door and face him anyway.

He's the hardest of them all to face.

I think it's the way he hasn't confronted me, hasn't tried to verbally knock me down or take a jab at me, he's just sat back and observed me, the look on his face always saying a lot about how much I don't meet his expectations.

His eyes flick over my outfit, my cheeks heating as I remember the fact that I look homeless, and then he steps into me like he's trying to force his way into the room.

It works, I scramble away from him like his touch would bum me, and he shuts the door firmly behind him. The lock is flimsy and he scowls at it for a second before flicking it anyway. I get the feeling, I'm not sure it would work to keep anyone out of here if they put some effort in.

"The healer did a decent job. I thought for sure you'd be bedridden from the pond bitch's bite."

I pull a face at him as my ass lands on my pokey

mattress. There's nowhere for him to sit except on the bed with me and I might die if he does. When was the last time I washed the sheets?

Why do I care about his opinion of my shitty room and the little sauce stain on my hoodie? Get a fucking grip, Oleander.

"She wasn't that bad."

As he leans back against the door, he stares me down, crossing his arms over his chest, and suddenly I notice just how freaking stacked he is. I knew it when he'd slid between Giovanna and me at Sage's party but the creaking noise of his leather jacket straining over his biceps is almost obscene right now.

My bond is a homy, needy bitch in my chest.

"She feeds on fear. Most Gifted go up against her absolutely shitting themselves because she becomes the worst nightmare they've ever had to live through. You gave her nothing, even after she spooked you. That's not a normal response."

Right, so this is an interrogation.

He's different from North's blunt commands or Nox's scathing barbs. Even Gabe's brooding, moody blowups are lightyears away from this calm, direct conversation and fuck if it isn't disarming.

I have to choose my words very carefully. "I never claimed I was normal."

If he doesn't stop staring at me I might just break down and bawl like a baby. Is this his gift? To just stare people into a complete mental crisis, because I can confirm that he's pretty fucking good at wielding this power.

"I think you made a mistake and instead of owning up to it and making amends, you've doubled down on it. You should have trusted us... whatever happened in that hospital room that made you run away, you should have run to us instead."

The terror of thinking about that day when I'd woken up in that sterile room is like ice through my veins. If I was facing the pond bitch now she would eat me alive, guzzling down the meal that those memories would make for her.

Gryphon's eyes narrow at me, the clear jade color of them striking and burning hot into my skin. All of the fight leaves my body at once, the despair and loathing at myself and the hell I'm stuck in overwhelms me until my mouth starts running. I'd say anything to get him out of here before I really lose my shit.

The tears welling up nearly blind me but I ignore them. "Those opinions of yours tell me I did the right thing and I'm not pissed about it. You can hate me all you like because at least you're fucking breathing, Gryphon. Please leave, I'm still exhausted from the healing and I can't do this right now."

I sleep away the rest of the weekend, waking up every couple of hours to guzzle down some water and hobble to the bathroom, but my body basically shuts down to process the healing Felix did on me. It's annoying but my brain becomes nothing but the need to *survive,* so at least I don't have to think about Gryphon's little visit.

The moment Gabe arrives at my door on Monday I can feel the difference in the air between us.

I'm still ready to hate him and bicker like the whole world is ending and it's his freaking fault, but he looks so freaking miserable and sort of like a sad puppy, even I'm not that much of a bitch to be kicking sad puppies.

As we walk across the campus to the dining hall,

he stays close to me, his eyes sharp as he takes in all of our surroundings, like he really is guarding me from something. My senses go on high alert right along with him and when my bond reaches out to his, brushing against him for reassurance, he startles and glances down at me. I get it, I've kept it on such a tight leash that he's never felt it before and I curse myself silently for letting it slip past.

His voice is a rough rasp, answering the question I haven't found the voice to ask yet, "Three more Bonded were taken last night from one of the gated communities about twenty minutes from here. My cousin was one of them."

Fuck.

My stomach drops so hard that if I had anything in it, I'd probably be puking on his shoes right now.

They're getting closer to me.

I've been meticulous about not letting my gift slip, not even a small burst of power, so I don't know if it's a coincidence that they're inching in on my location, or if that man has found a way to track me without using my gift as the beacon.

I'm too busy freaking the fuck out about the possibilities that Gabe gets us to the dining hall and fills me a plate of eggs before I make my way out of the panic to take the plate from him. It's rude of me to not offer him condolences but if I open my mouth right now, Lord knows what will actually come out.

Probably me freaking the fuck out and begging for him to let me go, let me run the hell away before we're all dead and rotting thanks to the Resistance and their never-ending mission for complete dominance.

We sit and eat in silence, Gabe's plate is almost completely empty before he breaks it. "When you first disappeared... we all thought you were taken. There'd been a lot of clusters in the area and, well, I was too young to know the details but my parents were both on the Council, so I heard enough to be scared for you. Every time we heard about bodies showing up, I thought it was you. Every time there was news about kids showing up brainwashed, fuck, I hoped it was you so we could get you home and save you, and all that time, you were just hanging out in some city, living whatever life you wanted."

It's a sad little story but there's a few very key things he's gotten wrong. Most of them I can't correct without causing a freaking shitstorm, but there is one thing I can set straight. "You know I was in the hospital because of a car accident, right? My entire family died in it. I was fourteen and completely alone in the world. I was terrified. It's not like I just skipped away into the sunset to live a happy and merry life by myself. Maybe you should try to see past your own story for once, and things might go a little better between us both."

He swallows and glances around the dining hall, but it's still a ghost town this early in the morning. It's why we both like it so much I think, neither of us have to worry about who is watching us eat.

"North told my entire family that you'd been spotted in Florida, working in a record shop, and without any markings or ties to the Resistance. He made it clear that all signs pointed to you just running away. How exactly am I supposed to just look past that?"

I shrug. "How would you take it if your whole family died in a single accident? If they were ripped away like that?"

He stares me down and then pushes his plate away from himself. "I don't have to imagine it. My dad was taken two years ago and we found his mutilated body a week later. My mom stepped down from the council the next day but she's still never really come home. If you're asking me to look past my *story,* then maybe you should look past yours as well."

There's nothing really that I can say back to that and I try to focus on finishing my breakfast, the eggs tasting worse than they usually do now that the room is full of our grief.

It was much easier to hate him when I thought he was just a pissed off, jealous asshole Bond without a story of his own.

When I finish up with my plate and grab my bag to head off to our first class, Gabe follows me, the easy grin back on his face as he greets guys around us with his usual carefree energy. I stop myself from brooding on how much I hate this place for a second and just watch everything around us both instead. The football guys all love him, the girls they're with all stare at him with heart eyes, and even the professors all greet him warmly.

None of them look twice at me anymore.

Sage meets us both at the doors of the Econ class, her eyes flicking between us, but she doesn't comment. When Gabe sits next to me instead of his usual three chairs away, she raises her eyebrows at me but doesn't say a word.

There's a reason she's my best friend.

I wait until the class starts and everyone is intently focussed on taking notes before I lean into him and whisper, "I don't want to bond but Ell stop going for your throat if you do the same."

It's the only olive branch I can give him right now, and it might be a bad idea to even go that far.

He huffs out a breath and doesn't answer me until the class is over, hovering over Sage and I as we pack our papers and books away.

"That's called being friends, Oli, and I'll give it a shot if you will too. We can figure out the bond shit later."

I scoff at him and sling my bag over my shoulder. "If

this is some 'nice guy' ploy of pretending to be my friend just to fuck me and get your bond, then I'll dick punch you right now and walk away without another thought."

Sage bursts out laughing, slapping a hand over her mouth that does exactly nothing to smother the peals of laughter shaking out of her body. Gabe shoots her a look but it's mostly exasperation. "At this point, Fallows, you'd have to beg me to fuck you. Friends with zero benefits, except that I'll be watching your every move and you'll be looking for a chance to run away from us all."

I shrug at him and knock shoulders with Sage as we walk out together. "Sounds fine, but the first rule of Reject Club is that we hate Giovanna and want to murder her. If you can't get behind that, then you're out already."

He shakes his head at me as Sage starts protesting, constantly putting herself down over that nightmare of a girl. "We don't want her dead, we just wish she'd hate me a little less."

I snort at her. "Fuck that, I want her dead. I've called dibs on her in the apocalypse. Gabe can take Riley out, and you can fuck Felix instead, he has my vote."

We turn the comer to find Felix standing there, grinning like a freaking devil, and Sage instantly turns beet red.

"I knew running off to heal you would work in my favor. Thanks, Fallows," he calls out as we pass by him, winking at Sage who is trying not to look as though she wants the ground to swallow her whole.

Gabe bursts out laughing with me and it's freaking eerie to be standing around with him and not planning out his death. I know it won't last, but even for a moment, it's a weird position to be in.

Sage digs an elbow into my ribs and mutters, "It's not up for a vote. We should hurry up, we're about to be late for History and Nox will start a whole new smear campaign against you, Oli."

Ugh.

Kill me.

I learn something very important the moment Gabe sits down with me in History and that is exactly how much power he has at this school. The moment people see us talking quietly with each other, there's an immediate shift, like they're all changing the way they're talking about me now that he's 'forgiven' me.

They don't need to know the details to change their position, and Zoey finds herself very suddenly alone.

Sage spots it first and points it out, murmuring to me, "Serves the bitch right."

I agree completely and when I nudge Gabe with a questioning look, he's a lot less subtle about it. "She broke the rules Vivian set. You deserved the win and he's already thrown her out of the class. Her parents are furious but Gryphon went to speak to them. You can't join a TacTeam if you have no loyalty to your team."

Well, damn.

It doesn't even matter to me that it's not really about me, it's all about her integrity, it still feels like a win. Maybe being interrogated wasn't so bad if this is the result.

My good feeling lasts ten more seconds before Nox walks in and sucks the good vibes right the fuck out. He looks good today too, hotter than Hades as he stalks into the classroom like some God of the Underworld, here to torment my goddamn soul.

I need to get out of this town before my hormones lead me straight to hell after him.

Nox's eyes flick over to where Gabe is now sitting with me but he doesn't react, no sign of whether he's surprised or pissed off to see us both sitting here together. He just plugs in his laptop and stands in front of the class and waits until the room falls silent, his appearance is all it takes to command the room.

"Someone tell me about the Tier System."

I'd rather die than raise my hand in any of Nox's classes but there's an entire row of girls all desperate to prove themselves to him, like answering this question will get him dropping his pants and feeding them his dick.

My bond squirms inside me at the thought but I torture myself with if for a second longer, like maybe I can convince it that he's a total fucking waste of space as far as I'm concerned.

He picks Amy, who's name I know because Sage loathes her, and even the sound of her voice has my hackles rising.

"When the three Councils of the Gifted communities came together to create the centralized Bonds network, they created a system of categorizing the Gifted and their abilities. The strongest Gifted have three levels of power; primary, secondary, and incidental. Most Gifted have primary gifts, some have a secondary as well, and very few have an incidental."

Nox nods at her and turns his back without another word, his constant strategy of 'treat 'em mean' that the entire room is forced to sit through. Okay, so I'm sure I'm the only one obsessively watching it and hating every second, but it is what it is.

"Right. So the blood tests and DNA sequencing can tell us more than just who your Bonds are, it can also give signs of what your gift is. Testing is then done within specially considered parameters to gauge what Tier your gift is on. Why is this done?"

More hands shoot up but this is actually something that interests me, so I keep my snarky thoughts locked away for a moment so I can hear his reasoning.

Not that I think he's always right.

There's always a sugar-coated bullshit pill given out to the general public and then there's the truth, and this is one case that I'm sure they'll lie about.

"Bragging rights. Everyone wants to know who the top dog is."

I don't know this girl but her shirt is so low that I'm sure Nox is getting a great view of her nipples right now.

Not that he's impressed. "You're guessing and you're wrong, don't waste our time here. Anyone else?"

A lot less hands are raised this time, but Nox picks Gabe to answer. I've never actually seen them interact with each other outside of the stupid bond dinners we're all trapped at, and I'm not enjoying having Nox's eyes on me as he stares us both down.

"TacTeams are picked with the highest Tier of the Gifted. The Council was originally picked from the strongest of our community, but these days it's also a tag-and-release system. If the Resistance takes someone, then we need to know how strong they are for when they're sent back brainwashed. Nothing more dangerous than a walking time bomb wearing your neighbor's face."

Christ.

How close I'd come to being one of those brainwashed zombies put back into the community with the sole purpose of finding other high Tier Gifted and dragging them back to the Resistance, killing anyone who attempted to stop me... it's terrifying.

The pen in my hand shakes as my fingers tremble.

Nox turns away and starts the lecture, highlighting everything Gabe said because my bond had gotten it right. Sage notices my mini ffeakout and shoots me a worried look, her hand knocking mine gently in reassurance, but there's nothing either of us can do or say in the middle of class. Not without Nox losing his shit at me in another public spectacle that I have no interest in, so I take a deep breath and just work through it.

As I take notes, my hand creeps up to the back of my neck, rubbing at the bump under my skin where the killer GPS chip is buried, like a reminder to myself that no matter how badly I want to run, it's not an option for me.

My only plans for spring break are to study and explore the campus grounds a little more to attempt to find somewhere I can get a job.

If I can earn some money, then I can take the risk of having my brain explode from the chip. At this point, I'm fairly sure North wouldn't actually kill me, not unless I did something terrible or became a danger to them all, but without money, I'm still freaking trapped here.

There isn't a person in this closed-off community who doesn't know who I am and the fact that a TacTeam dragged me back here, so there's no chance of me hitchhiking my way out of here. I need money and I need someone to dig the chip out from under my skin.

There's a cafe and the campus bookshop as potential jobs but when I drop off my CV, both of them shoot me down on the spot. I understand the bookshop because North probably forewarned them, but the cafe makes less sense to me until Sage shows up at my door to drag me to her place and tells me Gryphon's sister owns it and runs it.

I had no idea he even had a sister.

The woman who had served me looked at least ninety years old, so at least I didn't shame myself in front of his family member but, God, I guess I can't ever show my face there again now.

Sage laughs at my embarrassment, shoving a drink at me the moment we get into her room. Sawyer is already there drinking and even though I don't want to go to the party they're both attending, Gabe has already messaged me to say he got me a free pass from North to attend, and I don't want to have to speak to the domineering asshole to explain why I'd rather stay home.

Mostly it's because Sage is now obsessed with the idea of me and Gabe working our shit out. She's obsessed enough that the moment she starts her pre-party drinking, it's all she can talk about.

"You're going to end up Bonded to him. There's no way you're going to see Gabe shirtless at the party tonight and not fuck his brains out."

I choke on my own drink so hard that it goes up my

freaking nose, burning the whole way because Sawyer doesn't know how to make a cocktail without the imminent threat of alcohol poisoning, which is why his mixes are always my favorite.

Once I can breathe again, I give Sage's drunk ass a stem look. "I've seen it, and while there's no denying he's freaking *blessed,* I'm not fucking anyone anytime soon. I have cobwebs that no man is going to clear out for, you know, a century or two, at this rate."

Sawyer pulls a face at me without looking in my direction, all of his focus on the phone in front of his face. Sage kicks at him, already stumbling across the line of tipsy and right into wasted, but it's been a rough week for her.

Giovanna posted about her Bonded ring that Riley gave her.

Bonded rings are kind of a big deal at the best of times, the closest that someone in the Gifted community gets to an engagement, but the real problem here is that he gave her a family heirloom, one that he'd always told Sage he'd give to her. It was his grandmother's, smuggled into the country during a war, and apparently it's a Big Fucking Deal.

Just another freaking fracture he's caused her and he's now joined Giovanna at the top of my kill list. If they show up to the pool party tonight, I'm going to cause a scene.

From the look of Sawyer, he might be right there with me.

I don't know whether it's my charming ways or the fact that he's been forced to hang out with me every day during our cramming sessions, but I think Sawyer has finally warmed up to me. I mean, I'm still clearly not his favorite person, but he no longer winces at the sight of me or cringes when I speak, so I'm taking that as a sign that we're about to be best fucking friends.

My second phone buzzes in my pocket and I check it as I take another drink, the alcohol burning my sinuses.

Send me a photo of what you 're wearing tonight, Bond.

Atlas is also drinking, I can tell because he goes from sweet and kind to bossy and sexy in a hot minute. I can't believe I find it hot considering North's treatment of me, but there's something about his ability to just ignore all of my attempts at keeping us at arm's length that has me swooning a little.

If I get drunk enough I might ask him for a picture back tonight, but with far less clothing.

"If you and Atlas start sexting, I will confiscate your phone. If I'm doomed to be unloved and alone forever, the least you could do is keep that lovey-dovey shit out of my face," Sage pouts and I scoff at her.

"He's probably just homy, that's not love. Besides, I'm staying unbonded forever, remember? No dick for me. Not even if Gabe is the six-pack hottie of my dreams."

"Jesus fucking Christ, if the two of you are just going to get wasted and cry over boys and your sad sex lives, then I'm leaving you both here."

Sage giggles at him, a great sound to hear even if she's freaking plastered, and then leans forward to me to pretend to whisper, "Brothers are the worst. Sawyer's just mad that his boyfriend isn't coming tonight and he has to babysit us both without the promise of hooking up after we get back."

Boyfriend, *not* Bond. It's a small word choice, but a clear distinction in our world that makes all of the difference. Whoever Sawyer is fated to be with, he hasn't found them yet, and he's not waiting around for them. I get it, I found my own Bonds at such a young age, which skewed my own decisions on that front.

Sage also had her options ripped away from her.

"Who's your boyfriend? Someone I know? Is he hot? God, please tell me you're banging some freaking dreamboat so I can live vicariously through you."

He scoffs at me but then he's tapping on his phone and turning the screen around to show me a very hot hockey player with dimples and biceps bigger than my thighs.

"Holy shit! Sawyer you freaking *badass.* Please tell me his dick matches the rest of him."

Sage groans at me and collapses back on the bed. "Don't get him started on Grey's dick. I've already heard too much about it and all it does is remind me of how desperately alone lam... getting zero dick. Or flowers and candies and teddy bears."

Oh God.

When she'd seen the gifts from Atlas, I thought she was going to burst into tears over it. I felt guilty for half a second before she declared that Atlas was her favorite and we should take him with us when we run away. At this rate, we're going to have to hire a freaking bus because Sawyer clearly isn't letting his sister go anywhere without him and I wouldn't ever let him dump Grey's hot self just to come with.

Felix would chase Sage down, I'm sure of it.

I don't want to think about my Bonds or running away or the amount of dick that I'm not getting thanks to all of this shit, so I grab my glass and tip it back, finishing the liquid fire in two gulps before holding the glass out to Sawyer again for a refill.

He takes it with a smirk.

Tonight is going to be messy as fuck.

I'm not wrong.

Sawyer makes Sage and I both eat something and sober up a little before he drives us over to the Halliwell's mansion for the pool party. Apparently it's the social gathering to be at though, so we have to park down the block and walk up, cars double parked all over the streets. Most of the gated communities around here are full of Gifted families though, so no one bats an eyelid as we all pile out. My buzz is almost completely gone as the night air slaps me in the face. It's surprisingly warm out and my mouth dries out completely. I need another cocktail, stat.

The house would've looked luxurious and amazing to me a few months ago, but after spending so much time at North's place and then over at Sage's, the whole mansion spectacle has worn off on me. I really don't give a shit how many wood-paneled libraries and butler's wings a house has.

I care about whether or not the people in them are assholes.

Sage swipes a couple of bottles of wine on our way through the house and even though wine tastes like ass, it feels like a win. Neither of us want to be here or deal with any of these people, so we're both fully aboard the get-blackout-drunk train.

I decide straight away that the Gifted community is too freaking small because once again, there's council members everywhere, which means North is probably here, lurking in a comer somewhere and drinking alcohol he hasn't had to steal while he schmoozes with all of the other stuffy, condescending assholes here.

Sawyer tries to discreetly find wine glasses as we work our way through the kitchen and dining rooms but I'm not willing to wait around for that sort of luxury and drink it straight from the bottle, giggling with Sage like children when we find a storage room somewhere on the first floor to hide in until the council members all clear out of the house and into the garden.

We need to be as drunk as freaking possible before then.

Because we're in an obscenely luxurious mansion, there's a couch and table in the storage room. There's also some stacked barstools, and the wifi is so good in here that Sawyer just pulls out a seat and fucks around on his phone while Sage and I both chug the wine down like we're pros.

Sage clucks over her phone, "Felix can't make it, he's going to some study thing with the other pre-med students."

I snort at her because she's fooling exactly no one with her attempts at keeping him at arm's length. I'm proud of myself when my words come out without even a little slurring, "You should definitely bone him. Just once, give it a shot, and if it's not all that great, then go back to being awkward friends so you can both move on with your lives."

She groans and guzzles a little more of the wine. Her phone buzzes again and she gets back to texting Felix, totally engrossed with it because she's just as obsessed with him as he is with her. The only thing that's actually keeping them apart is fear and the damage that Riley has done to Sage. I think with enough patience and gentle prodding, she'll get past that and be much happier with the infatuated footballer.

Gabe finds us an hour later, cooped up and giggling over our phones together. He takes one look at us all and rolls his eyes. "Fuck me, that's a thousand dollar bottle of wine you're chugging back there, Bond."

I shrug and hold it out to him. "It tastes like swill."

He shakes his head at me, taking the bottle and then scoffing when he realizes it's already empty. I'm not sure that I'll be able to stand up and keep my legs under me if he insists we go out and socialize, but at least I no longer care about... well, *anything.*

"Did you guys bring swimsuits at least?"

Sawyer scoffs and rolls his eyes back at him. "Well, they didn't bring fucking floaties and they'll drown without them in this state."

I decide that this type of slander against my ability to hold my liquor is unacceptable and I pull myself onto my feet, slow enough that I'm sure I won't faceplant on the hardwood floor, and Sage groans at my decision to get a move on.

"If I've been forced to squeeze into one of Sage's swimsuits and come to this stupid council-circle-jerk party, then you bet your ass that I'm going swimming."

Sawyer has to help Sage get out of the storage room but when Gabe offers me an arm, I brush him off He huffs at me and I very kindly keep it to myself that I could've told him to keep his fucking bond the hell away from me while I'm not at full capacity because my own bond is still straining after him in my chest. If he touches me, I might end up fucking him in the middle of the goddamned party just to catch a break from all of this... pining.

Ew.

It feels wrong to even think that way but, God, the aching and the straining every time I end up near one of my Bonds is slowly driving me insane. Maybe calling a truce with Gabe wasn't a good idea because I'm barely holding my shit together.

When we walk past the kitchen, Sawyer curses under his breath and moves so he's covering Sage's tripping and stumbling ass. I startle when Gabe does the same for me, his shoulders somehow doubling in width and completely obscuring me from... whatever they've decided to protect us from.

I'm smart enough to keep my mouth shut about it until we're outside, but Sage is too far gone and Sawyer is forced to slap a hand over her mouth, muttering threats and cussing her out.

When we find a spot outside that isn't completely

writhing with bodies and booze, Gabe murmurs to me, "North and Sharpe are having a disagreement over the protocol now that the Resistance is getting closer to the campus. He's already made it well known that he's not above coming after you. Hate North all you want, but he's keeping you away from a whole lot of shit right now."

Dammit.

I don't want to owe that man anything, but even I can't deny that he's helping out big time with that shit

I pull the dress over my head and fold it up, carefully bending to slip it into Sage's bag because my tits are a little bigger than hers and there's a real danger of a nip slip happening tonight. When I straighten up, I find Gabe staring at me like I've grown an extra head and I have to glance down to make sure I'm not actually flashing the entire freaking party my goods.

"What? What the hell are you looking at?"

He grunts at me, shaking his head and muttering under his breath as he jumps head first into the pool, "I fucking hate you."

Well, what the fuck have I done to him now?

Sawyer knocks into me as he shifts around to cover Sage while she strips. "C'mon, Fallows, you're not that drunk. Give the guy a break."

I'm lost, utterly freaking lost, but then Sage steps up next to me and giggles, "Guess he had to cool down a little.

We might need to get you a swimsuit that actually fits your amazing tits."

I scoff at them both because it can't be that. There's at least ten other girls here rocking a better rack than mine, and Gabe has probably fucked them all, the looks they're all throwing his way are saying a lot on the subject.

We have a little bit of luck because Riley is nowhere to be seen, but then I spot Giovanna perched on one of the poolside recliners in a tiny bikini that makes mine look freaking supersized. To be honest, it's not even a bikini, she's wearing some red string that just barely covers her nipples and slit. It's the early evening, the outdoor lighting and bonfire are already raring, so it's not like she's working on her tan and I'm not trying to slut-shame, but it's just impractical.

Sage notices her the second we slide into the water, her happy and carefree joy just melting away until her arms are crossed over her chest and she's looking self-conscious again.

Fuck that.

"Sawyer, we need some cocktails. Who's dick do we have to suck to get them? I feel like you should take one for the team here, my friend."

He scoffs at me, clearly not on board with more alcohol, as he strips down and jumps in to join us. There's a huge tattoo spanning his entire back that I had no idea the little computer-nerd-slash-preppy-jock boy had.

I'm impressed. No wonder he's bagged the ice hockey hottie.

I keep half an eye on Gabe where he's talking to some other football players, laughing and joking with them only a few feet away from us. Even when they attempt to talk him into a beer pong tournament happening as far away from the council bullshit as it can possibly be, he says no, jerking his head in my direction without any further explanation.

It makes me feel like a burden and there's nothing I hate more than that shit.

"I don't understand why I have to be here," I whine, and it's totally a fucking whine because I don't understand why they're insisting on me being here if I'm just going to be everyone's problem. A pool party. A pool party full of Gifted, Bonds and Bonded. The Council. Riley and Giovanna and North and fuck knows who else?! It feels like a recipe for disaster.

Sage shrugs at me. "Apparently it's a rite of passage. I didn't want to come, but apparently this is supposed to be something we'll look back on, years from now, and be *so thankful* we attended."

I can literally tell which one of her parents had said it to her because Maria is so freaking obsessed with Sage being 'normal'. She's all tom up over the idea that Riley rejected her and now she's hanging out with me, what will that mean for the good Benson name?

It's fucking stupid and Sage deserves better.

"We should go find the drinks table, hopefully something is spiked strong enough to get our buzz back."

Sage chews on her lip, shooting me a half-smile, but it's clear that seeing Giovanna here has ruined her entire night. I'm suddenly overwhelmed with exactly how bullshit the entire situation is because Sage has literally done nothing wrong. Nothing.

As loath as I am to admit it, at least my own Bonds have a reason to hate me, and even if they're blaming me for something out of my control, it's not like I can tell them that.

The water around me ripples.

No one else notices, thank God, but it's a good reminder to me to *settle the fuck down.* So I stop looking at Giovanna and I stop thinking about Gabe and the burden I am to him. I stop thinking about all of the things wrong with this stupid freaking party and I have fun.

I drag Sage and Sawyer over to the other side of the pool where there's a waterfall and a slide. We sit on the edge and Sawyer manages to convince a couple of the seniors to grab us some beers. Sage is still quiet, but some of the gloom around her lifts and we can actually enjoy ourselves for five goddamn minutes.

When the crowd starts moving towards the food tables being laid out by the caterers, because of course this college party is being catered, we take stock of how we're feeling and decide food isn't a good idea right now. Well, the food is a great idea, but attempting to walk around isn't.

Gabe offers to grab me something, his shitty attitude over with, but I brush him off, watching as he hauls himself out of the water and walks over to the tables without bothering to grab a towel or cover up. Jesus, he really is too hot for words.

"You're drooling. Are you sure you can't just fuck him?" Sage whispers far too loudly at me and I splash her with the water.

Sawyer rolls his eyes at us both from where he's perched on the side of the pool. "Not without bonding to him and apparently that's off of the table."

I nod, pulling my face into the picture of seriousness. "Absolutely not, no bonding."

I glance over at Gabe and find him standing there with North, talking together before they both turn as one to look over at me.

Goddammit.

"Fuck yes, Grey just got back. We need to leave here, now," Sawyer says, standing up and waving his hands at Sage.

She giggles as she tries, and fails, to pull herself out of

the water, and it takes both her brother and I to get her out. The beers had given me my buzz back, but not so much that I can't get my shit together.

"I have to wait for Gabe, just to let him know you guys are getting me home safe... you are taking me back, right?"

Sawyer scoffs at me, "Of course, we're not leaving you here drunk and vulnerable."

I laugh at him, happy at how easy it's become between us now, he doesn't wince at my mere presence anymore.

"What a rack! Reject, I can see why you're so popular."

I freeze at the sound of his voice and when I finally turn around, yup, sure enough, it's fucking Martinez. Sage scowls at him but I hold out an arm to stop her from doing anything about him.

I just want to leave, some coward's opinion of my character or body means less than nothing to me.

"What the fuck did you just say to my Bond, Martinez?"

I turn and instinctively shove myself into Gabe's heaving chest. It's a bad move because we're both practically naked and my own bond has a freaking field day at all of the skin-on-skin action. He barely notices me though, the anger coursing through him is more than enough to distract him from me.

It's kind of hot and I have to remind myself that it has nothing to do with him protecting me and everything to do with his own reputation.

"Just when I thought Gabe couldn't get any more pathetic, he's simping after the girl who threw him away. How does that reject pussy taste, Ardem?"

Gabe moves around me so fast that all I see is the blur of his big body moving and then they're both on the ground. I bump into Sawyer as we both throw ourselves in front of Sage, which is dumb because she's the badass who could light us all on fire if she wanted to.

There's shouting over at the main house but I'm too busy backing Sage up against the pool fence, trying to keep her clear of the shifter brawl happening, to notice. I'm oddly proud to see that Gabe is kicking Martinez's ass, just pounding on his face like he could go at it all damn day.

It feels like karma.

Sawyer groans and then steels himself as he wades into the fray to pull Gabe off of Martinez, narrowly missing a fist to the gut himself. Gabe doesn't fight him but when they both straighten up, his eyes have a very feline look to them, his irises ringed with fire and still following his prey like he's imagining tearing flesh from bones and picking his teeth.

It shouldn't be so hot.

"What the hell is going on here? What have you done to my son?"

I glance around to find a crowd forming around us,

muttering and with a whole lot of phones pointed in our direction. I wish I had a towel around myself but that's the least of our problems now that Martinez's father is here with a savage look on his face.

He's shorter than Gabe and dressed in a suit, probably either on the council or works for someone who is. He looks a lot like his son, and he has the same gutless asshole air about him that sets my teeth on edge.

Gabe rolls his shoulders back, his jaw set like he's planning on just taking whatever this dickhead says to him on the chin, and that doesn't sit right with me at all.

"You always did have a vicious temper, I'll have you off of the football team for this—"

I jump in without thought of how it looks or which of North's rival councilmen surround us. "It was me. Gabe took a swing for me."

As if called over by my admission, the crowd parts and Gryphon and North appear. North is holding a plate of food, which my brain registers but doesn't really do much with because both of their faces are twin masks of thunderous, pissed-off Alpha males.

Great.

North's eyes flick over the entire scene and then he says, "What's happened, David?"

No one says a word, so I take the moment to butt in, throwing myself under the bus. Gabe took a swing for me and I'm not letting him take the fall for that. Football is his life, I have nothing left to lose.

"Martinez shifted in the maze during TT and hunted me down to use me as bait for the pond... girl. He started mouthing off and Gabe was defending me."

Gryphon's eyes shift between us both, Gabe's knuckles still bleeding from where the line backer's tooth broke the skin. I hold my breath, ready for him to call us both out and just be done with it, but then he turns back to the other and says, "You can't fault Gabe for protecting his Bond... even if he took it too far. "

David's eyes flick back over to me and when they begin to glow, Gryphon plants himself in front of me, his hands relaxed by his side, but the tension in his shoulders tell me he's ready to throw down with this Gifted man if he tries anything.

North shoves the plate of food at me and when he steps towards David, the crowd around us suddenly goes quiet, the fear rippling through everyone is so palpable that I almost choke on it.

Whatever he can do, it has them all freaking shaking.

"Take her home, Gabriel. Sage too, get them both out of here."

No one dares to question him. Gabe doesn't look fazed by the stem order either, he just grabs a towel and slings it over my shoulders while Sawyer does the same with

Sage, both of them ushering us out. My legs are steady underneath me and, surprisingly, so are Sage's.

When we get to the house, Gabe scoffs and shakes his head at me, leaning in close to murmur, "You're too fucking good at lying, Bond. Only a pro knows how to get past Gryphon like that, even North was convinced."

Be ready at 6.

The text from Gabe wakes me up at five in the morning and my head is still full of *pain* and *gross* and *no thank you.* I drink some water because I refuse to believe this is a hangover and dehydration must be to blame instead.

After yesterday, I can't bring myself to be angry at being woken up by him, but I'm still not excited about being around Gabe this early in the damn morning without even a goddamn reason.

He'd walked me up to my room after the party last night, seeing me safely to my door and not judging me for groaning and stumbling up the stairs, so I think we've found a real peace agreement, like now that I've proved myself by lying and covering for him, he's actually going to give this friendship a real go and stop lashing out at me every second he gets.

I get dressed in casual clothes because nothing on campus is open except the dining hall at this time in the morning so it's not like I'll need to impress anyone down there. I take notice again at the way my shirt is billowing on me now I've toned up a lot and I really, *really* need to find an income to get some new shit.

I can't even show off all my hard work, dammit.

I stomp down the stairs, making enough noise to wake the entire building up because they're all gossiping bitches anyway so no skin off of my nose if I ruin their last sleep-in of spring break. I get to the front of the building at the same time as Gabe does, bouncing straight over to his motorbike when he holds out his spare helmet.

I've become a pro at getting it strapped on right and swinging onto the bike behind him so in under a minute, we're flying down the road with a roar of the engine. The morning sun is bright already in the sky, but the chill of the early morning is still biting into the bare skin of my hands where they're wrapped around his waist. When we finally pull up in front of the TT center, Gabe kills the engine and holds his arm out so I can climb off without landing on my ass.

It's not where I was expecting to end up but Gabe has a key to get in and leads the way, turning lights on and ducking into the guy's locker room to grab out his bag. I duck into the ladies to do the same, the new pair of sneakers that magically appeared after the bloodbath of the maze still shiny and white, where I've only worn them once.

I didn't realize the college had a budget to replace damaged items but I guess Draven charges a shitload of money for tuition for a reason.

Gabe grins at me as I join him, looking way too freaking perky and I drawl, "You got me out of my dorms at the crack of dawn, before my curfew lifts, to work out? How did you get this past North's obsession with keeping me locked up?"

Gabe grins at the rough, gravelly tone of my voice as he slings his bag down on the ground by the wall and strips out of his shirt. I do everything in my power not to watch the rippling of his insane muscles but I'm only human, and fuck, he really is too hot for words.

Fuck. Nope, I need to stop looking before my bond comes out to play.

"North didn't enroll you into TT as a way to torture you, no matter how badly you want to believe that. Bonds are being taken off of the streets by the Resistance everyday. The ones we hear about aren't even *half*of the actual cases. You need to know how to defend yourself, especially since you don't have a gift of your own to use. You're doing well in TT, but we haven't actually covered anything about self defense yet and when I told North that I'm going to help you to train and workout, he agreed you need all the help you can get."

Ouch.

I mean, it's true but that doesn't mean those words coming out of that mouth don't hurt. Especially when he's standing there shirtless as he rifles through his bag for something. God, even his back is tightly muscled, how the hell do you even get that ripped at our age? Doesn't that kind of shit take time? Maybe the shifter genes do it for him and, God, am I enjoying the fruits of it.

"You're drooling," Gabe says, smugness dripping from every syllable, and there's something about this moment that makes it safe to flirt back just a little.

I know I look nothing like the perfectly toned and perky girls in this class but I've been shown enough interest in the past to know I'm not a complete hag. When I drop my bag down next to his and pull my shirt over my head, leaving me in just my sports bra, I make a show of bending over to dig my workout tank out of my bag.

He makes a strangled noise and then stops breathing.

I have to swallow the gloating cheer that works its way up my throat and when I pull the tank over my head, I arch my back a little more than necessary, my tits looking perkier than usual.

"That's just fucking mean. I'm here to help you and you're the one that took sex off of the table," Gabe chokes out, grabbing his water bottle and stalking over to one of the weight machines.

I snicker out a laugh, sounding like a depraved idiot, but too tired and smug to care about how I look to him right now. "I play to win, you should learn that lesson now before it bites you in the ass."

He shrugs and starts setting the machine up for me. "You've done enough damage that I'm bulletproof now, Fallows. What's the most you can bench now?"

Dammit.

I have to ignore his jab at me and I force my voice to be even as I reply, "Five pounds."

He rolls his eyes at me and then shoots me a glare. "I know you're being a brat right now but if we have to start at five, this is going to go on forever. You'll never get out of here."

I mean, I wasn't actually joking, but I don't argue with him when he adds twenty pounds on and then jerks his head at me to get started. I take my time, mostly to mess with him, but also because I have no idea if I can actually do this.

Half an hour later I decide that I'd rather just die.

I would rather lay down and die if the Resistance comes

after me because there's nothing in the world that could be worse than all of this working out. Fuck, and to think that I'd thought Vivian's training circuit was bad. Gabe puts him to utter shame and I start to regret ever extending that stupid fucking olive branch to him.

This is how he's punishing me for leaving them.

"I'm not doing anything else. If you attempt to put me on another machine, I'll scream murder and run out of here. I'm going to the police, the non-Gifted will definitely help me escape this kind of abuse."

Gabe rolls his eyes at my dramatics, and even though he's also sweating at the workout, his voice comes out steady and with none of the panting I'm doing, "You can bitch Gryphon out for this later if you hate it, he's the one who set the reps. He seemed to think you could handle it, but I guess I can call him and tell him you bitched out."

Fuck.

Goddammit, he's figured out how to play me like a fucking fiddle because that shit is a red flag being waved at me and instantly I'm back to lifting weights and hoping to die. It takes every distraction technique I've ever learned to get through it but I last the entire hour, my body collapsing on the mats the moment he mutters that we're done.

"I'm not carrying you back to the dorms so you better pull yourself together, Bond."

I curse him out but it comes out a garbled mess of

groans and panting that he just laughs at. There's no way I'm ever moving again so I just accept that I live here now, in this exact spot on the mats. I really need to change out of my gross, sweaty clothes, but my bag is at least four feet away from me and I almost cry at the very thought of getting over to it by myself. Gabe huffs at my whimpering and slings the bag over to me on his way through to the guy's locker room. I hear the shower cut on and I guess I have about ten minutes to heave myself off of the ground.

I need every second I can get.

I decide that being friends with Gabe might end up harder than it's worth if he insists on making me train every morning, but once I finally scrape myself off of the ground, he takes us over to the dining hall and we eat together in a pleasant sort of silence that neither of us want to break.

It's shocking to me how many students know and love him, and I spend half the time we're eating being introduced to someone new who's stopped past the table to talk to Gabe about some sporting bullshit. I'm polite but not friendly because, honestly, my circle is already looking a little too big for my liking. I was happy with just Sage but now there's Sawyer and Felix and Gabe and,/wcA:, Atlas, whose messages are still the first thing I see when I wake up and the last thing I read before I fall asleep every night.

I can't afford to have all of these people to miss when I leave them behind.

I make excuses to Gabe about needing to get assignments finished and he walks me back to my dorm without questioning the sudden shift in my mood. When I get back to my room, I text Sage and Atlas with the same story about studying and then I spend the rest of the day messing around on my phone and trying not to lose my goddamn mind over being trapped here with all of these people I'm starting to... need. Fuck, I need them all. I need their friendships like nothing ever before and I'm completely screwed.

I finally force myself into cracking open my textbooks in the afternoon and then I crawl into bed when my eyes feel as though they're bleeding around midnight.

I'm woken at four in the morning by my phone ringing.

I ignore it, because fuck whichever one of my Bonds is trying to ruin my week by waking me the hell up right now. I roll back over on the shitty, tiny bed and then shove a pillow over my head when the phone starts ringing again. I know better than to ignore it, I know they wouldn't be fucking with me like this and there's probably something major going on, but after the training with Gabe yesterday, I'm freaking exhausted.

The thumping on my door that starts ten minutes later

isn't as easy to ignore.

I might murder whoever the fuck is here.

I spring out of the bed and rip the door open, ready to spill some goddamn blood, only to find Gabe standing there, panting and freaking the fuck out. I forget my fury at the wake-up as I take him in. He's wearing nothing but a pair of basketball shorts, every inch of his golden skin gleaming in the glow of my shitty bedside lamp.

He's freaking magnificent.

A few of the doors down the hallway open, scowling girls popping their heads out to glare at me like it's my fault Gabe has shown up like a raging goddamn bull in a china shop at the ass crack of dawn.

"Where's your phone? Why the hell didn't you answer it?" Gabe croaks but I'm too busy trying to restart my now very broken brain to reply, all of my usual sass and sarcasm just freaking gone thanks to the sight of him, and as he brushes past me to stalk into my room, I notice his bare feet. My brain might not be at full function but something does click for me.

He shifted and ran here.

"What's happened? Fuck, Gabe, what the hell is going on?" I shut the door and lean back against it, trying desperately not to look at him as he paces around, eyeing everything like he's expecting to have to defend us both against an entire freaking army that's lying in wait behind my shitty, cracked mirror.

"Twelve Gifted were taken tonight. Three of them were from this building, heading back from a party and taken outside. North said your GPS hadn't moved but... I had to check for myself."

Fuck.

Fuck. This is getting out of hand, if they don't let me go soon then I'm going to be caught and that'll be the end of everything. The fear has me snapping at him, "I don't need a fucking babysitter!"

He spins back around to snarl at me, "Then answer your *fucking* phone!"

I'm more open than I would normally be because it's actually too freaking sweet to think he ran the whole way here just because I didn't answer my phone, but I'm still freaking the hell out over having friends and ties holding me here. "You just said North checked the GPS, there's no reason for you to be rushing over here and waking the whole goddamn building up!"

His eyes narrow at me and then his chest heaves as he takes a deep, calming breath, the type that probably means he's trying to find a little patience to deal with my bullshit. "You said we were friends... well, this is what friends do, Oli. When you didn't answer the phone I had to be sure that you weren't taken. This is what friendship with me looks like, take it or leave it."

I have no choice but to take it because I'm so fucking tired of arguing with him. I can't change our situation, and I definitely can't let my guard down around him, but all of the fight in me that I usually have for him is just gone.

"Okay. Alright, fine, now you know I'm alive and I promise I'll answer my stupid phone next time. Go home and let me get a few more hours of sleep in."

I slump down onto my bed, finally realizing that I'm wearing nothing but a pair of ratty old shorts and a tank, but Gabe hasn't noticed or commented on exactly how homeless I look, thank God. I lay back against the terrible pillow and attempt to get comfortable but it's impossible to do with the way he's just standing there watching me like I'm so fucking interesting here in my shitty room with absolutely nothing personal. Not even a decent set of sheets or a blanket.

I give him a look which he completely ignores as he slides down onto the floor, his back pressed against the door and his eyes glowing in the darkness just a little, the only proof that he's struggling with his gift at the moment.

I really can't be fucked fighting with him, my voice wrung out and exhausted, "I'm still tired, Gabe, please just leave me to sleep."

He shrugs and glances away to look out the tiny, grimy window. "I'm not leaving you alone here while there's fucking Resistance snatching people. Just go to sleep and in the morning I'll head over to the dining hall with you before class."

I huff and pull the blanket up to my chin but it's too freaking weird to attempt to sleep with him sitting there so I give up before I really give it a try. "What's the Council doing about this? You can't tell me they're just sitting around letting people be kidnapped."

I hear Gabe exhale in a long stream but I keep my eyes on the ceiling. "Some of them want to do exactly that. They're too fucking gutless to form a plan and go after them, spouting some bullshit about higher ground and keeping the peace."

Fuck that, there's no such thing as higher ground when it comes to these people. They'll take any weakness or show of morality and they'll use it to destroy you.

I know this for a fact.

"And what does North think about it? What's he doing for the community with all of that money and power of his?" My voice is scathing and Gabe doesn't answer me for a minute, the room settling into a charged silence that's full of all of our secrets.

My phone buzzes under my pillow and, without thinking, I pull it out to see Atlas' message.

I heard about the abductions. There's been seven here overnight as -well. I'm going to push for a transfer, I'm not going to sit by and leave you alone to face this shit.

I swallow because I really don't want him to come. He's the tiny bit of joy that I allow myself because of the distance between us. If he shows up, then I'll have to put that same distance between us that I have with the others and that feels fucking devastating to me right now.

"Whose phone is that?"

Fuck.

I drop it down onto the covers but there's no use hiding it now, Gabe's seen it and realized it's definitely not the older model iPhone that North had given me. Nope, it's the shiny and brand new one that Atlas had couriered to me. It's on his phone plan and I allow myself to accept that from him because he's the only one I ever message on it.

"Oli, where the fuck did you get that?"

I roll my eyes and then turn my back on him because he's once again proving to me that they all think they own me and have a right to take away every last one of my freedoms. "Atlas sent it to me, now run along to snitch on me to North like the good little lapdog you are."

There's silence again and then he mutters quietly, "Fuck, you're a bitch, Fallows."

He still doesn't move to get up and eventually sleep claims me.

We're thrown right back into our classes like nothing happened and it's so fucking strange.

Gabe pretends that we hadn 't argued over his impromptu trip to my dorm and our fight over the phone, and we start spending every morning at the training center working out and going through Gryphon's self-defense training routine. North doesn't show up at my door to snatch it off of me so I have to assume Gabe kept his mouth shut about it. No one else seems worried about the abductions, though I do notice the extra security on campus, subtly watching over us all as we move through the buildings.

Sawyer glues himself to Sage's side, only leaving her to go to his own classes, and I'm sure he only does that because he knows Gabe is shadowing us both. The more I look around the hallways, the more I see that everyone is moving in clusters, like all of the Bonded groups are sticking to each other for safety, so maybe they're not as unaffected as they first seem.

On Friday, Gabe and I split off from Sage and Sawyer to head to TT and even with the extra workouts we're now fitting in before class, I find myself dreading going back in there with the other students. I'm waiting for Vivian to take us down to the maze again, my body still feels the aches and pains from the last time.

He doesn't.

Once I'm dressed in my workout gear and I step back out into the training area, I find a lot of TacTeam guys standing around. Half of them turn to get a good look at me which is really off-putting, especially when it becomes clear that I know them.

They're the ones that grabbed me and dragged me back here.

I'm about to walk over to one of them, the guy who had tackled me and slammed me into the ground at the cafe I'd been working at, and kick him in the balls so hard his goddamned ancestors feel it, when Vivian calls out to start the class, "We're going to be working on self-defense techniques and head back to the mats."

I'm expecting the same sort of groaning that the

basement had pulled out of everyone but instead there's a buzz that goes around the room instantly. The girls all start looking each other over and the guys start flexing like this is an opportunity to impress.

I stay in my usual spot at the back of the group but Gabe comes over to stand by me, a couple of his football friends joining us with a respectful nod in my direction. I bump Gabe gently with my shoulder and point out the Tac guy I want to murder in cold blood and ask, "What's his name?"

He frowns at me and leans down to murmur quietly in my ear, "Kieran Black. He's Gryphon's second and he's got a temper, so stay away from him."

I nod but I think he's forgetting that I also have a temper and it's been ignited, burning inside me and ready to bum that asshole to the ground.

"Let's see how much you've all forgotten, shall we? Hanna, Ty, get on the mats and run us through the stances, hits, and blocks we've already gone through."

One of Gabe's football buddies walks over, as well as one of the girls. Hanna isn't a gossip or a flirt, and her shoulders are so muscular and defined that I think she's going to crush anyone who goes up against her, because she's clearly a badass. It's almost enough to make me feel intimidated as hell.

Well.

Except the thing is, I've already been working on these positions, thanks to my time with Gabe, but I'm not stupid enough to say that to anyone. I just watch as Hanna and Ty go through the motions like I'm soaking in something new.

Hanna is much better than I am, obviously, but Ty's footwork is sloppy. I spot it at the same time Vivian does, his mouth turning down, and when he kicks out Ty's ankle, the pair of them go down in a breathless, groaning pile.

I smother a giggle that earns me a scowl from Kieran. Gryphon doesn't attempt to look over at me, which I already know is thanks to his belief that I'm a worthless brat, so that bums a little.

Once they're back on their feet, Vivian steps up into the empty space and calls out in his booming voice, "The rules are simple; first one to get their opponents shoulders onto the mat, wins, and under no circumstances are you allowed to use your gift."

Ah, perfect, the exact type of competition I actually have a chance at winning and with the stances and throws Gabe has been going over with me, I'm quietly confident I'll beat... someone. Even if it's just the first person who underestimates me, it'll be good for my confidence and mood after the shit-show of a week we've had.

Maybe my Bonds will back off a little if they know I can defend myself even without a gift. I doubt it but, hey, here's hoping.

"Fallows, get on the mats. I need to see how far behind you are with this so I can figure out how the hell I'm going to catch you up."

I roll my eyes at Vivian before I shoot him a grin. "If you keep picking on me, people will talk, old man."

The TacTeam guys in front of me all stiffen up like they're in shock that I'm talking to their beloved trainer like this, but Gryphon just shakes his head, his eyes still anywhere but me.

I hate it so much.

"Quit your shit. I'm not letting you off just for running your mouth. Off you go, take Hanna to the mats and I'll be impressed enough not to make you run suicides for giving me lip."

I scoff at him even as I start moving over. "If you think that's lip, you haven't seen me at my best, but fine, throw me in the deep end for your own sick enjoyment."

Gabe grins, ducking his head down at the mats so Vivian doesn't get an eyeful of him enjoying me sassing the old trainer. I get the feeling that he wouldn't get away with as much as I do.

Hanna is ripped, and the closer I get to her, the more that I hesitate because I wasn't expecting her to be so solid looking up close. She doesn't smirk or attempt to egg me on, she just waits for me to slip my shoes off and step up. We stand there and stare at each other until Vivian decides to start the sparring.

"Go."

Her first mistake is that she immediately goes on the offensive, rushing at me and striking, but after a full week of Gabe doing the same thing, I'm prepared for it. It's as easy as breathing to use her own momentum against her and flip her over my shoulder and plant her onto the mats.

Gabe is easily twice the size of her so I'm a little too rough with it, but before I can ease up and apologize for being an asshole, her gift shoves at me and sends me flying across the room, smacking me into the wall.

The squeak that rips out of me is embarrassing, but there's no way I can stop myself at the shock of her breaking the rules just because I very efficiently beat her.

"Jesus Christ, can we ever get through a class without one of you damaging Fallows? The kid is going to need a fast pass to urgent care at this rate," Vivian grumbles, but I heave myself to my feet and wave a hand at him.

"I'm fine, don't get your panties in a bunch over the paperwork."

The students around me break out into a nervous sort of chuckle, like they think they'll be murdered for laughing along with me.

I rub at the back of my head but I wasn't saving face, I really am fine. I'm shocked when Hanna appears in my eyeline with a frown.

"I'm sorry, I can't believe I just did that! I haven't lost control of my gift in years. I have no clue how that just happened. Are you okay? Do you need help to the med bay?"

She sounds sincere enough and I wave her off. "It's not the first wall I've been thrown into, you're fine."

She nods and straightens up, turning to face Vivian, but staying close to me like she's expecting me to pass out on her or something. I attempt to pull my focus back to the class but it's like the air in the room has shifted and now there's tension leaking out everywhere. I glance around but there's no signs of where it's coming from so I force my attention back onto the sparring that's happening on the mats.

I'm forced to sit out for the rest of the session but there's a rough sort of competition that starts and it's too freaking cool to watch. Round after round, we watch as the groups get smaller and smaller. There's a weird, Bond sort of pride in me that Gabe wins every fight until he's the last one standing.

Vivian grunts a 'well done' at him but Gabe preens like he's been given endless praise, and it's freaking weird. We all head back to the locker rooms to change and Hanna sticks a little too close to me the whole time. I start to think her apology was just a smokescreen and she's about to throw a punch at me while I'm standing around in my underwear, but then she takes a deep breath the second the locker room door swings shut.

"Holy shit, I honestly thought I was about to have my life ruined by Shore's entire TacTeam for throwing you off. I swear to you, I didn't mean to do that. I have no idea why my gift went haywire."

Her words come out in a rush and it takes me a second to remember that Gryphon's surname is Shore. "It's fine, they were probably just shocked you'd stepped out on Vivian's rules. I'm not hurt, don't sweat about it."

She groans and strips down to pull her jeans and tee on. I'm a little more awkward about changing in front of everyone but only because half of my clothes don't actually fit me anymore and it's embarrassing to not look the way I want to style myself.

"We all know what happened to Zoey, I know better than to lose my shit around you. I'll never let it happen again."

I frown at her but she's still muttering to herself and I have to butt in to say, "Zoey lost her spot because she went against a teammate, it had nothing to do with me. Chill out, Gryphon honestly can't stand me. You're good."

She stops, staring at me for a heartbeat, and then shakes her head. "He went to her family personally. I was at her place to finish up an assignment we had together and it was the most terrifying thing I've ever seen. Personal shit aside, you're still his Bond, and Gryphon Shore is not someone you just decide to piss off on a whim."

She slings her bag over her shoulder and rushes out before I can decipher half of what she's said. I'm left standing there in the locker room as it clears out, my hoodie clutched in my hands, as everything I thought I knew about these Bonds of mine is questioned.

When Gabe and I arrive at North's mansion for our bond dinner, I'm still a twisted, messed up pile of emotions. I don't like feeling like this, like I don't really know where I stand with any of them, and Gabe keeps staring at me like he's worried I'm about to burst into tears.

I mean, it's not that far off because I might.

He unlocks the front door like always ,but when we step in, we're immediately stopped by two of the house staff and North's driver. Gabe doesn't seem worried, but I feel so uncomfortable because I've seen these people dozens of times and yet I still don't know their names. It feels ciassist and like I'm some asshole for not introducing myself to them properly.

The driver inclines his head at me respectfully and gestures to the house staff. "Miss Fallows, Councilman Draven is attending a dinner in the city tonight and you will be joining him. He's on a call at the moment, but he's left instructions for you to be ready in the next hour, so we must move quickly."

Oh, fuck no. Absolutely not. "I'm not—"

"Miss Fallows, you really must hurry. Councilman Draven won't be available to speak with you for some time and there's so much to do."

I'm about to turn on my heel and run screaming back to the campus on foot, but Gabe plants a hand on my back and gives me a gentle shove in the direction of the house staff, propelling me into this entire farce of a night.

I'm led through the maze of a house into a bedroom somewhere on the second floor and immediately there are women 'working' on me, stripping me and working to turn me into the pretty, obedient, and voiceless Bond North wants for the evening.

I realize that it's not the woman tugging me into a stunning Dior gown's fault, or the timid girl clucking over the lavender tones of my hair either, so I seal my mouth shut and let them do their work. I can murder North's assuming, pretentious ass when he crawls out from whichever rock he's hiding under.

The staff are far too good at knowing how to out-maneuver me, so instead of leading me downstairs to wherever the fuck North is, they take me straight down to the garage in an elevator I didn't know existed and deposit me straight into one of the Rolls Royces, locking the doors so I can't escape.

I have to use a variety of meditation techniques I've learned over the years to calm myself back down because I'm about to stab someone. It doesn't help that I'm due for my period and all of the extra hormones have me so insanely bloodthirsty that my gift is *begging* me to let it out to play.

I'm safely encased in an ice-cold demeanor by the time North finally arrives, sliding into the seat next to me without so much as a greeting or an apology, and I ignore him entirely.

I'm going to ruin him during this dinner.

The trip into the city is silent and as uncomfortable as hell.

I do my best not to fuss with my dress, but I've never worn something so fancy in my life. There's a part of me that's worried that I look like an idiot, like a child playing dress-up in her mother's closet, and North's complete dismissal of me doesn't help a single bit. He doesn't even have his phone in his hand as an excuse, he just scowls out the window like we're some old married couple who enjoy nothing more than stilted silence.

It's not until we're stopped at a red light in front of the restaurant that he finally speaks to me. "This dinner is about more than your attitude. If you really care about the

Gifted community as much as you say you do, then you'll be on your best behavior, whatever that looks like."

I hate him.

I hate him and all of his manipulations. Every part of this experience has come from him watching me and learning about me without my notice, only for it all to be used against me to get exactly what he wants.

I loathe him.

The driver stops in the valet drop-off area and North waits for him to open the door for us both, adjusting the Rolex on his wrist and rolling his shoulders back like he's preparing to go to war.

I get a hold of myself and prepare to do what's right, I can wait until the night is over before I scratch his eyeballs out for being the single worst human I've ever met, and I'm including the scumbag he calls a brother in that assessment.

North helps me out of the car and then directs me into the restaurant and over to the table with a firm hand on my back. The skin underneath his palm feels warm and tingly and I have to tell my bond to settle the fuck down because we hate him. He doesn't care about me, he hasn't brought me here as his beloved Bond, I'm just a pawn in his chess game.

The other council members all stand from their seats when they see us approach. My knees begin to shake because this is a lot of goddamn pressure to have thrown at me without any warning or coaching. He's just expecting me to know what the fuck to do here and honestly, I'm probably going to fuck it up without meaning to.

There are at least twenty people attending and all of them know my name, greeting me as they greet North, and I feel like an idiot standing there with him in the gown, makeup on, heels, and lavender freaking hair!

They all look me up and down, assessing every inch of me, and it makes me feel like a prized sow at a country fair. Every one of them wants to take in all of my attributes— the length of my legs, the blue tones of my eyes, exactly how straight I'm standing— and to give me a mark accordingly. I can tell which of them find me wanting and that violent rage sparks in me again.

North pulls out a chair for me and I murmur a quiet 'thank you' as I carefully sit, smoothing the dress down over my thighs as I attempt to settle myself down.

I just about jump out of my own skin when North leans down to press a kiss to the top of my head as if I'm some precious person to him and I have to bite my tongue. This is all an act, a display of unity and control so that there's no question of his power and integrity.

I know exactly how much torture I can withstand and there's no one in this room that could force this truth out of me; North is actually a freaking great councilman.

Every little scrap of gossip about his policies and planning that I've heard since being dragged to the Draven campus is stuff I agree with, like the Gifted community doing more to help out the non-Gifted or finding better solutions for orphaned Gifted children now that the Resistance has been kidnapping and killing so many of the Gifted. He doesn't want to sit by and watch people get hurt, he's proactive about safety and leveling the wealth gap between the higher society families and the Gifted in lower earning areas.

I have no choice here but to play the obedient Bond.

I plaster a sweet smile on my face and make eye contact with every person at the table. When North takes his seat next to me, I slide my hand into his on the table where everybody can see, because if he's allowed to put on a show then so am I.

He doesn't react other than his fingers tensing slightly under my touch, and I try not to think about my Bond being repulsed by the feel of my skin on his. Fuck, how am I going to make it through this dinner without breaking the hell down or snapping at him? It's freaking hard but I keep the smile glued to my face, even as my own bond begins to mourn inside me.

"So all is well in your world again, Draven?" says the older, distinguished-looking man at the other end of the table. He's handsome enough but there's something off-putting about the smile on his face.

His Bonded is a thin, desperate-looking woman sitting next to him with a sneer pointed in my direction. She doesn't even try to hide her disdain for me and I find myself sitting straighter, pulling myself into a fighting pose because there's nothing like a look of disgust to get me ready to rumble.

"Oleander needed some time to find herself. She has a wild streak that none of her Bonds wanted to stifle, though we are glad to have her back with us once again." His voice is smooth and rich, gesturing at my hair as if the color only proves that I'm a lot to handle and not that I am simply a nineteen-year-old girl with agency and my own sense of personality.

I smile and bat my eyelashes at him as if he has complimented me and we're perfectly in sync, no trouble here, absolutely *thrilled* to be trapped together for all our lives because of this stupid bond.

His fingers tighten around mine again and I don't know if he is warning me to cut it out or showing surprise at how easily I have decided to go along with this bullshit he's forcing on me.

"I, for one, am very happy to see you two together. North has done too much for our people to be left behind by an unruly child," says the woman sitting to my left.

Her eyes bore into mine and I do my best not to look

away, not to cower to this show of power she's attempting. She's perfectly made up, her hair pinned up carefully and her dress cut across her chest so that hints of her tits are showing through the emerald green lace, making her the picture of elegance. She mixes her cocktail with her gift, swirling her finger above the rim in an effortless flex of power that quite a few of the Councilmembers at the table are watching warily.

It makes me wonder what they're all capable of.

North chuckles under his breath and pulls my hand under the table so our joined hands rest on his thigh. The woman's eyes follow the movement and I see the flinch. Oh my God. Oh my *fucking* God, this is another one of his ex-lovers here to mess with me because she's pissed that I'm his Bond. She's sitting there snarking bullshit at me not because I left my bond, but because she's pissed that I've come back and now she has to compete with me.

Well, jokes on her, I want nothing to do with this coldhearted bastard. My smile turns into a baring of teeth. "I'm aware of just how *great* my Bond is, thank you."

Can this dinner be over now, please?

Something as simple as finding out that my Bond has been having it off with one of our dinner guests is enough to change my plans of presenting a united front.

North can sense the change in me immediately, and I wonder if it's simply an innate ability to read people or if it has something to do with whatever gift he's hiding underneath those perfect suits of his. His fingers squeeze mine again and I tug them out of his grasp.

If he thought I was a petulant brat before, he has no idea what his dinner has brought out in me now. I might be willing to grit my teeth and struggle through this for the greater good but the second we're out of this place, I'm going balls-to-the-wall on this asshole.

Dinner goes from bad to worse very quickly but I manage to keep myself out of the fray completely. It's not an easy task, especially with North insisting on ordering all of my dishes for me as though I'm not capable of choosing anything for myself. It's so insulting and demeaning that I really do have to talk myself out of stabbing the asshole in the throat with my fork.

The salmon en papillote is to die for and I hate him for choosing it for me because how the fuck does he know that I prefer fish and seafood over anything if given the option?

Two of the councilmen spend the entire dinner arguing with him in that polite 'boys club' way they all have. I keep my mouth shut, only speaking when addressed directly, and smile prettily at all of the servers because no one else here uses manners to them at all.

By the time we get back into the car, I want to die.

Not just because the entire evening has sucked the will to live right out of me, but also because I'm cramping like a motherfucker and there's a good chance I'm bleeding all over this ridiculous gown right now. I ask North to stop the car at a drugstore on the way back and he completely ignores me, directing the car back to the dorms and leaving me there without a single kind word or, I dunno, *saying fucking thank you* for dealing with this night so well.

I really fucking hate him.

I strip out of the gown the minute I get back to my room and, sure enough, there's blood fucking everywhere. I wrap a towel around myself and walk to the shared bathrooms, even though it's peak hour and they're all giggling and laughing at me for my state.

I don't care about their opinions but, fuck, a friendly face would be nice right now. I do my best to ignore them, and all of the bullshit I'm going to have to deal with because of this, and instead crawl into my small, uncomfortable bed. The thin blanket scratches at my oversensitive skin, but I'm shivering and need whatever help I can get to regulate my body temperature.

The pain in my stomach is so bad that I can feel it radiating through to my fingers and toes, not a single inch of my body spared from the ache. I quickly check my phone to see if there's any drug stores close by that I can make it to before my curfew with no luck. Every single one of them in this small college town would be at least a half hour round trip.

I don't think North would consider this a good reason for breaking my curfew, especially since he wouldn't even stop at the drug store for me. All I'd get from him would be a lecture about how I deserve to feel some discomfort after what I'd put them all through.

I try to rest but instead I slip in and out of sleep, the pain waking me up more often than not, and I don't know how long that's been going on when I'm startled by a knock at the door. I consider ignoring it because getting up is going to cost me. I lay there and try to figure out if I can even get up, and then I hear the door unlock.

Who the hell has a key to my door?

It swings open and Gryphon steps through. He is the last of my Bonds I expect to be here. He stands and looks over me critically, his eyes taking in every inch of my disheveled form. I've never been so aware of how much of a mess I must look. He's standing there dressed in his ripped jeans and biker boots, with a leather jacket slung over his shoulders and his hair curling around to his chin. His jaw keeps flexing like he's grinding his teeth and he looks as though he's fuming.

"I'm going to need you to be really honest right now, Oleander. The girls downstairs are saying this is a botched abortion. I checked your GPS tracker and I know that it can't be unless you did it in a bathroom stall by yourself over lunchtime. So, what's going on?"

Hot tears of rage fill my eyes and I think about risking the wrath of North by running away from this fucking place. "Does it even matter what I say to you? It's not like you will believe me anyway."

His eyes follow the silent tracks of tears down my cheeks and I wipe them away hastily. Damn him for seeing me at such a freaking low point!

"Just tell me the truth."

I roll my eyes even though it hurts me to do such a small movement. "Well, it's not a fucking abortion and it's not a miscarriage. I have my period and I'm in a lot of pain. It's like this every time I get it but normally, I can get pain medication that will help. I don't have a bank card to get it delivered, and all of the drug stores are too far away to get back in time for curfew. I'm here for the long haul tonight and tomorrow, I'll just have to be late for classes to get the damn Midol."

His eyes widen. I guess he wasn't expecting that sort of honesty from me tonight. Either that, or he doesn't believe me, which, to be honest, I'm in enough pain that I don't care. I just want him to leave me the hell alone until I'm feeling up for this sort of interrogation.

He nods at me slowly and then he hits the lights, the whole room plunging into darkness. My breathing becomes a little unsteady which, again, hurts a whole fucking lot. “What the hell are you doing?”

He doesn’t answer me. He steps up closer to the bed and then I hear the rustling of his clothes. I swear to God I could laugh in his face. I just told him that I’m in complete agony and he wants to bond?

“You need to leave. I can’t give you what you want right now.”

He scoffs at me and I feel his hands moving me on the bed so that I’m teetering on the edge, then he slides in behind me. My heart begins to race so hard I can hear it pulsing in my ears.

“Gryphon, what the hell

“Just shut up,” he snaps.

He pulls me back into his chest so that I’m laying a little more on the bed, and then one of his hands splays out on my bare stomach underneath my thin nightshirt. His palm is warm but it becomes scalding hot as his power flows through his skin and into mine.

The pain stops.

I start to cry all over again.

I stay stiff in his arms, mostly to stop the sobs from taking over my entire body and letting him know exactly how freaking pathetic I am. It doesn't bother him, he starts to move me, just little adjustments until I'm more secure in his arms and we're both comfortably wrapped up together.

I wait until I think my voice will be steady and not drenched with my tears before I croak out, "Thank you."

He hums under his breath dismissively. I feel like the world's biggest fucking bitch and it's because of that, or the warm drugging sensation of his power, that I add, "Leaving you was the hardest thing I've ever had to do. This pain is nothing compared to that."

His arms tighten around me until I think I can't breathe, but it only makes me feel... safer.

I fall asleep easier and more deeply than I have in years.

I wake up alone in my bed.

My cramps are back but much more manageable, thank God. I feel bloated and cranky and ready to rip the faces off of any bitches that start on me today. I go and take a shower, thankful that the shared bathroom is blissfully empty.

I do have a little chuckle at the thought of North's face if he found out I'd gotten into a fight with some of these girls. I can only imagine how terribly embarrassing that would be for the great Councilman himself. Then I remember his complete dismissal of me when he'd dropped me back here last night and the smile just falls straight off of my face. It doesn't matter what they think. I'll keep telling myself that until it sinks in.

I dry off and head back to my room to pull my clothes on for the day. I aim for comfortable *and* cute, needing what little armor I can have against these people, and I have my shirt halfway over my head when Gryphon unlocks my bedroom door and walks through. He doesn't look up at me or notice my state of undress as he grabs the door to shut it and lock it behind him.

I manage to get the shirt over my bra before his eyes finally touch me. He doesn't show any sign of being shocked, but he does take his time in dragging his eyes over my bare legs. I'm glad I chose cute underwear today because usually I stick with comfort while I'm on my period. The black bikini briefs are simple but sexy enough.

He glances at me. "I grabbed you the pills you need. I also grabbed a heat pack and some junk food. My sister lives on candy when she's PMSing so I guessed you'd want that too," he says, holding the plastic bag out to me.

I just stand there and blink at him for a second. "Why would you do that?"

He puts the bag down on my bed when it's clear I'm not going to take it. I finally remember that I'm not wearing any pants and stumble over to my bag to grab my jeans, forgetting my plans for yoga pants now that Gryphon is here looking as hot as hell. I turn away from him to shove my legs in and try not to wince as I do them up. Why can't they make cute jeans that don't squeeze your uterus like a damn vise?

"I'm going to ask you a question and I want you to answer it honestly."

I grimace and give him a side-eye. "And why would I answer it for you?"

He scoffs at me. "I helped you last night, didn't I? It's a simple question, nothing too revealing."

My eyes narrow as I take him in. He did help me, he helped me more than he knows. It wasn't just the pain I was feeling that he helped with, I was starting to feel like I couldn't keep going here, but he changed that with a single act of kindness. I guess I do sort of owe him something.

I shrug. "I'll answer what I can. I can't promise you any more than that."

I grab the Midol out of the bag and take it without any water, the pill dragging down my throat a little, then I sit on the bed to pull my shoes on. I don't have long until my classes start and I need to eat something before or I'll have to wait until lunch and that sounds like another form of torture. I really don't want one of the Draven brothers up my ass today. I'll be too likely to throat punch one of them and I need to hold onto my control.

It's getting harder and harder to do.

"Did you want to run away from us, or were you forced?"

It's an open question, open enough that I can answer it honestly without completely fucking my life up, so I sigh and give him a wry smile. "I'll answer, but you won't believe me anyway. I had no other choice. I can't say any more without risking you and the other Bonds and, despite what you all think, everything I've done is to keep you safe."

His eyes bum into my skin, hotter than his power had been on my stomach last night. "Tell me who is threatening you."

I shake my head. "I can't tell you. I can't tell anyone."

I watch as he grinds his teeth again, something he clearly does when I piss him off. We've barely spent any time together and yet I already know this about him. "What if I promise not to tell the other Bonds, would you tell me then? We could keep it between us and I'll deal with the issue."

I laugh at him as I stand and sling my bag over my shoulder. "Nox is your best friend, you sit through all of his bullshit at the stupid dinners. There's no way you wouldn't tell him. It doesn't matter anyway; I can't tell you."

The glare on his face gets darker and when I step towards the door, he doesn't move away. I'll have to brush against his body to get past him but as I move to do so, his arms shoot out and grab me. My breath leaks out of my lungs.

Too close. He's too close and I'm too close to breaking the fuck down.

He stares into my eyes for a second before pulling a credit card out of his pocket and slipping it into mine. "That's yours. You'll use it for anything you need from now on. Order in food, pills, a new fucking bed, I don't care. Just use it."

Holy shit.

My brow furrows at him and I struggle to find the right words. "Why would you do that? I don't want to take anything from you. If you could just get North to let me find a job, I can take care of myself."

The hand he still has wrapped around one of my arms tightens. "Tell me you will use it if you need it."

I roll my eyes at him for ignoring me. "Fine."

I pull my arm out of his grasp and take another step towards the door, but he clearly has no intention of letting me go. He grabs me again, spinning until he can pin me against it with his body. A gasp rips its way out of my throat and he leans down, his eyes still hot with that intense heat of his, and he whispers, "Say it and mean it. There's nothing worse than a liar."

I swallow and gasp out, "I'll use it if I have to but I still want a job of my own."

He lifts one of his hands to trace the side of my face. "North will never risk losing you again. I don't think he will ever let you find a job, but if you ask him directly, I'll side with you."

I can't breathe with him this close to me, with the hard lines of his chest pressed against me, and he doesn't make a move away from me, just holds me there against the door. The buzzing of his phone in his pocket pressed between us breaks the spell, and he curses under his breath as he steps away.

"Grab your shit, I'll drive you down to the dining hall."

He steps out of the room without another word, hovering by the door until I get it locked. The hallway is full of girls, all of them staring at him like he's a slab of meat, but he doesn't acknowledge them. He walks slowly enough that I can keep the pace without running, not that I would today with how freaking bloated I am, and then I realize that he knows that and is adjusting for me.

I don't know what to do with that sort of consideration.

I'm just as awkward getting into his car this time around as I was the first time. I shoot Gabe a text to tell him where I am and then I shove the phone back into my bag. Gryphon doesn't say a word and the three minute car ride is silent.

When we pull up at the dining hall, I clear my throat.

"I really appreciate-"

"Are you going to try running off again?" he cuts me off, his eyes scanning the campus like he's expecting me to be snatched off of the curb in broad daylight.

I frown and rub at the back of my neck, the little bump of the GPS chip still easy to find. It still kind of aches and I push at it to really feel the bum. "No."

Gryphon's eyes drop to my fidgeting and he says, "Would you run if we couldn't track you?"

He can smell my lies so I go with the truth. "I would have to run. It's better that way."

He nods slowly. "You could tell me, you know. It might change a lot of things for you around here."

I shrug. "We both know it won't. Your bestie has already told me there's no excuse good enough for him to accept. I'm trapped here, and because of that, bad shit is going to happen. I'm doing everything I can to stop it but... it's probably going to happen anyway."

His fingers drum on the steering wheel. "The problem is that I know that you believe that. I just also know that whatever it is, you should have come to us about it instead of running. You should have trusted us."

I laugh at him, dark and freaking desperate. "Oh yeah? I was fourteen. Did you know my parents both died right before I was tested? Did you know I lost everything and... it happened? I'd just found out I was going to have Bonds and everything was going to be ok. I'd lost them, you know? I'd lost everything."

Gryphon's hands tighten so hard that the leather of the steering wheel creaks. "Did you want your Bonds? Back then?"

I blink back the tears that always come when I think about that time. "More than anything, that's what I wanted."

He nods. "And now? Do you want your Bonds now?"

I reach for the handle on the door to escape. I have to get the hell out of this car before he gets another truth out of me, the only truth here that eats at me every time I find myself trapped with one of them.

"Oli, answer me. Do you want your Bonds or not?" he growls, pushing the lock button to stop me from getting out.

I glance back at him, glaring at him for doing this shit to me. "There's no point in answering it. I can't have these Bonds. You all hate me, and I know it's too dangerous to try. I'm better off alone."

I get out but I hear his words before the door slams shut behind me. "That might be your truth, but it's not mine."

I need to stay the hell away from them all.

Gabe questions why Gryphon was driving me into the campus but I brush him off easily, still mad that he had a hand in getting me to the Council dinner shit show with North. He doesn't notice how pissy I am though and just shadows me like usual.

It's not until we're sitting with Sage and Sawyer at lunch in the dining hall, that he hears the rundown of what actually happened and he realizes just how angry I am at him over it.

"I only found out about the dinner when you did! How the hell is it my fault you had a shitty time? If interacting with girls your Bonds have fucked is enough to ruin your day, I have some bad fucking news for you."

I jab him in the ribs, not that he notices because he's made of muscle stacked on freaking muscle. "You shoved me at his people and left me to it! I almost died, and then I had to deal with the complete bullshit that is the gossips of my dorm because North wouldn't stop at a freaking drug store for me."

Sage winces at me. "I heard the rumors too. Obviously I didn't believe them, and I told Grade if she ran her mouth about it I'd tell her mom about her panting after someone else's Bonds."

Gabe frowns at her and glances between us. "What rumors? I haven't heard anything."

Sawyer scoffs at him and finally looks up from his phone. "Of course you didn't, they're talking shit about the Bond you've just called a truce with. You think Zoey and her little crowd of bimbo bitches would tell you to your face that they're accusing your Bond of a self-administered abortion?"

I feel his control over his gift slip and it doesn't take a genius to work out that he's not lying about having no idea. I keep my eyes on my food because I don't need his white knight bullshit.

"That's why Gryphon brought you in. He heard—"

I cut him off, "Yeah and I had to convince him that it wasn't true—"

"Well, of course it's not fucking true! Who said it?

Which of Zoey's friends? I'm going to fucking kill—"

"You're not going to kill anyone—"

Sawyer cuts in, "The two of you better not start fucking on the table here in the dining hall because this all feels like really angry foreplay to me and, honestly, I just want to eat my pizza in peace."

I shoot him a look but almost instantly I have to shift my focus back to Gabe who is about to flip a table over this. I guess this is cutting a little too close to whatever the fallout of his Bond disappearing was and now he's out for blood.

"Just forget about it. I honestly don't give a shit about what some petty, jealous girls think of me. As long as it doesn't cause me any grief with the Dravens, I don't care."

Sage winces again, mostly because both North and Nox terrify her, and I shoot her a grateful look. I'm thankful she's here, listening to me whine and not judging me for being a grumpy fuck about it all.

Gabe shoves the last of the grilled chicken from his plate of sadness into his mouth and says, "Gryphon will clear it up with North. Nox might still bring it up because he's... like that."

I shove my bag on my back and stand up, ready to get this day over with. "That a nice way to say he's a total asshole who'll bring it up over the dinner table for the next fifty fucking years."

We make it through the day and even though Sage invites me to her place for tacos and textbooks, I bail on her, my stomach still a bloated, aching mess. I just want to mope around in my room and hate my life quietly for the night. She gets it, because what girl doesn't, and leaves me behind with a hug and a promise to check in on me tomorrow.

I eat dinner early and then head back to the dorms to shower and get into something comfortable. I text Atlas back, just a general text to tell him about my day and let him know I'm okay, and then I hit the books hard.

A little after midnight, I'm still pouring over my textbooks for the next assignment Nox has us doing when my door unlocks and Gryphon steps through it, a bag dangling from one hand.

"You're not even going to attempt to knock at all anymore?" I say, my voice tired and my hand shaking a little as I take notes because I'm so ridiculously freaking tired. I should have stopped hours ago but my brain doesn't want to stop yet.

"I was expecting you to be asleep, not cramming. I didn't think exams were for months."

I shrug and watch as he kicks his shoes off. I have no fucking clue of what's happening right now. "I'm a high school dropout, remember? I have no choice but to spend all of my spare time with my nose in my textbooks."

He pulls his jacket off and throws it over the peg on the back of the door, covering the cracked and shitty mirror. I watch as he pulls his hoodie off as well, standing there in his low-slung jeans and a soft black tee, looking like sex on legs.

Shit.

"Are you hungry? I brought a burrito, but I can split it."

There's literally a Twizzler hanging out of my mouth so I shake my head at him. Honestly, I'm still trying to get my exhausted brain around what is happening right now. He's here, in my bedroom, offering to split food with me without any sort of a reason that I can tell.

It feels like a trap.

"Stop staring at me like that, Oli. I'm here to make sure you're okay. You sobbed in my arms for hours last night, even after you fell asleep."

Oh God, that's embarrassing. "I'm fine. It's better with the drugs and you made sure I have a great supply of those. Seriously, go home and forget about me."

He grunts at me and parks his ass on the floor, a mirror of Gabe only a few weeks ago, and he tears into his food. I shift my focus back onto my books and lose myself into the history of the blood tests, and how the Bond markers were discovered.

The next thing I know, I'm waking up to Gryphon's hand gently moving me onto the bed. I try to mumble a thank you, but it comes out as a garbled mess. He huffs at me, pulling me into his arms and that magic freaking hand of his slips onto my stomach.

I could get addicted to this so freaking quickly.

This time when I wake, he's still stretched out in the bed next to me, wearing nothing but a pair of black boxer briefs. The bed is too small for me to roll over so I just lay there, too afraid to breathe in case it wakes him up and I lose this moment.

I'd get this all of the time if I was allowed to Bond with him.

This moment I think it, I hate myself because my bond starts immediately straining towards him, desperate to have him. I'm rough as I yank it back, my frustration coming out.

There's a sharp knock at the door that startles Gryphon awake. He bolts out of the bed, instantly on high alert, and he pulls a gun that I had *no freaking clue* was in the room out of his boot as he takes the two steps over to the door.

My brain hasn't even caught up to the fact that someone is here, when he grabs the door handle and yanks it open, shirtless, bed-rumpled and in all his early-morning glory.

Sage and Sawyer look at him in twin images of shock.

It would be absolutely hilarious if it wasn't also completely freaking shameful. There's no way I'm getting out of this without them making some comment that is going to make me want to die because one look at him, and they have to assume we've spent the whole night fucking like horny rabbits.

"Well, excuse the fuck out of us! Sage, we need to leave. Now. Move it."

I groan as Gryphon stares him down, finally lowering the gun and stepping away to let them in, except Sage is cemented to the floor in shock. I climb cut of the bed and rush over to attempt to explain that this is definitely *not* what it looks like.

I hear Gryphon rummaging around behind me so I assume he's getting dressed, thank God, but the moment I open my mouth, Sawyer cuts me off, "We need to swap dick stories because there are a lot of rumors about him and I need to know which ones are true."

Sage elbows him in the gut so sharply he actually groans and I grin at her. "Sorry, I forgot to set an alarm. I'll be a minute while I throw some clothes on and we can grab food on the way, right? I'll explain—"

Gryphon nudges me out of the way, his keys in his hands as he scowls around at the entire hallway full of gaping girls. "What's there to explain? You're my Bond."

He then stalks off like he didn't just casually confirm to the girls here that he fucked my brains out last night, and I want to die. Not that there's anything wrong with us hooking up, but I've been so adamant about hating them that this feels like I've suddenly just bent over for him because he asked.

I sigh and usher the siblings in, groaning as I shut the door behind them.

Sage awkwardly stands there like she's trying not to touch anything but Sawyer slumps down on my bed. "Dammit, I really thought you'd finally fallen into bed with one of them. I'm strangely disappointed."

I quickly start throwing clothes on, crowing inside a little when I find Gryphon's hoodie that he's left behind. "Sorry, he was just here as pain relief. I didn't think you'd believe me. I'm shocked at your trust, Sawyer."

He rolls his eyes at me and picks at the sheets. "There's no sex smell. I know the scent of a good fuck when I smell it."

That's oddly disgusting and when I finally sling my bag onto my back, I find Sage looking at me with concern. "Are you sure you're okay? Should you be going to classes if you're in that much pain?"

I'm fine now and there's no way I'm calling North to get a sick pass. "Let's just forget this happened. Gryphon still hates me, he's just also a decent human being. He won't be back anytime soon."

A week later, I've almost forgotten what my bed feels like without Gryphon in it. He's much more discreet about his stays in it, always coming in after I've fallen asleep and leaving before I wake up in the morning, but there's always little signs that he's been here.

I get up and try to ignore the fact that my bed is empty again. I wish he'd stay to wake up with me, just once, but I also know how dangerous that is because he's chipping away at my resolve to keep them all at arm's length. I can't afford to let that happen, no matter how desperately I want him.

The shared bathroom is full of girls and I have to grit my teeth to ignore all of the looks and whispers. You'd think they could all find something better to do than gossiping about me and my asshole Bonds, but nope, they love nothing more than talking about how great they all are in bed while I scrub my body like I'm trying to scour the devil from my skin. Just once I'd like to get clean without hearing about how amazing Nox is with his tongue or how big Gryphon's dick is. Just freaking once!

The Gryphon comments bum a little more these days.

By the time I get back to my room, I'm so angry about how freaking rude every girl in this damn building is that I don't even bother looking at my phone for my usual good morning text from Atlas. I just shove my legs into a pair of yoga pants and throw a hoodie over my head, nothing but a bra underneath. The hoodie is one of Gryphon's, the one he wore here last night, and I tell myself I'm only wearing it because it's cold out and not because I've become addicted to the smell of him. If Gabe spills something on me at lunch and forces me to wash it, I'll freaking... stab him, or something. Hell, I'll ask Sage to set his ass on fire.

I won't tell her why I'm pissed though.

As I'm giggling to myself about setting one of my Bonds on fire, there's a knock at my door and I roll my eyes, expecting it to be Gryphon coming back to steal back his hoodie or bitch me out over something, but when I fling the door open with a frown on my face and fire in my soul, I'm ready to unleash my shitty mood on him. I find my breath knocked out of my chest instead.

The photo Atlas sent me of himself did not do him justice at all.

I am stunned as I stand there and take him in. Tall, dark, and handsome. I check to make sure I'm not drooling at the freaking sight of him towering over me. He fills the entire door frame, his shoulders wide and defined in the tight tee he's wearing. Hot-freaking-damn! His arms are covered in tattoos that creep up his neck to tuck under his chin and my eyes follow them up obediently. It's only when I get to his face that I see the cheeky grin plastered across there at my swooning and I blush.

"Well, damn! You look even better in person and I

can tell you, I was fucking impressed with your photo," he drawls, and I scoff at him, recovering from my embarrassment now that his smart mouth is starting up.

"You could have called ahead and let me know you were coming! I'm wearing yoga pants, for fuck's sake! I could have at least attempted to look cute."

He chuckles at me and grabs my hips in his big hands, walking me backwards into my room and kicking the door shut. I swear to God, my heart skips a beat or five.

"If this isn't your cute, I don't think I'm prepared for it."

I blush and grab my bag, the blush deepening when Atlas takes it from me and swings over his own shoulder like a lovesick teenager.

"I can carry that, you know," I say, hoping the words sound flirty and not snappy. My mind is still whirling with the shock of him being here and the unspent rage of dealing with the other girls.

He grins and shrugs. "Yeah, but you'll let me do it today. I was kind of hoping we could stay here for the day, let you get to know me a little better, but if you insist on going out, then you'll let me take care of you a bit instead."

The sweet grins he's giving me make it even harder to look at him. "I'm not allowed to skip classes. The GPS tracker means North will know and he will personally come here to punish me."

All of the teasing and playful joy melts off of Atlas. He goes from looking flirty and sweet to having the stone-cold glare of a beast who has smelled his prey. "Yeah, I'm going to fix that for the both of us pretty soon. North may be on the Council on this side of the country, but my family controls the Council on the East Coast. If he is going to a be a dick about this, then I'm taking you home with me and they can fucking rot here for all I care."

A shiver takes over me. "If I thought we could get away with that, I would totally agree. But I get the feeling North Draven doesn't ever lower himself to compromise."

Atlas smirks at me, pushing the hair away from my shoulder and kissing my cheek softly. "Sweetness, I don't give a fuck what *North Draven* wants. If he gets in my way or upsets you, I'll royally fuck him up."

Ok, now I'm definitely swooning.

I have to remind myself that I'm trying not to get too close to these guys and I take a half step back. "We should head to class. I don't want to fall behind."

He doesn't look pissed off at me for pulling back, instead he holds out a hand and threads his fingers through mine. When he opens the door to lead me out, we find Gabe walking up to escort me to class, the smile on his face directed at the girl poking her head out of the room next to mine. It slides right off when he sees Atlas standing there, holding my hand and my bag.

Oh shit.

A giddy sort of giggle bubbles in my stomach, but I hold that sucker in. Atlas squeezes my hand gently and leans in close to whisper in my ear, "Lock your door, Sweetness."

I side-eye him, he totally did not have to get that close to me to say that, but I do as he says, turning my back on them both to lock up with the extra-secure lock Gryphon installed.

A snarl rips out of Gabe and I fight my instinct to spin around to face him, trusting Atlas to watch my exposed back against my shifter Bond. I make sure everything is secure and then turn slowly, as if the idea of a freaking wolf tearing my limbs off isn't at all concerning. There's a whole lot of interest in what's about to go down here. Every door is open and there's girls everywhere. Even a few guys standing with their own Bonds and girlfriends, watching.

Atlas laughs. "Oli has no need for her pouting jailer today, Ardem, so fuck off."

Gabe's eyes start to glow and I suck in a deep breath. Who the hell do I call if he loses it? I grab my phone, Gryphon is going to be my best backup, but he never freaking answers my messages. Nox is a dick, and I'd rather gouge my own eyeballs out than speak to North. Well, fuck.

"Don't fucking tell me what I can and can't do with my Bond, Bassinger," he spits out between clenched teeth and Atlas drops my hand to instead sling his arm over my shoulders.

"No one wants a sulking dickhead trailing after them, so beat it, Ardem. Do it before I make you. You *really* don't want me to make you."

Gabe struggles to get control over himself, the shift rippling over his face as his eyes glow and the skin of his arms darkens into a soft pelt. I've never seen him actually lose control before, even when Martinez went for him, he'd kept his gift under tight control.

I really don't want to do this, and certainly not in the hallway of my dorm with all of the gossiping girls here. "Can we just head to class, please? I don't want to be late and I'm assuming you'll need to get your timetable together, Atlas?"

He shrugs and holds out a hand for me to take. I hesitate for a second, because this time it feels like more than just a little sign of affection, but it doesn't bother him. "You wanna go slow, then we're going slow. Take my hand, Bond."

Deep breath.

And then I take his hand.

Eating lunch is usually my favorite part of the day, but being jammed between Atlas and Gabe, with Sage and Sawyer dying of laughter at their vicious jabs at one another, kind of ruins it for me. Atlas had picked up a timetable that slotted him into all of the same classes as Gabe and me, grinning at me when I questioned him about it.

"You're in the general courses, if I have to repeat, at least we're doing the easy shit."

I roll my eyes at him with a huff, mostly because it definitely doesn't feel easy to me, and our relaxed familiarity pisses Gabe off. He then shadows us both, scowling and snapping at us whenever Atlas leans in to me or makes me laugh with his easy going humor.

I'd taken my bag back and kept my hands to myself as soon as we'd made it out onto the campus grounds, but Atlas hadn't commented, just accepted the boundaries I was putting in place like this is all going exactly the way he expected it to.

Sage and Sawyer had accepted Atlas in without an issue, both of them already rooting for him in the 'Bonding race', as Sawyer has so nicely dubbed the mess that my life is.

When lunch is over, Sawyer heads off to his computer science class, and I have an awkward moment of trying to get around Gabe to walk with Sage to our next class, but he's not willing to just step back and let me walk with her. Atlas smirks at him when I finally shove at him to get him moving, and I decide that I would rather drop out and deal with North's scathing reaction than deal with this every day until I get out of this place.

We arrive at our Econ class to find Gryphon's second, Kieran, on watch outside the lecture hall. He's my least favorite of all the TacTeam security, and I struggle to keep the disdain off of my face when I realize he's the one checking over the students' ID's to get in and I'll be forced to speak to him.

I forget that Atlas has no clue about any of the history between us and when he gets an eyeful of the look on my face, he instantly shifts to tuck me into his side, curling a little so he's covering me.

"Who the fuck is that and what did he do to you?"

I shake my head at him, because I have no idea of who is around us and what their powers are, but Gabe, who is watching us both with a moody sort of obsession, murmurs, "He's on Gryphon's TacTeam. She just hates him."

Sage scoffs and darts a look at Kieran, like he's venomous and she's afraid of being hit with that acid. "He's the one who caught her, tackled her to the ground in broad daylight like she was a criminal, and then dragged her back here to have all of her freedoms and liberties taken away by Councilman Draven. As glad as I am to have Oli here, I hate him for doing that to her too."

Atlas' arm tenses around me for a second but then he relaxes, that grin back on his face again, and I'm learning very quickly that the grin spells out danger.

We have to wait in the line as the ID of every student is checked. I fumble to grab mine out and Sage curses as she digs through her bag, loose sheets of paper rustling at her rough treatment. Gabe stands there like a brick wall, scowling and huffing under his breath at the wait.

When we finally step up to the door, I have to take a deep, calming breath, checking in on my gift and my bond to ensure they're locked down tight. Kieran is huge and kind of terrifying this close but he acts like I don't exist, grinning at Gabe and clapping him on the shoulder as he ushers him through without question, completely ignoring the frown on my Bond's face. He checks Sage's ID but only because she already has it out, waving her through quickly as well.

He holds out an arm when Atlas steps up, pulling me along with him.

"Who are you? There are no extra seats in this class for a bystander."

Even his voice has my jaw clenching, but Atlas just flashes his own ID at him. "I just transferred in. You should move your arm."

Kieran's eyes narrow at him until they're nothing more than dark slits, but he doesn't move his arm. "Bassinger. You're related to Athena Bassinger of the East Coast Council?"

"My aunt. I'm not going to ask you to move again."

Gabe takes a step back through the door and says, "He's telling the truth, he's Oli's other Bond."

Finally his eyes dart down to me and the disgust on his face is palpable, like a sharp slap to my cheek, and I immediately flush scarlet as though I've done something wrong.

Atlas doesn't like that reaction at all and when the grin drops away, Kieran finally figures out that Atlas isn't just a grinning, arrogant kid. He's a Gifted making threats.

Because things can only get worse for me and because that is exactly what I need in my life, Gryphon turns the corner and stalks towards us, reading the malevolent atmosphere perfectly. "Move aside, Black. They're late for class, and I know you weren't about to use your gift on campus grounds, Bassinger. That's rule number one here."

Atlas smirks and shrugs. "I have an exemption, Shore. I can't turn mine off, it's a part of me. Your thug here didn't like that I'm not worried about him. Honestly? I think he didn't like that I'm not a Gift-less girl half the size of him that he can throw around."

Oh God, I don't want to be around for this dick swinging competition and I definitely don't want my entire life aired out and picked through in the hallway with way too many eyes on us all.

"Fuck this, I'm going to class. If you guys wanna whip them out and measure them to get this over with, then go right ahead, I'm not sticking around for it."

Kieran scoffs at me and snaps, "Of course you're running away. Oleander Fallows is exactly the type to just disappear when things get hard."

I walk away because there's nothing I can say back to him. I don't want to see any of the reactions from the others and Sage immediately moves to tuck her arm in mine, stalking over to the back row of seats where we normally sit together, as if the entire room isn't listening in on the drama happening at the door. Literally, the entire class is waiting for my Bonds to sort their issues out and sit down so the professor can start the class.

I want to scream.

"Ignore it, this has nothing to do with you. They're all just on edge because Gifted are being taken and Atlas has shown up to rock the boat," Sage whispers, shooting Zoey and her giggling friends a look when they all stare back at us.

I block them all out. When Atlas finally takes his seat next to me, he's still looking calm and steady, pulling out textbooks and his laptop to take notes as though nothing has happened. Gabe sits next to Sage and seethes the entire time, a walking timebomb today. I'm sure he's planning on destroying me with the temper tantrum that's brewing.

When the class is finally over and we're all heading to the library to study, Altas slings an arm over my shoulders as we walk out. Kieran is nowhere to be seen, and his replacement doesn't so much as glance at us as we walk past.

The library is busier than it usually is and when we finally wade through the crowd to our table, we find Sawyer and Felix already waiting for us. I smile at them both and introduce Atlas to Felix, who accepts him into the fold as though this is all completely normal and there's not a seething sort of rage radiating off of Gabe right now.

I'm set on ignoring it and just focussing on my damn assignments, but I'm also prepared for Sawyer's shit-stirring ways by now.

"I heard about the spat this morning but the real question here is, which one of your Bonds has the biggest dick? Tell us so we know who won, Fallows."

Sage groans and buries her face in her hands. "For the love of God, can we please stop talking about dicks for five fucking minutes?"

Sawyer grins like he's going to torture his sister but Gabe buts in, "Kieran might be an asshole but he wasn't wrong, was he? It's hard to defend someone when everyone knows their rap sheet."

Atlas slips his hand into mine on the table, threading our fingers together where everyone can see. I think it has more to do with claiming me than showing me any sort of affection.

Gabe's eyes drop down and glue themselves there and Atlas smirks at him. "Oh yeah? Well, unlike you, I'm not afraid to tell the others to fuck off and keep my Bond to myself. I don't care what's happened in the past, that shit is over with. She's mine and you've chosen for her to not be yours."

Gabe's nostrils flare. "It's not as easy as saying *she's mine.* There's more going on-"

"I don't give a fuck," Atlas cuts him off, and then

resolutely ignores him for the rest of the afternoon, no matter how badly Gabe wants the fight.

We study until the dining hall opens for dinner, the table falling into a tense sort of quiet while we all cram as much knowledge into our skulls as possible.

Sawyer, Felix, and Gabe leave to go to football practice together. I notice how much calmer and less stressed out Sage is about hanging around Felix now and I give her a raised eyebrow about it as we head to dinner together.

She glances at Atlas and then murmurs, "I told him I just wanted to hang out as friends... for now. He hasn't pushed the subject and— I mean— it's been nice to have him back. I'm still positive he's going to find his Central and leave me but... well, maybe it wouldn't be such a bad thing to enjoy the time until then."

I tuck my arm into hers again and whisper back, "You absolutely should. Why should you be alone forever if Riley has made his decision? He doesn't own you, Sage. You can do what you want."

She shrugs at me with a little smile, glancing over at Atlas who is very kindly pretending he can't hear a thing we're saying and has no interest in what we're gossiping about. I've vented out my anger about Sage's Bond situation to him before, just general shit and none of the personal details she's trusted me with, so I'm sure he's got a pretty good idea of what's going on.

We eat dinner together, a very dry and flavorless lasagne, which Sage gives up on two bites in thanks to the luxury of having a car, money, and access to a fridge at home. Atlas eats all of his but doesn't look happy about it.

I choke the entire plate down and try not to be pissed off all over again and my lack of options.

Sage hugs me before she heads home for the day, leaving Atlas and I alone together for the first time since he opened my bedroom door to find Gabe heading our way this morning.

I'm suddenly completely unsure of what to do.

Atlas grabs my hand again and gives it a squeeze. "I'll walk you back up to your room, Oli, unless you want to head somewhere else first?"

I shake my head and try not to look like I'm completely shitting myself, which, to be fair, I absolutely am. This is why I've kept everyone else at an arm's length... okay, not really, because the Draven brothers have been the ones to put distance between themselves and me. Gabe is an anomaly because I think he's both desperate to bridge the gap between us, but also completely unwilling to let go of the damage my supposed abandonment did to him. Then there's the small fact that not only does Gryphon sleep in my bed every night now, but I'm also wearing his hoodie right now and just wallowing in his scent like it's a drug I'll die without.

My legs move on autopilot while I try to figure out what the fuck I'm going to say to him, what explanation I can possibly give him for not being able to do anything with him, no matter how much I like him.

The moment we get to the dorms, my skin starts to crawl at the eyes that follow us both the entire way up to my room. News has clearly gotten around that Atlas is the last of my Bonds, come from the other side of the country to be here with his defective Central Bond, and the attention we're getting is enough to get my back up in a big way.

I fucking hate this place.

I usher Atlas into my room without thinking, desperate to get out of sight of the entire freaking building. I flick the lock and throw my bag down onto the bed, wincing at the fact that I didn't make it this morning and it looks messy.

I also don't want to admit that I don't like to make it because I can still see the indent in the shitty mattress of where Gryphon slept, which is very pathetic, stupid, and a little too heartsick for what I'm trying to project here.

It's clear I've forgotten how bleak the room really is because it takes me a second to realize why Atlas' lip curls as he looks around the room. "How the fuck did I not notice how bad this is this morning? Pack a bag, Oli. You're moving in with me."

A nervous laugh creeps up my throat. "I can't do that! This is where the Council put me, they're paying for it. I don't have any money or anything. They won't let me get a job."

I feel shame curling in my stomach. I hate admitting just how freaking bad my situation really is. I have nothing, no money, no job. The education I'm getting is just to keep me under their thumbs and not to actually help me find a job I want. I'm freaking powerless and it sucks.

Gryphon's card sitting in my bag is taunting me, but I've already decided that I'm not using that little plastic rectangle unless someone is dying.

"Pack a bag. Looks like they haven't let you have anything here anyway, so it'll all fit in your duffle. You're coming with me now and I'll deal with the Council if they have questions. You're my Bond, I'll take care of you."

My cheeks flush with shame. "You don't need to do that, I can take care of myself. Well, I could if North would let me work. I'm kind of... bored sitting around here all day."

Atlas gently moves me over to the bed with a hand under my elbow. "Pack. We can figure out how to get you a job later, once you're out of this shithole. It would be my honor to take care of you while you find your feet, Oli.

Wouldn't you do the same for me?"

I answer without thinking. "Well, of course, but the others will be pissed you're doing this and... I can't bond with you. I can't give you any reasons why either, this is a fucking mess."

He scoffs. "We'll figure out our bond when we're ready, you don't owe me a goddamn thing and, Oli, I need you to understand that I don't give a fuck what they think. I care about our bond. I care about getting to know you and us making decisions together. My place isn't swanky or anything, it's just an apartment, but it's better than this. We can eat real food too, not the cafeteria crap we just had to choke down."

There's no arguing with him and he's right, it only takes me a minute to pack everything into the small duffle bag I have. Honestly, the only reason it looks reasonably full is because I have two other hoodies that Gryphon left behind and they take up a heap of space.

He takes my duffle off of me and slings it over his back, smirking at one of the girls when we step out together in the most arrogant, cocky way that has me giggling. She looks shocked and a little shaky as she darts back into her room.

"Come on, Sweetness, let's get the fuck outta this shithole."

He leads me down to the small parking lot behind the

dorm that I've never stepped foot into because everyone always picks me up from the loading zone out the front. I know which car is his immediately because there's no car that screams BDE like the black Dodge Challenger Hellcat, and the grin he shoots at me when he unlocks it is total smug asshole. It's cute, and also a little gross, how well he pulls this off without looking like an utter douchebag.

His apartment is only a few blocks away, still within walking distance of the campus. He drives as confidently as Gryphon and a little less *crazy suicidal* than Gabe on his motorbike.

The apartment is on the top floor and he was definitely underselling it when he said it was nothing fancy. Sure, it's not North's mansion, but there's a view of the entire campus and two bedrooms in the place. The kitchen is full-sized with granite countertops and the bathroom has a tub.

The dorm feels like a dirty little hovel compared to this place.

When Atlas finishes the tour in his bathroom, he drops the duffle down onto the bed and scrubs a hand through his hair and blows out a breath. "I can take the couch."

I glance out of the open doorway and then give him a look of disbelief. The couch is a two seater and there's no way in hell he's going to fit. Hell, I won't fit on it either. "It's fine, I don't mind sharing. I mean, we're Bonds, right? We have to get used to it sometime."

He smirks at me, the dimples flashing at me. "I was hoping you'd be a little more enthusiastic about sharing a bed with me but we can work on that."

I scoff at him and shove at his chest a little. "It's not that, I just... I still feel bad about mooching off of you by being here. I don't know what to do about finding a job. North can track me, if I even get close to the edges of campus, he calls me and scolds me."

Atlas clutches dramatically at his chest where I pushed him and stalks past me to the fridge, pulling us each out a bottle of water. "There's shit you can do online, that way you can stay here and North won't ever know about it. Money *and* secrecy, it's a win-win."

I perch on the couch, still a little uncomfortable. "What, like a cam-girl? I guess I could get my tits out. Do you think I have a voice for sex work?"

I'm joking, there's no way I'd ever have the confidence to do that kind of thing, but the glare Atlas shoots me is kind of awesome. I haven't had any sort of possessive actions from any of my Bonds like this so having him care about my tits... is pretty great.

"Over my dead fucking body, Fallows. Never, and certainly not before I've even gotten to see them."

I giggle and wiggle my eyebrows at him. "Play your cards right and I might get them out later."

Again, I'm joking. I've known him in the flesh for

about ten hours, but the look he gives me melts my panties right off of my body. "I'm playing to win, Oli. This is one hand I refuse to lose."

Fuck, and I'm pretty sure he will too because I'm struggling to keep my cool right now and he's not even trying to seduce me. I'm not going to be able to handle anything he throws at me right now. He notices all of my brain-melting and grins lasciviously even as he flicks the TV on and changes the subject.

It's awkward at first to just sit around with him and hang out but he's the perfect gentleman, never pushing me or questioning me, and I spread out on the floor in front of the TV with all of my textbooks to work on my next assignment to hand over to North. It's become my obsession, but I will prove that man wrong even if it kills me.

When we both finally head for bed, there's an awkward moment when I want to be embarrassed about the old, oversized cotton tee I have for pajamas and the silky boxer shorts, but I'm not exactly a lingerie kind of girl. Atlas's eyes trace over me appreciatively anyway, as if I was only standing here in lace, and I find myself getting addicted to the heat in his gaze.

"Is it cool with you if I sleep in just my boxers? It's too hot for a shirt," he mumbles as I pull back the covers and climb in.

I shrug. "Whatever is comfortable for you."

I don't mention Gryphon and his penchant to do the same. There's an ache in my chest over the thought of him showing up to my dorm room tonight to find it empty so I flick him a quick text to tell him where I am instead. I already know he won't answer, but at least I've tried.

BROKEN BONDS

The sound of a door being kicked in wakes me.

Atlas rolls over me, bracing himself as he goes so he doesn't hurt me, and then leaps out of the bed on my side, standing between the bed and whoever the fuck has just arrived. It's all a little too smooth for me, he's definitely had training and I'm jealous of how quickly his brain has come online because I'm still trying to figure out what the fuck is happening right now.

"Who the fuck— are you kidding me? What the fuck is your problem, Draven?"

My eyes finally adjust to the light streaming into the room from the kitchen and I find that it really is North here, storming into the apartment with an entire fucking

TacTeam because I dared to break his stupid rules... by sleeping in Atlas' apartment, two blocks away from the dorms.

It's probably because of the two am wake up, but I suddenly want to burst into tears of rage and hopelessness. Atlas squares up on him, staring around at the men all dressed in their riot gear like he's going to take them all on for showing up here.

I don't feel a tug to any of them so at least Gryphon isn't here to see this mess.

"She has a curfew and she knows it," North says, his voice sounding the same as ever, cold and unaffected, but I can feel the difference in him. I've been forced to spend enough time with him to know that under all of that ice, he's fuming, pissed off that I would dare defy his rules.

I feel like a freaking child being scolded and the scowl on Atlas' face says he's feeling the same way. "She's my Bond and if I want her to sleep in my damn bed then she will. She wasn't running off or doing anything else you've put on your no-no list. I'll go to the Council myself if you try to stop her from coming here."

North smooths a hand down his tie. "Good luck getting the rest of the Council to go against me."

He finally looks over at me, his eyes calculating and unimpressed at the disheveled state of me sitting there in my old, ratty pajamas. ''We're leaving. Get up, Fallows."

I pull my knees up to my chest as I stare around at the men all standing there. “I’m not even wearing a bra, I don’t want to-”

“I wasn’t asking what you wanted to do. I’m telling you to walk downstairs and get in my car, Fallows.”

My heart climbs up my throat and tries to choke me. “Atlas is one of my Bonds as well. Why can’t I stay here?”

North doesn’t budge and his mouth is sealed shut in a disapproving line. Well, fuck. Atlas shifts forward like he’s going to attack them all and I really don’t want a part in that. I can’t afford for that to happen, if it triggers my gift then it’ll be a big game over for me so instead, I sigh and get out of the bed.

Tears prick at my eyes as I leave without looking at Atlas. I don’t need to see whatever it is that’s showing on his face, it’ll only push me over the goddamned edge. Maybe he’s figured out that I’m too much fucking trouble. Maybe he’s finally realized I’m no fucking good for any of them.

Fuck.

I think about running but it leaves me as quickly as it comes. North will find me, no matter where I go, he’ll find me.

The elevator is freezing and I cross my arms over my chest when the TacTeam member glances over at me, escorting me down as though I’m about to run screaming into the night in my freaking pajamas.

More useless tears threaten to fall and I choke them back.

The driver pulls the door open as I approach and I tighten my arms across my chest to try to hide my lack of bra a little. I smile and thank him but he ignores me completely, shutting the door firmly after me. Great. Everyone fucking hates me, even North's freaking driver.

I sit and wallow in my own bleak misery until the door opens and the man of the moment climbs in, sitting opposite to me so we're facing one another. The car starts and we take off down the street, in the wrong direction.

I fidget nervously, unable to sit still in the suffocating silence.

North is, as always, unaffected. Completely at ease as he looks out at the college campus.

"If the housing provided to you is inadequate, then I will have you moved into my residence. You can commute from there."

Dear God, no. I can barely handle the dinner there one night a week. "The campus is fine. I can go back there. I can call a cab, just let me out."

His eyes are so sharp I'm sure I must be fucking bleeding. "Is there something wrong, Fallows? Some reason you don't want to travel with me? I will provide everything you require."

I swallow. "I was going to stay with Atlas so I could be with one of my Bonds. The campus is fine, I can go... home to there."

The word home gets stuck in my throat but I force it out, anything to get out of this fucking car.

"You're in luck. My house has three of your Bonds living there, so you will have one of us with you at all times."

I glance out of the window so he doesn't see the useless tears starting in my eyes. Perfect. I've gone from a shitty, but solitary room, to something that's probably over the top in it's luxury but full of the men who hate me.

"Anything else you'd like to say, Fallows?"

I blink back the tears. "No. Thank you."

My voice comes out thready, but clear enough. North gets his phone out so I guess that's the conversation over with.

The moment we step out of the car in North's garage, we're greeted by three of his house staff. I keep my arms crossed over my chest tightly, as though no one will notice I'm standing around looking homeless if I just keep my chest covered, but none of them look my way anyway.

"Councilman Eversong has arrived, he's waiting in your office."

North curses softly under his breath and takes the folder from one of the men, speaking to me in the same cold tone he has all night without so much as a glance in my direction, "Evelyn will show you to your room, Fallows. I'll collect you from there in the morning to take you down to breakfast, I expect you to stay there until then."

Perfect.

Great.

Fucking wonderful.

I've gone from a limited existence to a freaking cage and there's nothing I can do about it. This beautiful, obscenely ornate mansion is now more than just a place I come each week to be tortured... now it's the hell that I'll be trapped in until I freaking die.

Maybe the Resistance finding me wouldn't be the *worst* option.

North and both of the men walk away without noticing the seething rage I'm trapped in, leaving Evelyn and me behind to head off to my new prison cell.

"If you could follow me, Miss Fallows. Your room is on the third floor."

I want nothing more than to lash out and tell her to fuck off, but then I glance over to find her staring at the ground in submission. I have no freaking clue how North treats his staff, but they all tiptoe around like we're monsters they've been enslaved to and it makes me feel as uncomfortable as hell.

So I keep my mouth shut and spare the poor woman the vitriol that's running through my head.

I need to start keeping track of directions in this place because after two turns, I'm already completely disoriented and lost. When we make it down one of the long halls to the elevator, I startle at the *ding* because I honestly thought the elevator was on the other side of the building the last time I was forced into it.

Evelyn doesn't speak, she doesn't look around at anything or fuss with her clothing in a nervous tick. She's the picture of a subservient housemaid in a mansion who sees *everything* and *nothing.*

I have exactly none of her composure. I twitch and pick at my skin like I can feel a million crawling insects moving through my veins.

We turn another corner and come face-to-face with the real reason I don't want to stay in this fucking house because my worst goddamn nightmare is headed right towards us, dressed casually in black slacks and a soft cashmere sweater. Nox's eyes flick over to Evelyn and he dismisses her with a simple, "Leave us."

That's it.

Two words is all it takes for me to be stranded in a hallway with the only one of my Bonds that I'm positive wants me dead. Evelyn just scurries away without a word.

Once we're alone, he doesn't waste time going for my throat. "Why are you dressed like a common whore? Did North have to hunt you down at some frat house? You sure know how to piss my brother off, don't you, Poison?"

Poison.

Of course he'd be the person to link my name up with the terrible position that I've inadvertently put us all in. I'm the poison that's been spread into his family.

I will not cry, and I certainly won't let him know how much he's getting under my skin. "A girl has to get her fun where she can, Nox. Why do you care so much? It's not like you want me. You have more than enough on your plate, right?"

He steps forward, crowding me against the wall. "Maybe I should bond with you, Poison. Maybe I should try you out so the next time I fuck my girlfriend, you'll know all about it and you'll feel like your heart is being ripped out of your chest. It might help you to understand what you put the rest of us through when you ran off."

He steps into my body, the size difference between us means he looms over me and I have to force myself to stand my ground. He's never been this close to me before. I'd once thought the burning rage in his eyes was hot, but it's nothing compared to the heat of his body as he presses me into the wall. I feel his bond skim over my body and I pull mine in closer, fighting against it as it strains for him. There no fucking way I'm ending up tied to this man.

I'd rather have any of my other Bonds over him. Fuck, I'd take North with a smile and a 'thank you, sir' over this asshole.

"You can't hide it, Poison. You might not have a gift, but I can feel your bond and it wants me."

I couldn't give less of a fuck what my bond wants, I will not bond with him.

I want to plant my hands on his chest and shove him the fuck away from me, but it's taking every fiber of my being to keep my bond under control. My hands are balled into fists at my side, my jaw clenched up tight, and my knees are locked to stop them from shaking.

I can't say a word as his hand comes up to wrap around my throat, his fingers flexing there like he's imagining squeezing the life out of me, and then we're moving backwards together, his body pressed against mine as my back hits the wall. I'm trapped in every way that I can be; my bond is wrapped up tight, my mind is stuck holding the threads of my sanity together so I don't tie myself to him, and physically, there's no way I can fight him off.

He pushes one of his knees in between my legs and I suddenly become acutely aware of the fact that I'm only wearing my old pair of silky boxer shorts, a thrift shop find of new-with-tags that at the time felt so mature and edgy, but now I'm trembling like a freaking lamb at the way he's pushing into me, his leg rocking and grinding. Fuck me, this is the hardest goddamned thing I've ever done because the moment I come, my bond is going to unleash, binding us together for all of time, which sounds fucking terrible but it's not even the worst part of this situation.

If my power grows we are all *fucked.*

His hand around my throat flexes a little and then he leans forward again, his lips brushing against my earlobe as he whispers in a dark rasp, "I want my power. I want what you owe me. I have waited five years for this. I'd been waiting five years before then. An entire decade I've been waiting to have my full power, and you're just going to come here and say no to us all? I don't fucking think so, Poison."

I struggle to pull away from him, there's no way I'm going to bend over in a hallway for this arrogant asshole, but it's nothing for him to just jerk me forward and catch my lips in a biting kiss.

My bond reacts immediately.

It's never left like this before, the surge of power within me almost taking me to my knees, and it takes everything inside of me to stop the bonding from happening, the tying of our souls together forever.

As Nox bites my lip and forces my mouth open, our tongues tangling together while he makes use of my inability to protest or move, my bond tries to pull free harder than ever before but I leash it, shoving down until it's contained.

I'm so goddamned focussed on stopping my bond from claiming him as my own that my body moves into autopilot, becoming pliant and easy for him to move and control however the fuck he wants. There's nothing soft or sensual about what he's doing. He knows exactly what it takes for a bond to occur and he's utterly ruthless about moving through the steps.

Somewhere, in a dark and faraway comer of my mind, I'm almost impressed at how quickly he's able to work me over. Kissing, stroking, the knee between my legs pushing into my body until my hips rock all on their own, there's no way I can fight him and my bond at the same time.

When his bond slams into me, a force all on it's own, I almost cry because I want it so badly. Fuck, my brain isn't even my own anymore. All I know is the bond. All I can think about is the bond and I want it so fucking badly.

I accept that he's going to make me come.

I hate him and I hate that he's doing this to me, but the lesser of two evils right now is keeping my shit together. When his fingers touch me, skimming down the old, ratty shirt and shoving the silky shorts down my legs until he has full access to my traitorous pussy, I almost give in to the bonding. I almost lose control and just kiss him back because why the fuck shouldn't I lose myself to the pleasure? Why shouldn't I give in to the power coursing through me, desperately trapped within my skin because I won't let it touch his bond where it's caressing me?

Then my brain comes back online and I remember all of the devastation that's already come from my power. I cannot let myself get any stronger. I can't become the evil that the Resistance wants me to be.

I can't even shove him away because if I move a single muscle right now, my bond will take over me and then it's all over. Everything I've worked so goddamn hard to stop, it'll all happen and I'm not letting that happen with the worst, most arrogant and entitled of my Bonds.

He has too much experience with women, clearly, because he has no problems finding my clit, slicking a finger through my wet folds and using it to circle and stroke and work me over like a goddamned pro.

It's almost insulting how easy it all is for him.

His fingers are merciless as he takes me higher and higher, and for a second I think he's enjoying this as much as I am.

When I break away from his lips to moan and pant, desperately fighting to control myself, he leans back in to croon in my ear, "Well? Let's see what you've got then, Poison."

As the orgasm rips through me I have to force my

ability down, to keep it hidden, and the pain that comes with it bums my skin and muscles until I think I'll burst into flames for real. A sob tears out of my throat and my knees finally give out. Nox doesn't even attempt to hold me up, his lip curling as he steps away from me, and his bond slips away from my skin as he realizes that he's not getting what he wants from me. I slide down the wall until I'm on my knees before him, my entire body burning with the pain of holding back the bonding.

Nox scoffs at me, his voice still that same scathing, furious tone of his that cuts through my skin right down to the bone, "Fucking pathetic, Poison, you can't even bond right. You're nothing but a liability."

And then he stalks off down the hall, leaving me with my shorts around my ankles and my pride in tatters around me.

What have I done?

Okay, no, I did nothing wrong here. So why exactly do I feel like the worst goddamned person on the planet right now? I did the right thing. I didn't bond, that was the right thing... wasn't it? This is his fault.

A soft voice startles me out of my misery, "Miss? I can show you to your rooms."

Tears do track down my cheeks as I glance up at the maid hovering over me, pointedly not looking at my very exposed lower half. She's younger than Evelyn was, but

I'm not sure if that makes it better or worse.

I lurch to my feet and get myself covered as I croak out, "Thank you, I would very much appreciate that."

She nods and waits for me to get myself back together, then leads me down the hall. My room is tucked away, about as far away from the sea views as possible, but it's quiet and private, and that's all I really need.

The maid hovers for a second after I walk in and then says, "The door locks from the inside and only Mister Draven has a copy of the key to open it. Mister North Draven, that is. You'll be... safe here, Miss Fallows."

Oh great, she's seen enough of what happened between Nox and I to be worried. "Thank you... Sorry, I'm so rude, I didn't even ask for your name."

The maid smiles and waves a hand. "Don't worry about that, Miss. I'll be in to clean in the morning, just leave me a note if there's anything you need. Mister Draven has instructed me to ensure you have everything you need."

Freedom, independence, and a plane ticket out of here. "My bag was in North's car, it has my clothes in it."

She nods. "I will have it here shortly. Goodnight, Miss."

She leaves me to it and I check out the bathroom quickly before climbing in the shower to wash off the guilt and awful feeling Nox has left me with.

I have no choice but to get dressed back into my pajamas, leaving the boxer shorts in the laundry basket. I'll never freaking touch them again. I should really bum them. I absently wonder how much it will cost to replace them and suddenly becoming a cam-girl is looking even more tempting.

Someone out there must want to pay to see my rack, right?

My bag is sitting on my bed when I get back to my room and it reminds me to flick the lock on the door before I climb into bed.

I grab my phone and find Atlas' text message waiting for me.

I've already called the Council and put in a formal complaint. They 'll probably rule in North's favor, but I'm pushing to have you here a few nights a week, Oli. I'm sorry, I didn't realize how fucking irrational he is about you. Sweet dreams, sweet girl.

I'm not sweet though. I really am fucking poison, just like Nox said. I'm everything that's wrong with our bond. If I wasn't bom... wrong, this would never have happened. I'd never have to leave them again and we'd all be whole right now instead of being these broken people.

Nox is so fucking damaged by what I've been forced to do, I don't think he'll ever forgive me.

I know I won't forgive him.

I won't even be able to look the guy in the face ever again.

Fuck.

My phone buzzes in my hand again.

I can see you've read the text, Oli, tell me you 're okay. Because if you 're not, I'm coming there right now, fuck the Council.

I rub my finger over the photo of him in my contacts. Fuck it, we're bonds right?

Nox is pissed and he tried to bond with me. It didn't work and he's told me I'm defective. You should probably be warned that you're trying to solidify a bond with someone who isn't... worth it. I'm turning my phone off to go to sleep. Goodnight, Atlas. You're the best guy I've ever known and I'm so sorry you 're stuck with a defective Bond.

I switch my phone off the second the text shows as delivered. I don't need to know what his answer is, I just need to forget about this absolute shit-show that my life is and pass out.

I can't run from this forever but I can for tonight.

The house shakes me awake.

I'm sure it's an earthquake and I panic because I know exactly nothing about what the hell to do in an earthquake. Then I remember that I'm at North's house and I don't even know how to get the hell out of this place usually, let alone during a natural disaster. What the fuck am I supposed to do?

I turn my phone on, ready to start calling my Bonds until someone picks up and tells me what the fuck to do right now, only to find thirty messages from Atlas.

When the house rumbles again, I realize the shaking is absolutely related to my Bonds and I immediately hit dial on his number.

"Oli? Where are you? Which floor? I'm taking you home."

I scramble out of the bed and stumble over to the window, yanking on the curtains until I can see out onto the street. Sure enough, there he is.

The gate is also rubble.

"What the hell— okay, never mind. The third floor, but good luck getting past—"

He cuts me off, "Fuck the Dravens. I will take the entire fucking house down to the ground if they try to stop me. That asshole North told me you'd be safe here and then he can't even protect you from his own brother? I'll kill the cunt."

Jesus have mercy. "It's not exactly like that, Atlas. Please just listen—"

There's the sound of a key in my door and I almost drop my phone before I remember the maid's words. Only North has a key, so at least it's not going to be Nox storming in here to tell me again how worthless I am as a human and a Bond.

The door swings open and North flicks the light on, glancing at the bed and then around the room until he finds me. I'm too shocked at his appearance to say anything because I've never seen him out of a suit before and yet there he is, sweatpants slung low on his hips, and holy good goddamn. Are they all stacked? Who would've thought he was hiding all of *that* under the Tom Fords?

"Oli? Oleander, what the hell is happening up there?" I jolt at the sound of Atlas' voice in my ear and North's eyes narrow at me.

"You called him here?"

Before I can say a word, Atlas snaps, "Put me on speaker, Oli."

There's no way out of this without my reputation, sanity, and will to live being absolutely shredded, but I do as he says.

"Open your fucking door, Draven, because I'm not leaving without my Bond. And while you're at it, tell your scumbag, rapist brother that I will kill him the second I find him."

Oh fuck.

Oh God. I open my mouth but there's nothing there, no words to give either of them as North stares me down. He looks furious, freaking fuming, and I flinch away from him when he takes a step forward. I'm not actually scared of him but my ego is too bruised right now to have someone else take a verbal swing at me.

His jaw clenches and then releases, his voice pitched low and a little warmer than it usually is when he says, "Come downstairs, Oleander. I'll let Atlas in while I speak to Nox."

"Hurry the fuck up," Atlas snaps and then I hang up

because I need to figure out how the hell to explain to the both of them that it— it wasn't— fuck, it was definitely something that happened, but it's maybe not the scenario that they're both thinking.

Isn't it?

It wasn't. It definitely wasn't.

Fuck.

"Grab a sweater, the house is cool overnight."

I could argue with him for the demand because he's once again bossing me around, but I have nothing left in me. No fire or fight, just the hollow shell trying to figure out to say I made a decision tonight that I'm sure they'll all shame me over even though I did the best I could.

Fuck.

I wish North would put a sweater on because the moment I follow him out the door, tucked up in the extra layers, my bond wakes up *again.* I'm furious at it for this ridiculous situation I'm now in so I shove it violently away.

Violently enough that North glances back at me with a frown, as though he's questioning whether he actually felt the ripple of power that my frustration let out. I try again to say something to him, this time managing actual words.

"I can talk to Atlas and sort this out. I just need a minute, you don't have to intervene."

He presses the button on the elevator without looking at me. "No, I'll be getting to the bottom of this mess before it gets out of hand. There's too much going on for me to deal with, without adding a feud in my Bond to the list. I will deal with Nox if that's what's required."

The elevator is too small to deal with all of my panic. Why am I so panicked? I didn't do anything wrong... except that the Bond I hate more than anyone or anything kissed me, pushed me against a wall, encouraged me to grind all over his leg, and then added fingers to the mix until I came so hard it hurt me.

I also didn't complete the bond.

They're all facts, and I only had control over some of those things and certainly not the orgasm... so why can't I just tell him that now before Atlas loses his mind over that stupid text I'd sent?

Of course he'd come here to get me.

Of fucking course, he's always been protective and possessive, even from the other side of the goddamned country.

The elevator opens and North steps out, pausing to make sure I'm following him, and then he leads me out to the foyer. I try to make some notes about where we are but within a minute, I'm as lost as ever.

North's driver is standing at the door with three other men, all of them staring out at the mess Atlas is making of the front lawn.

"I've called the authorities and the HOA, we're on top

of damage control, sir."

North nods at his driver. "Thank you, Rafe. I'll take it from here."

I make a note of Rafe's name, because I can't just keep calling him the driver in my head, and then I watch as North stalks forward to open the door, his body blocking the way, but I can see just enough of the carnage out the front to wince a little over the damage bill.

I should've just kept my mouth shut. I should've never texted Atlas and confided in him.

The moment North steps aside, Atlas stalks into the foyer, clearly intent on pulling me into his arms, but I'm barely holding my bond at bay and I step away from him.

The mood in the room gets malevolent.

I realize what I've done immediately, and because the world is against me, Nox chooses this exact moment to arrive, walking out through the door from the garage, the smell of whiskey clinging to his clothes.

He glances up to look right at me, his mouth twisting into a sneer, and I instinctively lurch forward to grab Atlas's arm. With one action, I probably saved Nox's life.

The smirk stays put as he looks over Atlas, his entire body radiating smug dickhead energy, but it falters a little when he sees North standing there in all of his half-naked, sleep-rumpled glory.

"What's going on?"

North glances over at me and this is the moment where I want to run screaming from the room and away from the shame of this moment, but still I can't figure out how the fuck to explain anything going on in my head.

Atlas doesn't wait for any of the careful family politics that is very clearly happening around us. "What's happening is that you attempted to force a bond with Oli, and you think being a fucking Draven means you can get away with it. I'm going to torture you and *then* kill you."

Well, fuck.

I cringe a little because I'm expecting an immediate scathing retort or for a punch to be thrown, if not some sort of gift use, but the room goes strangely quiet again.

North stares at Nox for a second and then says, "Did you do it?"

I've only seen them interact at the dinner table and North always just leaves him to tear strips off of me with his words, never once interrupting or telling him to leave me the hell alone. This seems... weird. He's acting as though Nox is a broken man, kid gloves and calm words in his direction. That's not at all the man that I know and loathe being around.

Nox smirks and raises an eyebrow back at him. "She didn't say no. Not once. She came on my hand so no, brother, I didn't rape her."

Could the ground just open up and swallow me whole?

That would be great, thank you. I don't want to live through this at all. Nope, give me death's sweet embrace because fuck this.

I'm expecting Atlas to turn some of his anger onto me, to demand an answer or just storm out of here, but he doesn't. Nope, he takes a step in front of me until he's covering me entirely, a very obviously protective move.

"You literally teach Gifted 101, we all know that you used her bond against her. You knew exactly what you were doing, and I'm not going to let you treat Oli like that. You're not so fucking intimidating when you're facing someone with a gift, asshole."

A smirk stretches over Nox's face and his eyes turn entirely black. "You sure about that? C'mon then, try me."

My brain shuts down for a second because his eyes are black. *Black.* I've never seen someone with the same depthless voids as mine are, and then Atlas' turn white and the danger of the situation finally hits me. I'm about to find myself in the middle of a fucking Gifted fight with no way to protect myself.

Atlas smirks back at Nox and I start to look around for something to hide behind or an exit to magically appear.

"If either of you throw a single attack at one another in *my* house in front of *my* Bond, I'll be finishing this and neither of you want that."

I glance over to North and almost pass the hell out,

because not only are his eyes black, but his hand, which is outstretched and ready to throw whatever the hell he can do at them both, is slowly turning black too.

I really should've been more insistent about finding out what the fuck they can all do because... well, what the fuck is he threatening them both with that even has Nox hesitating? What other gifts would give them both black glowing eyes, so close to my own?

"Bassinger, you're welcome to stay tonight with Oleander. We can discuss living arrangements tomorrow but for right now, we all have places to be in the morning."

Even Nox can't argue with that.

North walks Atlas and I back to my room without a word and then locks the door after himself. I'm still writhing with shame over the entire ordeal, but Atlas just immediately strips down to his boxers and climbs into the bed like this is all very normal and not the worst night of my life since I arrived here.

I sleep like shit and every time my eyes open overnight, I find Atlas frowning at the ceiling, so I know he hasn't slept a wink either. At six in the morning, I wake to a text from Gabe saying he'll pick me up for our morning workout and I decide to just get up and start my day.

I take a quick shower, excited as hell despite myself that I have a private bathroom with no gossips to talk shit about me while I get myself clean. When I'm dressed and ready, I walk back into the room to find Atlas dressed and waiting for me on the bed, his face still solemn.

I panic a little and my mouth runs away from me a bit. "I've been working out with Gabe, it's a brutal routine Gryphon put together, but it's been helping out with TT. Vivian has been impressed with how far I've come since I got here. You'll like him, he's grumpy and tries to get us all killed in the basement maze, but I like the old guy."

"I'm well aware of who Vivian Wentley is, Oli, but I'm more concerned about you at the moment. We need to figure out our game plan here because I've already spoken to my family. They want us to head back to Philadelphia, get some miles between us and the fucking Dravens until we have the chance to get to know each other a little better... You have a lot of options here, I don't want them making you think that this is it. You're not a prisoner. You're not property that Nox can just abuse."

I cringe and rub a hand over my face. "You heard what he said, it wasn't what you're thinking. I could have shoved him off and I didn't. That's on me."

Atlas stands up and blows out a breath. "You heard what I said too, Oli. He knew what he was doing. You're a Central, literally every fiber of your being wants the bond and he used that against you."

I don't really like what he's saying because it's making me feel like he thinks that I'm helpless to the bond within me and I think I proved last night that I'm not. I clawed myself back from the edge like a freaking machine and even if the aftermath wasn't all that great, I'm pretty freaking proud of myself for it.

"I don't want to talk about it anymore. Can we just... go to the workout and then decide everything else later? I'm just— I'm tired."

He lets out another breath and nods, rubbing a hand over the back of his neck and holding out the other for me to take. It doesn't matter if I'm a little sore over his words, I still take it because at least I know he's trying to do what's best for me.

No one else can say the same.

The moment the door shuts behind us, I realize I have no freaking idea how to get us downstairs but when I blanch, Atlas chuckles and pulls me along. "I memorized the way last night."

I huff at him for being too fucking good with directions, but I'm glad we don't have to call North and ask him to come direct us. When we get to the foyer, Gabe is already there waiting for us both, dressed in his workout gear with a frown on his face.

Atlas jumps on the offensive, always ready to fight

with someone who isn't me. "If you were hoping to have Oli on your own, you're shit out of luck because I'm not trusting her with any of you after last night. Fuck no."

Gabe's eyes flick over to me but I avoid meeting them. Honestly, I just want to get today over with as soon as possible. I want to jump on a treadmill and get some alone time to figure out what the hell I'm going to do.

Should I go to Philidelphia with Atlas and start a new life there? Should I carry on with my plan to run away from them all?

Gabe doesn't say a word to either of us, clearly he's already heard someone's version of what happened last night, and instead he walks back out to his motorbike and shoves his helmet on.

Atlas grabs my hand and leads me out to his car, opening the door for me and helping me in like the perfect gentleman. My head is a jumbled mess and I really don't have it in me to make small talk with him this morning.

We listen to music on the way over, neither of us speaking, and it's only when we get to the campus and find roadworks blocking the entrance that Atlas curses softly under his breath. "Do you know where else I can park that's close?"

I direct him over to the other side of campus and we find Gabe already waiting there for us, as well as a dozen other cars.

The next hour is a special type of torture.

Atlas makes it his mission to beat Gabe at everything, the two of them snarking scathing remarks to each other the entire time, and I've never wished for headphones and loud pop music so badly in my life.

When Sage messages me to meet her for breakfast in the dining hall, I'm ready to kill them both and just take off by myself. They both follow me out, flanking me like my own scowling guard, but I don't have it in me to attempt to lighten the mood.

Hopefully Sawyer is with Sage and he can pick up the slack.

We're halfway over to the main building when my gift starts squirming in my gut, the early warning from within me that something is very, *very* goddamned wrong here. Both of the guys stop, grabbing my arms to get me to halt with them.

Atlas raises an eyebrow at me but Gabe's eyes flash white as he looks around, using his shifting ability to enhance his eyesight, and then he curses viciously under his breath, his phone out in a second and his fingers flying across the screen.

"Run. We need to get to shelter right the fuck now."

He doesn't need to say it twice.

We take off for the main building, my sore legs unhappy at running again, but I'm much faster and more resilient now that we've been training for so long. I silently send Vivian a thank you for all of the time I've spent on the treadmill thanks to him. I can see Atlas forcing himself to keep pace with me, obviously he's faster without me to watch out for, but Gabe is used to sticking with me. He grabs his phone out without missing a beat, tapping on it and then shoving it back in his pocket.

"North is on his way and Gryphon is already on the campus, we just need to get you to an evac point," Gabe says, his voice pitched so only we can hear it over the pounding of our feet on the sidewalk.

Atlas nods at him, ready to follow his lead even after they've been at each other's throats all morning because he knows more about this place than either of us do. As we make it to the dining hall, there's an explosion on the east side of the campus, the sound so loud that my teeth rattle and Atlas immediately grabs me, pulling me off of my feet and curling around me like a human shield. I can't breathe for a second and then Gabe is shoving us both off of the path and behind a building.

"Is this an evac point? I thought we had to get to the main building.?" Atlas snaps, but Gabe is barely listening.

"Dara? Fuck, I can't see shit here, you must be around."

He's literally talking to a brick wall and I'm about to start checking his head for injuries when the air around us shimmers and then suddenly there's a group of students standing there together, as white as sheets and murmuring amongst themselves about what the fuck is going on.

"Thank God! Ardem, where are Shore and the Dravens? We've seen at least eight groups of Resistance, there must be fifty or sixty of them here!"

Fuck me, I recognize the voice immediately and, sure enough, it's fucking Martinez. I try to convince myself that now probably isn't the best time to be holding onto grudges, but I also can't help hating the guy.

"TacTeams are already neutralizing them, we just need to keep a low profile and wait it out," Gabe says, his voice confident and clear. The change in the group is instant, some of the worry and panic easing like his word really does mean something to them all. I wish I felt the same, the fear is still coursing through me, but my head is still clear enough to see what's happening around me.

That isn't necessarily a good thing, especially when another group of Resistance comes jogging past us dressed in riot gear. I seal my lips shut, smothering my own breathing in case I inadvertently make some noise and give us away.

Then the doors to the building across the courtyard open and students come running out in all directions. The Resistance turn and immediately move in after them, one of the guys in the front sending out a wave of fire and I have to look away because there's no way I'm watching people being burned alive right now.

"Ardem, do *not* leave Oli's side," Atlas snaps, and then he's gone, sprinting through the shield and heading right for the Flame just as the screaming of his victims starts up.

Gabe curses under his breath, glancing around at who else is in the group with us, but none of them are moving to help out. He looks at me again and I nod at him. "Do it. Go help him, I'll be fine."

He hesitates again for a second and then grips both of my arms. "Dara is the best Shield I've ever seen, no one will know you're even here so long as she's with you. Don't move from this spot, Oli. Promise me."

There's another explosion sound and then Gabe is tearing his clothes off, kicking out of his shoes and shifting so fast I can barely say I've witnessed it. One second he's standing there, all golden skin tight over his muscular frame, and the next there's a huge wolf standing in his place.

I've never seen a shifter up close.

It's fucking incredible.

I stand there with absolutely no intention of moving. I can't, not without using my gift, and there's no reason for me to do it right now. I can't help the people burning, and I trust Gabe and Atlas to do what they can to stop the fighting. They're both more useful than I am right now and I have to believe that the others are on their way to us right now.

Then I hear it, Grade's screaming coming from behind us.

"Oh my God, Sage! SAGE!"

No.

Absolutely fucking not. Over my dead fucking body am I standing by for something to happen to the one person who accepted me without any reason or expectation.

"Fallows, are you fucking stupid—" I don't wait around for the rest of Martinez's bullshit opinion, I leave at a sprint. There's smoke everywhere but I follow the sound of Grade's screaming until I literally run straight into her, my vision completely impaired by the aftermath of the explosion.

"Oli? Oh my God, please, where are your Bonds? They've got Sage, they're—"

I grab her arms and shake her, as if I can shake the information I need out of her. "Where, Gracie? Where the fuck is she?"

She doesn't get to answer me because I hear a voice I was hoping to never hear again in my goddamn life call out, "Power surge! Grab that one."

I already know that Sage is strong, I've heard stories about how she came into her power, and her elemental control is elite. It's for this reason that I don't immediately run away screaming as Olivia's voice cuts through the chaos.

Olivia Turner.

The Resistance's sniffer dog is here to find the Gifted worth taking, which means they've already gotten Sage and now they've found me. I can't help Sage unless I let them take me too.

It's stupid and reckless and I don't give a fuck because she's my best goddamned friend.

So I stand there, shoving Gracie away from myself as I snap at her, "Run," and then I let them take me too. The smoke is too thick to see them until their hands are already closing around my arms and I thrash a little as if I want to get away as they tug me along. The two men holding me both have masks on, completely covering their faces, so they've come prepared for the exact warfare they planned today.

When we stop at the back of a convoy truck, I look up to lock eyes with an absolutely terrified Sage, bound and gagged in the back. Her eyelids peel back and she starts to sob at the sight of me. It's not relief at having me with her. Nope, she's freaking out that I'm in danger now too.

If I wasn't sure before that I was doing the right thing, I am now.

"Get her loaded, the Dravens are clearing the courtyard and if we're not out in the next thirty seconds, we're dead."

I duck my head at Olivia's voice. Fuck, I hope she doesn't get an eyeful of me right now, and then the men holding my arms get me trussed up and thrown in the back with Sage. One of them slides in after me and then we're off, the truck taking off too freaking quickly,and we all bump and jostle each other as we attempt to stay upright without arms to balance or hold on with.

There's another shout and then the truck swerves on the road, hitting a bump that almost sends us into a ditch, but the driver manages to correct and keep us all alive. I look back out of the opening to see Kieran sprinting behind us, a gun in his hand already, but there's no clear shot for him to take, not without risking hitting one of the captives or causing the truck to roll.

The last I see of him is with the phone pressed to his ear.

I work out very quickly that we're not dealing with the lower level grunts in this vehicle.

There's a Dampener sitting on the other row who is rendering everyone they've captured gift-less and there's definitely a Shield on board because we weave through traffic and red lights without a single hitch or horn blaring at us, and after my forced captivity on the Draven campus, I have no idea of where we are or where we're heading. Sage keeps her head ducked but I can see her discreetly checking out the view and keeping tabs on where we are, so I'm hopeful we'll be able to find our way back once we figure out how to escape this mess we're in. I'm very aware that neither of us are Bonded and there's only the

GPS chip in me to help us be located.

It could be worse.

There aren't a lot of ways it could be worse but neither of us are badly injured or dead, no one is attempting to torture or rape us yet, and there is some way for us to be located, so I focus on that.

The guy who tied my arms back is sitting between Sage and I, his mask still secured over his face as if he's worried one of us is about to emit noxious gas and knock him out or something. Dammit, where is Zoey when we need the bitch?

There's three other students in the truck, all of them bound and gagged, and two more of the Resistance. No one speaks, the sounds of the engine and the road outside too loud to make out much in the open back. When the view starts to quickly change from buildings and parking lots into open pastures and sparsely wooded areas, I start to get nervous. I was hoping they had a shielded building in town to keep us in for a few days. That's their usual MO, waiting until the heat is lifted a little before transporting their cargo of humans.

A field means they're planning on testing and taking out.

Sage will survive and be transported. If I don't access my gift, there's a good chance they'll attempt to kill me which will only trigger my gift to protect me and then, again, we're all fucked.

In or out, I have to decide now.

The truck suddenly veers off of the road again without slowing down and my body slams into the guy next to me, knocking the air out of my lungs. The guy grunts and shoves me away as though it's my fault the driver is clearly fucking insane and I have no free hands to catch myself with. One of the guys on the other row of seats goes flying and ends up sprawled on the ground in front of us all, blood pouring from a wound on his head.

My stomach curls and I have to remind myself that head wounds bleed like a motherfucker and he's probably not hurt that badly, but it's hard not to puke over the sight of it anyway. No one attempts to help him up and when we hit another bump, he groans with the pain of being thrown around.

The truck comes to an abrupt halt and the guy in-between Sage and I grunts, slamming a fist on the metal paneling and yelling, "For fuck's sake, Daniels, get your shit together before you kill us all!"

Daniels.

It's an old habit but keeping track of as many names as I can has saved my life before, so I slip right back into it. There's doors opening and slamming around us but no one moves until the back is opened up. It's frustrating to me that they all have those masks on still because I don't know if any of them recognize me.

I won't know until it's too late.

One of them speaks, but it's impossible to tell which one. "Get them out, we're being transported in five and we're not taking freeloaders or charity."

The guy on the ground is moved first, pulled and dropped onto the ground, and finally one of the Resistance takes her mask off to look him over. She's got blond hair cropped close to her skull and a tattoo of a rose under one of her eyes. She doesn't look evil but I've already learned that even the sweetest and kindest looking people can be monsters.

"He's strong, an elemental. I'd keep him."

One of the others pulls off his mask and snaps, "Elementals are more trouble than they're worth. We need fighters, not someone to make sure it's a nice day out."

She shrugs and moves the guy to the left, pulling a gun out and shooting him point blank in the head. One of the Gifted across from me in the truck screams, the sound muffled by the gag, but ear splintering all the same.

It occurs to me that this is where my own trauma shows because there's nothing about the fragments of skull flying everywhere or the blood and brain matter that bothers me. It's as though the version of me who was queasy over some blood earlier is long gone and has been replaced by survival me. The girl that once... well, let's just say my hands aren't as squeaky clean as I'd like them to be.

There isn't much difference between me and biondie with the gun really.

Nothing but what side of the dispute we're on.

One by one we're brought down to be tested. Sage gets an instant pass, shoved along to stand and wait for the rest of us. The other girl is a shifter and she passes. The last guy is also a Flame but he's not as strong as Sage. They argue for a minute before deciding to keep him. I'm shoved in front of the tester last and my breath catches in my chest.

This close, I recognize her.

I have to force myself not to panic. The plan hasn't changed, if she recognizes me then I let my gift out and use every ounce of control I have to stop Sage or one of the other Gifted from ending up as collateral.

Then, I run.

Carlin, the biondie with the gun who was a brunette without a face tattoo the last time I saw her, frowns as she takes me in. She doesn't recognize me, but she also has no idea of what I am or what I'm capable of.

The guy without the mask snaps, "Well? Are we keeping her or not? Because transport is now in less than two minutes, we need to move."

Her lips curl and she snaps, "She's too powerful to toss but I can't see what she is. She's... blank."

"We're not taking freeloaders, kill her."

Carlin holsters her gun and shakes her head. "Did you not hear me, Daniels? She's literally leaking power out everywhere, you don't kill that kind of potential."

He huffs at her and grabs my arm. "I can't feel it but fine, you can poke and prod her later to figure out what's going on under the hood."

Of course he can't feel it, only people like Carlin could sense the power I'm desperately tamping down to keep them from knowing about it. I've seen her hold toddlers and accurately assess their abilities, she's stronger than most at what she can do.

She'll be furious when she realizes who I am.

We're moved along to an open field, the truck and the Gifted's dead body left behind without thought, and even though I can't see a marker, we stop in a very specific spot. Then the Resistance all remove their gloves and grab each other and each of us until we're all touching, skin on skin.

There's a popping sound and then out of thin air a woman appears, slapping a hand on Carlin.

The next pop is louder and my stomach lurches as we're transported.

I fucking hate this shit.

We could be anywhere now. Literally anywhere. I was once moved to Egypt for two weeks to get away from a particularly good scouting TacTeam. The feeling of being moved in this way makes me sick and the moment our feet are back on the ground, I slump down onto the ground, gagging and trying not to actually vomit.

Daniels grabs me and pulls me to my feet roughly, shoving me along with him, and I have to fight the chaos in my head to get a good look around at where we are.

I don't recognize the camp, but I've been in one of these before. It's a limbo, a way to sort out stock and sift through the Gifted that have been abducted until they find the ones they really want. I spent two weeks in one when I was first taken and I think that was more about scaring me because they knew before they took me that I was valuable.

We're all moved to a tent and when we're dragged inside, we find the cages and the babysitters.

By some stroke of luck, Sage and I are shoved into cages next to each other, our hands unbound and the gags removed before the doors are firmly locked behind us. I wait until they clear out before I look around properly.

The babysitters are ignoring us, as though four new faces mean nothing to them, and I'm sure we really don't register to them at all. Their job is to knock us out if we start trouble and to listen to everything we say, collecting information that could be used against us.

The tent flaps open again and three huge guys walk in carrying another bound and gagged Gifted between them. My eyes squeeze closed as I hold my bond down within myself, forcing it to not react and lash out because I *cannot* let them know that the Gifted they're dragging in and I are Bonds.

I squeeze my eyes shut tighter as I hear them drop him to the ground, grunting and lashing out at him as they swing the cage door shut behind them.

"He took out eighteen men, he's a dead man walking."

Chills run up my spine but Carlin purrs at them from the doorway, "He's one of the Bonds in the Draven family, if any of you touch him, I'll personally deal out your punishment. We're close."

Daniels looks in each of the cages, his eyes not seeing anything special when he glances at me. "He gave himself up. Once we've got all of the fresh meat in here, we'll need to find whoever it is that he came after because I'd bet we have his Central somewhere in this group."

Well, fuck.

Fuck.

Fresh meat.

It's been years since I've thought of that lovely term, five years since I had to have that label attached to me before I wised up and knew how things worked in the Resistance camps.

I'm going to use that shit to our advantage today.

If I can escape once, I can do it again. I've already accepted the cost of that.

I close my eyes and finally, *finally,* let my gift fill my

veins, my entire body feeling sharper and more capable the moment I unlock that door inside of me and let it take over. It's as though I've drunk an elixir of pure light, every cell in my body transforming and coming back to life. It's been three long years of learning how to exist without this, slowly losing myself as my body adapted and became nothing more than... human. Ungifted.

Normal.

Sage's eyes fly open as she looks at me, her own senses on high alert as she feels my gift radiate out of me. There's too much power pulsing in my veins for her not to feel it, the curse of my life being that all Gifted can sense how dangerous I am. We all have that power detection built into us to know when danger is close by.

I hold a finger up to my lips to motion to her to keep quiet and she subtly jerks her head in a nod, careful not to attract any more attention from our captors, but they're all busy moving all of their fresh meat around. Five more Gifted are brought in but I don't recognize any of them.

I keep my eyes downcast and focus on Gabe's breathing.

The second he wakes up, we're getting the fuck out of here.

It only takes ten minutes before the Gifted start talking

amongst themselves, whispering and freaking out with each other about where we are, what they're going to do to us, or how we're going to get out of this mess. When Sage glances over to me, I press a finger to my lips and she nods, both of us glancing over at the babysitters again.

We have to just be patient and pray Gabe wakes up soon, because neither of us can carry him and our gifts won't help with this either. So we wait. We sit there and wait while the day stretches on. There's shouting and screaming outside a few times, but no one else comes into the tent. My fingertips begin to tingle with power, like my gift is pissed that I've called on it but done nothing yet, and Sage's eyes widen at me when she feels it.

When Gabe finally groans, I can't help but let out a pulse, my relief pushing out in a tangible wave that has the entire tent falling silent.

Both of the babysitters glance over at me, their attention finally piqued enough to come over.

"ft was the anomaly, Fiona. You should go deal with her so we don't get our asses kicked for playing with her."

Fiona unfolds herself from the cot she was slumped on, her dark eyes flicking over me before they start to shine.

Nothing.

I don't even register her attempting to knock me out and my power crows a little, smug all on its own that we're finally not at the mercy of everyone anymore.

I'm less smug because I know better than to be excited about being *me* again.

"Too strong for you? Well, we can't have that can we," the man speaks again, standing up and walking over to me.

His eyes flash at me but when nothing happens, he curses under his breath, "She's a void, I can't knock her out either."

It's as easy as breathing. The same plan I used the first time to get away from the Resistance. I groan and bend at the waist to clutch at my stomach, feigning an injury. They're not going to attempt to help but, sure enough, they step closer to get a good look at me.

There's another groan and a grunt and I glance over to see Gabe awake, his eyes open and staring right at me. I falter for a second, my power stuttering in my veins, because I could maybe convince Sage to keep this quiet, but there's no way that Gabe would ever keep my gift a secret.

But I stare into Gabe's eyes and I decide that enough is enough. I can't lose anyone else, God-fucking-dammit.

It doesn't matter that I haven't touched my power in years, the well is still there, waiting for me. It's like finally taking a deep breath after shallow gasping for all this time, to feel the true power within me come to me as I call on it.

I feel whole again.

Gabe finally notices it, he can smell it on me, and his

eyes flare wide. He's smart enough, and coherent enough, to keep his mouth shut, but I can see the shock etched into his features.

I grit my teeth and focus, my hand trembling where it hangs at my side, but I need to get this right. If I don't funnel it right, I could lose my best friend and my Bond, and I've lived through enough pain and despair. I don't need to add their deaths to that list, even if I did want to get the hell away from them all.

Fiona finally notices it, and recognizes the power, her eyes peeling back. "Holy fuck. Ho/v *fuck,* what is she doing here?"

The man steps forward as if he's trying to get a better look at me, only my power lashes out and floods their bodies, grasping at their souls. My gift wants to take everything but I hold it back, triggering the darkness in them instead.

It's still as horrifying as the first time I'd done it, watching the worst of their nightmares and fears and the ugly parts of themselves wash over them until they're writhing on the ground, their minds irreparably broken.

Trapped in their own horrors, they'll never escape it until someone puts them out of their misery.

I thank God that neither of them make a sound, usually there's at least a strangled scream or something as they go down but now that everyone is staring at them in both shock and absolute horror, there's not a single sound in the tent.

"Oli, what the fuck was that? What the fuck did you do to them?" I glance over again to find Gabe struggling to sit up with his hand still bound behind his back, his eyes wide as he stares at me, but time is now working against us.

Anyone could walk in here and see what I've done.

I reach out until I get my hand around the leg of the guy and, bless her fucking soul, Sage immediately moves to help me pull him over. It's freaking hard but we manage to frisk him through the bars until we find a set of keys.

"What the hell are you two doing?"

I startle but it's only the guy in the far comer, finally come out of the stupor that seeing my Gift in action put him in. Instead of answering him, I lift a finger to my lips to signal to him that he needs to shut the fuck up before he gets us found out. He blinks at me like he's never been told to shush before.

Fucking idiots.

I get my cage unlocked and then Sage's, moving quickly over to Gabe while one of the other girls starts sobbing. I hope it's relief and that she'll get the fuck over it quickly because there's a long way to go before we're even close to safe.

Sage gets his cage open, moving on to the next person, while I slip in to get him freed and out of there. He blinks at me blearily, his eyes struggling to focus, and my heart clenches in my chest at the sight of whatever the fuck they've done to him.

When I crouch down to him he croaks, "How did you stop them from knocking you out? I've seen Zoey do it a hundred times."

I fumble with the rope around his wrists as I struggle to get him free. "You saw Zoey knock gift-less me out. I'm a little more supercharged right now. I don't have time to explain this, can you hulk out and get these off?"

His head sort of rolls around on his shoulders and I start to get properly worried that he's concussed or taken too much damage to that pretty head of his. "One of them drugged me, I can't access my shift. How the fuck are you still conscious, Oli?"

I huff at him and give the rope one last tug, almost whooping with joy when it finally comes undone, "You obviously haven't paid enough attention in Gifted 101. I'm higher up the food chain than those little bitches, so far higher, that they're nothing to me... the exact same way you are and they had to resort to drugging you. Can you stand? We need to move now."

I help him up and out of the cage. Thankfully he can carry his own weight, he just needs some help staying steady on his feet. When I have to catch his arm to stop him from tipping over, his jaw locks up and I watch as he pulls himself together, blinking furiously and rubbing at his face like he can force the drugs out of his system through sheer will alone.

I clear my throat to grab the attention of the room, all ten of us now out of our cages, and then I mime out that we *need to get out of here.*

I'm slow, watching each of them to make sure they're getting what I'm saying. Then I mime, *who can still use your gifts?*

Sage can, and three others. We have a Flame, a Shifter, and two others who can't accurately mime for shit because I think they're either mental abilities, or saying they've taken a hit to the head.

Great.

I shut my eyes and cast my gift out and let it create a map for me. This is dangerous, but only if I hit Carlin or another tester with her level of ability. Then, something fucking magical happens.

I find Gryphon.

I feel him startle when my gift hits him. I feel his disbelief and then the surge of adrenaline, relief that I'm alive and here. Wherever we've been taken, either it was close by or he also has a transporter. Kieran is with him and I can't even be mad at that douchebag being here.

Then I find Nox.

Okay, I'm less happy about that one, especially when

his gift reaches out for mine. He's trying to figure out what the fuck I can do, how I'm mapping them all out, and every other secret I've ever kept from them.

I pull away from them.

My eyes pop open and I push up onto my tiptoes to press my lips to Gabe's ear, whispering so softly it's barely more than my breath, "Calvary is here."

When he starts to rock on his feet, I sling Gabe's arm around my shoulders and wrap my arm around his waist as I move us towards the tent opening. I slow my breathing down enough to use my heightened senses.

Fuck, it's good to have them back.

I'm happy for exactly half a second before the gunfire and sounds of fighting break through.

My Bonds have been found.

One of the girls stops us from immediately leaving the tent, the panic in her so bad that she collapses to the ground sobbing. I try to remember that she's never had to face this sort of thing before, probably never experienced this sort of terror or loss before, but it's hard not to lose my temper.

"One of you is going to have to carry her or we're leaving her behind. We have to move now." I pitch my tone low and even though Sage looks over at me, she's not shocked or disgusted by my words.

She's looking at me like she's waiting for instruction, a perfect soldier in a crisis. She should really be in_TT with a backbone like this but I'm not going to talk her into joining the torture sessions with me.

One of the guys squats down to murmur to the sobbing girl, pulling her into his arms and standing back up. He presses her face into his chest and smothers the sounds. I wait until I know she's secure enough in his arms, and then I nod at him.

He's probably just saved her life.

I glance at Sage and she moves closer immediately, taking up Gabe's other side like she's ready to defend my drugged Bond with me the entire way out of this shithole, and I shoot her a look of gratitude.

She shrugs back at me. "You'd be the first one to defend Sawyer... or Felix."

Damn fucking straight I would. There's no way out of all of this unless we're all pitching in and doing the team thing. I glance around for a second before I murmur to her, low enough that only her and Gabe can hear me, "I need to know if you can use your power if you need to... that you can take someone out if our lives depend on it. I'm not pressuring you or judging you, I need to know so I can cover you if you need me to."

Gabe stiffens in our arms but Sage just stares at me, steady as ever. "I can do it, Oli. I'm already going to need a shit-tonne of therapy after this, why not add some homicide to the mix?"

I fail miserably at keeping a smirk off of my face, but

I don't feel guilty about it because fuck the Resistance. "Atta girl. I'll teach you how to compartmentalize like a pro when we're home safe."

Gabe's arm tightens around me and he murmurs, "We're going to talk about that when we get back, Oli. We're going to talk about a lot of shit."

I roll my eyes and then shut them to cast my power out to double-check that we're still in the clear to get out of here, immediately startling and jerking forward to open the tent flap.

Kieran jogs towards us.

"How the fuck did he get here so quickly?" I hiss and Gabe sighs in relief at the sight of my least favorite TacTeam member.

"Black's a Transporter."

We step back to let him into the tent, the entire space shrinking the second he stalks in dressed entirely in his full uniform with a whole lot of firepower strapped to his body.

He glances at Gabe, who waves him off. "I was drugged but I'm fine. You're getting faster at finding civilians."

Kieran gives him a look and then jerks his head at me. "Fallows' gift is like a beacon. I followed it over here to you all. Any injuries? We need to mobilize and move. Shore can only hold them off for so long, even with Draven helping out."

His eyes finally hit Fiona and her little pal where

they're both still jerking and fitting on the ground over by the cages. The blood is starting to slowly drip out from their ears and eyes, but I'm trying not to look too closely at either of them. If I do, my gift starts getting a little too excited and I need to be careful not to let it take over, to consume me and tear everyone and everything in my path apart, whether they're friend or foe.

I watch him process their state, his shoulders rolling back a little and when he looks at me again, he's wary, as though he's expecting to be next on my hit list.

I enjoy the feeling a little too much.

"We're ready to leave," Sage answers him for us all, drawing his attention away from me and squaring her shoulders up as she readies herself for a fight.

From Kieran or the Resistance, I'm not sure, but either way, my money is on her.

"Fallows, stay behind me and with me the whole way. You're my top priority, and if anything happens, my only order is to get you to the evac point alive, whatever the cost. If you want Ardem and the Flame to make it through, you need to keep your ass in line, because I'll abandon them in a second to get you out of here."

This fucking man and his tripping over my trigger points... I'm going to end up taking him out before we make it back to my Bonds.

My hands tighten their hold on Gabe and my lip curls

back at him. "Good luck getting me to leave either of them behind, I'd have you screaming on the ground before you ever got your hands on me. It doesn't matter, we're all following you. I won't step out on the rules, let's get the fuck out of here."

Kieran moves so quickly out of the tent that I don't have time to get nervous or worried, my legs just move on autopilot to keep up with him. Gabe stumbles a little with the first step and then he's rock steady, barely needing the support both Sage and I are giving him.

I don't look back to check if everyone is following us, we've done everything we can for the others and all they need to do is keep up, but my eyes are busy taking in the changes in the campsite since we were first dragged through here a couple of hours ago.

There's blood everywhere, bullet holes and scorch marks littering all of the tents and grass around us. There's bodies too, screaming and gunfire from every direction, and I have to force myself to breathe normally.

"We need a fucking Shield," Gabe mutters, trying to pull away from me, but I hold on tighter. Keeping him moving is a freaking great distraction from the carnage around us, and it also means that I know where he is at all times. My bond is thrumming in my blood, a constant stream of *protect them all* that I have no control over.

I need him to be safe.

Kieran has to take out three fleeing Resistance to get past the tents and it feels too easy to me, until we round the comer and I see what the fuck they're running from.

It isn't really a battlefield, it's a massacre.

Thick, black fog covers the entire field except it's... sentient. Sentient and filled with barely formed creatures that look more like nightmare demons than anything that exists in nature. My feet stumble and Gabe grunts as he catches me, muttering back to me, "It's Nox, they won't touch us."

Uhm.

I feel like Nox would definitely let his gift take a chunk or two out of me and when Kieran shifts to secure his mask back over his face like he's also concerned about wading in there, I decide I don't freaking wanna.

"Oli, evac is on the other side. We have to move—"

Kieran cuts Gabe off, "Get her moving, Ardem, or she's going over my shoulder the rest of the way."

I have no choice but to follow them in.

I thought I knew how bad it was, but I had no idea. The moment we all breach the dark, covering our eyes to adjust to the murky surroundings, I can see all of the Resistance trapped in here being mauled and tom apart by the creatures.

I don't even realize I've stopped again until Kieran grabs my arm, the one not wrapped around Gabe, and snarls at me, "We don't have time for your breakdown at the *delightful creations* of the Dravens. I get it, he's a monster, but you need to keep your ass moving."

I cringe away from him instinctively, but I can't get far with the tight grip he has on me. He refuses to let go of me, dragging me across the field until we meet back up with the TacTeam, complete with Nox and his black void eyes as he destroys every last member of the Resistance that his smokey horror touches.

If the Dravens are monsters, then what does that make me?

Kieran transports us out of the Resistance camp and this time, I vomit all over his shoes.

The look he gives me as everyone starts to move away from us is savage and after I wipe my mouth with the back of my hand, 1 give him a smirk because if f had to ruin someone's shoes, I'm glad it was his.

Then Gabe lurches out of my arms to collapse on the grass and I have more important things to think about. "Do we have any Healers here? Fuck, please don't die."

Gryphon stalks over, that glowing hand of his pressing into Gabe's forehead and almost instantly he regains some color in his face. Sage comes over to tuck her arm in mine, a show of solidarity as always.

Nox has already turned his back on me, pretending like always that I don't exist.

I look around and realize I have no freaking clue where we are. More empty fields for miles, we could be anywhere in the world right now.

"Where are we?" My voice is croaky and raw thanks to the puking, but Gryphon hears me well enough, glancing over to me. Nox doesn't bother, his eyes staying fixed on the skyline.

"Kieran couldn't get us all back home in one go, and rather than leaving some of the others behind, we've made it to a rendezvous point. We'll be picked up from here in a few hours. Find somewhere close by to sit until then."

I walk back up to Gabe and park my ass next to him, ready to just whittle away the hours there, and instantly my eyes start to droop. I've gone too long without using my gift that it's exhausting to use it now, like taking months away from the gym and then dying after your first session back.

Gabe's head moves slowly until it's resting on my thigh, his breath evening out. Gryphon finally moves away from us both, standing back up and walking over to Kieran to talk amongst themselves.

I lose time in the haze of my exhaustion, only rousing when a female voice calls out, "Are we expecting any ground cover?"

My eyes flutter back open, the light blinding, to a lot of movement around me. It's hard to see from the ground, but I can just make out the army convoy through the legs.

An entire freaking convoy.

"Fuck. Samual, get us covered and fast."

Instantly there's a shield covering us all, all of the TacTeam shifting into position at the edges of it like they're waiting for the opening to unleash hell on these worthless excuses of humans. But when the vehicles open up, the streams of bodies piling out never seem to end, and my stomach drops out at the realization.

We're outnumbered, at least ten-to-one.

"Get Oh out of here now."

My head jerks up to see Gryphon and Kieran checking over their weapons together, their hands moving quickly over their bodies. Kieran doesn't look happy at this suggestion. "I don't have enough energy to come back, we'll find another way."

When he glances over at Nox, Gryphon shakes his head at him. "Draven can't go again, he's drained and I'm not going to let him push past his ability."

I glance over to him, shocked that he's tapped out when he looks completely fine, but as soon as I look at him, actually look at him, I can see it. There's a tightness around his eyes and shadows across his face.

It seems obvious now that Gryphon has said it, he just took on dozens of Resistance and dealt with them himself. Gifted aren't *usually* limitless.

Not even Top Tier Gifted.

There's another shout and then one of the cars is lifted and thrown at the shield, bouncing off of it without any damage, but then Samual's nose starts to bleed and we all know we're running on borrowed time.

It's time for a Hail Mary pass... we're going to die here without one. I scramble up to my feet, stepping towards the shield.

"Stand behind us, Oleander," Gryphon growls, but I shake my head. Healing light isn't going to help us here. The TacTeam are checking their weapons, assessing how much ammunition they have left, but we're not in a great spot.

"There's no use dying here, Poison. You'll only have yourself to blame. Gift or not, there's at least a hundred men," Nox spits out, still intent on hating my guts.

Gabe moves to stand up as well, swaying on his feet, and Sage looks so pale as she helps him stay upright. Pale but ready, as though she's already made her peace with whatever end we're going to find here today.

I take a deep breath. Those two mean something to me, they're worth protecting, no matter the cost. Gryphon... I can't let him die, there's something there. The potential for something maybe.

Stubborn, bull-headed pride means I can't leave Nox here to die either, if only because I want to prove him wrong.

I roll my shoulders back and let my power out, gently and carefully, the tendrils of it spanning out like a net casting out into the ocean. It touches every last one of the Resistance, all of them unaware of my touch.

All three of my Bonds here can feel it though, no hiding this shit from them, and know what I'm doing. I turn to stare Nox in the eye, a challenge and a show of exactly how badly he's underestimated me, his Bond, the one he's supposed to adore and protect.

Then, all at once, I trigger the terrors and nightmares within them. Ninety-two men and women writhing in agony in the blink of an eye.

And I feel *nothing.*

Nox's eyes flare but he doesn't look away from me, just keeps his eyes glued to mine. The others around us aren't so restrained.

"Holy fucking shit."

"Did she do that? I thought she wasn't Gifted?"

"How the fuck did she take out that many at once?"

"Monster."

Gryphon moves to stand in front of me immediately, blocking me from the view of his entire team and the others who were rescued. Gabe grabs my hand and yanks me into his body as though he's worried I'm about to be attacked by our own people. I have to break my staring contest with Nox, but I think I've proved my point.

I pull away from Gabe, my gift is still a little too excited about being let out to play and I can't have him touching me right now. He frowns at me, but then follows my eyes down to my fingers and gulps when he sees the fine tremble in them.

Finally he takes a step away, stumbling a little only to be caught by Nox, both of them looking like the walking dead at this point.

Nox, ignoring Gabe's groans of pain, snaps, "Don't think we've forgotten about your idiot decisions either, Ardem. What the fuck were you thinking? You would've been more useful to us if you'd stayed behind and kept Bassinger muzzled. Fucking useless."

My gift explodes out of me.

I can't stop it or contain it, the wave of it hitting everyone around us, and the entire group scrambles away from me, leaving only Gryphon there with me. The entire TacTeam takes cover as though they can outrun me, but I barely even think of any of them, every fiber of my being is honed in on where Nox is holding Gabe's arm and berating him.

I don't like that.

"Nox... let him go," Gryphon says, pulling the attention away from me as everyone looks over to what has set me off.

Very slowly, as if he's cautious not to spook me, Nox's hand slips away from Gabe. My body moves without thought, stalking over to Gabe as if an invisible force is shoving us together, and I plant myself in-between my two Bonds.

I have no fucking clue what I'm doing, but my bond finally calms the fuck down a little once my back is pressed against Gabe's chest.

"Incoming, the plane's here."

There's a whoop of joy and the TacTeam recovers from my little bond-tantrum moment, moving around us to prepare for our pick up. I stand there with Gabe and watch the descent without a word between us. When the plane hits the runway, landing perfectly, with the roar of the brakes and engine reversing, we both exhale as though we've been holding our breaths for hours, *days* at this point.

"How the fuck do we tell North about this? I don't even know what to call it," Gryphon mutters to Nox, his eyes flicking over his shoulder to me, and I take a deep breath.

I can't say a word to him because he always sees through my lies, and how could I explain this situation away to him? How do I tell him that the nightmares are horrible but the least of our problems?

If only they were the worst thing I can do.

SIGN UP FOR MY NEWSLETTER TO HEAR ABOUT UPCOMING RELEASES

Also by J Bree

The Bonds That Tie Series

Broken Bonds

Savage Bonds

Blood Bonds

Forced Bonds

Tragic Bonds

Unbroken Bonds

The Mortal Fates Series

Novellas

The Scepter

The Sword

The Helm

The Trilogy

The Crown of Oaths and Curses

The Throne of Blood and Honor

The Mounts Bay Saga

The Butcher Duet

The Butcher of the Bay : Part I

The Butcher of the Bay : Part II

Hannaford Prep

Just Drop Out: Hannaford Prep Year One

Make Your Move: Hannaford Prep Year Two

Play the Game: Hannaford Prep Year Three

To the End: Hannaford Prep Year Four

Make My Move: Alternate POV of Year Two

The Queen Crow Trilogy

All Hail

The Ruthless

Queen Crow

The Unseen MC

Angel Unseen

About J Bree

J Bree is a dreamer, writer, mother, and cat-wrangler. The order of priorities changes daily.

She lives on the coast of Western Australia in a city where it rains too much. She spends her days dreaming about all of her book boyfriends, listening to her partner moan about how the lawns are looking, and being a snack bitch to her three kids.

Visit her website at http://www.jbreeauthor.com to sign up for the newsletter or find her on social media through the links below.